96 WORDS FOR LOVE

RACHEL ROY and **AVA DASH**

FOREWORD BY JAMES PATTERSON

JIMMY PATTERSON BOOKS
LITTLE, BROWN AND COMPANY
New York Boston London

Copyright © 2019 by Rachel Roy and In This Together Media
Foreword © 2019 by James Patterson

JIMMY Patterson Books / Little, Brown and Company
Hachette Book Group
1290 Avenue of the Americas, New York, NY 10104
jimmypatterson.org

First Edition: January 2019

JIMMY Patterson Books is an imprint of Little, Brown and Company, a division of Hachette Book Group, Inc. The Little, Brown name and logo are trademarks of Hachette Book Group, Inc. The JIMMY Patterson Books® name and logo are trademarks of JBP Business, LLC.

The publisher is not responsible for websites (or their content) that are not owned by the publisher.

The Hachette Speakers Bureau provides a wide range of authors for speaking events. To find out more, go to hachettespeakersbureau.com or call (866) 376-6591.

Library of Congress Cataloging-in-Publication Data
Names: Roy, Rachel, author. | Dash, Ava, author.
Title: 96 words for love / Rachel Roy; Ava Dash; foreword by James Patterson.
Other titles: Ninety-six words for love
Description: First edition. | New York; Boston: Little, Brown and Company, 2019. | "JIMMY Patterson Books." | Summary: While exploring her grandmother's past at an ashram in India with her cousin Anandi, seventeen-year-old Raya finds herself and, perhaps, true love in this modern retelling of the legend of Dushyanta and Shakuntala.
Identifiers: LCCN 2018023834 | ISBN 978-0-316-47778-9 (alk. paper)
Subjects: | CYAC: Coming of age—Fiction. | Ashrams—Fiction. | Cousins—Fiction. | East Indian Americans—Fiction. | Human trafficking—Fiction. | Folklore—India—Fiction. | India—Fiction.
Classification: LCC PZ7.1.R817 Aah 2019 | DDC [Fic]—dc23
LC record available at https://lccn.loc.gov/2018023834

10 9 8 7 6 5 4 3 2 1

LSC-C

Printed in the United States of America

To those who have gone before,

Those finding their way,

And those yet to begin,

May we move in peace, love, and joy.

Foreword

I love a good retelling. As an author *and* a reader, there's something so satisfying about taking a favorite story or character and asking *"What if?"* What if Romeo and Juliet were part of rival gangs the Jets and the Sharks? What if Poseidon had a son named Percy Jackson? What if King Arthur were a girl? It's a great way to look at our favorite tales through a modern lens, and it's also a way to experience incredible stories from different cultures—stories that otherwise we may never have gotten to know.

In *96 Words for Love,* I was excited to find a superb retelling of the greatest star-crossed love story from Indian mythology. In the epic tale of Dushyanta and Shakuntala, a king is cursed to forget his beloved bride—and you won't forget one word of this surprising and inspiring novel.

—*James Patterson*

96
WORDS
FOR
LOVE

one
∞

DYING GRANDMOTHERS AND DECISIONS

My acceptance to UCLA was giving me insomnia.

Talk about first-world problems. I sighed out an annoyed breath and rolled onto my side, wondering if maybe it was time for a new pillow. "Siri, play rain forest noises," I pleaded.

Instantly the sounds of dripping water and cawing birds filled my bedroom. They basically helped not at all, and I was still wide awake twenty minutes later.

It was the third night in a row I hadn't gotten any sleep. Usually I'm the girl who can pass out standing up and sleep for ten hours without even waking up for a bathroom break. But not anymore. I punched my pillow for, like, the thirty-fourth time that night while I decided this was all my best friend's fault. Lexi had definitely kicked off this bout of nonsleeping the moment I'd gotten the e-mail from the UCLA College of Letters and Science.

"Ahhh!" she'd screamed, as she read over my shoulder. "Raya, you got in, you got in, you got in!" We'd been standing in the middle of our school's courtyard area, where most of the seniors hang out between classes. Some rando in the corner gave us a weird look, but no one else seemed to even notice. College acceptance celebrations and crying fits had become the new normal for us in recent months.

"I got in! Yes!" Lexi and I hugged and danced while I mentally planned my newest status update. *GOT INTO UCLA! BRUINS 4 LIFE!*

Or maybe I'd try to come up with something more original. I'd never beat Lexi's college acceptance status update. When she'd gotten into Berkeley, she posted a picture of herself surrounded by about fifty teddy bears (the Berkeley mascot is also a bear), a life-size cardboard cutout of Olympic swimmer Daria Eldridge (she goes to Berkeley), and the caption GUESS WHO I'M GONNA BE HITTING ON AT MY NEW SCHOOL?!

Lexi totally admitted that half the reason she'd applied to Berkeley was her crush on Daria. She'd had a thing for swimmers ever since second grade, when she decided she wanted to be just like our swim instructor, Coach Morales. Unfortunately, Lexi had the worst backstroke the school had ever seen, and the poor woman cringed every time Lexi jumped into the pool.

"You applied to be an English major?" Lexi was still reading my acceptance e-mail over my shoulder. She sounded surprised.

"You knew that," I told her. Lexi is the only person in the world who knows everything about me. When we were six, she was the only one I told that I accidentally broke our classroom hamster cage and let Little Midgie escape. I've never kept anything from her since.

"Nuh-uh. I thought you were going for prelaw."

Where had she gotten that idea? "Why?"

She shrugged. "Because your mom is a lawyer, I guess. And you never said what you were going to study, so I just thought… Why would you study English, anyway?"

"Because I like writing." And I did. My Tumblr blog, where I reviewed new indie rock albums and concerts Lexi and I went to see, had a few hundred followers. Not great, but not bad, either.

"Oh, okay." Lexi perked up again. "I mean, of course you do. I just didn't realize that's what you were going to *do* do, you know. Like forever. C'mon, let's go celebrate! We'll grab lattes before sixth period."

Just like that, she was off and running. As Lexi usually was. But all I could do was stand there and think of the two words she'd said: *Like forever.*

It hadn't really occurred to me that whatever I studied in college would be my *life.* College had always been the long-term goal. UCLA had always been my first choice. Both my parents had gone there, and I knew it was my dad's dream that I did, too.

I liked school and getting good grades and learning new stuff, so it wasn't difficult for me to work toward that kind of dream for thirteen years of school.

Only now the thirteen years were over, and I was signing up for a life path. Did I actually want to study books and writing theory for four years? And what was I even going to write after that?

I went to get the latte—mocha, skim, half whip, decaf—with Lexi, but already a new kind of anxiety was filling a corner of my head. And I hadn't slept through the night since.

So there I was, not sleeping and contemplating whether my subpar piano talent meant I should major in music, when Mom showed up in my doorway.

"Raya," she whispered. "Cousin Prisha is on the phone. She doesn't think Daadee will last the night. . . . She's saying good-bye to us."

Bile rose in my throat. *No.* I wasn't ready for this.

My grandparents both lived with us when I was little, until Daada died and Daadee went back to India because she missed it. I was only twelve when she announced she was moving there, and at first I was so mad at her for leaving. I even refused to speak to her for a week. I might have held out longer, but she made *kachoris* and refused to give me one until I caved.

I didn't stand a chance. *Kachoris* are this Indian snack that's almost like a samosa—dough that's stuffed and fried, basically. Daadee's *kachoris* are this perfect combination of sweetness and spiciness that takes over your whole mouth and makes you want to eat forever. Once, I managed to eat eight in one sitting.

"Daadee?" I said into the phone. My voice sounded weird and breathy, like I'd just run a marathon. Daadee had only gotten sick a week ago, and Mom had thought we'd make it back to India before she passed. I'd been so certain that Daadee would never die without saying good-bye to me in person that I hadn't seen this moment coming at all. Hadn't even imagined the possibility that I might have to say good-bye to one of the most beloved people in my life through cell phone towers.

"*Nini baba nini…*" a voice was singing on the other end of the line.

Tears immediately started falling down my cheeks. "Nini Baba Nini" is an old Indian lullaby. When I was little, Daadee used to sing it to me. I hadn't heard it since I was eight or nine years old.

"I wish I was there with you," I told her. "I wish I was there with you so much, Daadee." Mom cuddled up next to me on the bed and put her arm around my shoulders, and I curled into her like I was still five years old and she and Daadee were tucking me into bed together, just like they always used to do.

"There are so many things I wish, my Raya," Daadee answered. "So many plans I had for us. So many things I wished to show you and Anandi."

I might not be ashamed to cuddle with my mother, but I was ashamed to say that jealousy churned in my stomach just then.

Anandi was my age, my second cousin, and Daadee's great-niece. Daadee lived with Anandi's family in India, and I knew they'd gotten close since Daadee moved in with them.

Which was cool with me, usually. I liked Anandi. We'd spent time together when my family visited India to take Daadee back over there, and we were friends on Snapchat and WhatsApp. But I sort of didn't need my dying grandmother telling me that she wished she could spend more time with me *and* Anandi.

I know—jealousy only hurt the person holding it. Whatever. It was what I felt.

"What I wish the most," Daadee went on, "is that I had time to show you both my ashram."

Really? I thought. Daadee used to tell me stories about her childhood in India all the time, but she never said much about the few months she'd spent living in an ashram, which was like a Hindu monastery. The ashram of Rishi Kanva was in the Himalaya Mountains somewhere, high in a part of India no one in my family had visited since. Daadee had lived there before she eventually came to America, but she never talked about going back.

"Uh...I'll see it someday," I told Daadee. If my grandmother asked me to, I'd climb the Himalayas myself. Barefoot. In the snow. "I promise. For you."

"You will," she answered. "That I am sure of. When you need the ashram, it will call to you. I have left things there, Raya. Things you and Anandi should have. Things you need. I am sorry I did not tell you sooner. I realized much too late why I was leaving these items behind...." She trailed off.

"What are you talking about?" Daadee hadn't been in that ashram since before my mother was born. What could she possibly have left behind that would still be there?

"I'm sorry I can't tell you where to look, my Raya. My memory right now...it isn't what it was, my *baba*. I have forgotten...." Daadee trailed off again. "You will know where to find them— you and Anandi. When the ashram calls you, do not ignore it. If you wish to find what I have left, simply search what you know." She began coughing then, and it was several minutes before she stopped.

I couldn't worry about ashrams and left-behind objects just then. It was becoming clearer that Daadee didn't have much time left.

"I love you, Daadee," I said. The words felt thin and painful in my throat. "Thank you for always loving me as much as you did. Thank you for everything you taught me. For everything you did for me. Good..." I stopped, unable to finish. For so many years, Daadee had been one of the most important people in my life. When my parents were first moving up in their careers, she was the one I came home to every day after school. She was the one who had listened to stories from my day, cleaned scrapes off my knees, and laid cool cloths on my forehead when I was sick. Nothing in our house had been quite the same since she went back to India.

Now she was leaving me. I couldn't bring myself to say the word *good-bye*.

"I love you, my Raya. I will never forget you." Her voice was soft, and it sounded like it was getting harder for her to talk.

My sobs got fairly hysterical at that point, and eventually Mom took the phone out of my hand.

And then, for the first time in three days, I slept.

I woke up with my eyes stuck shut, a crick in my neck from where I'd fallen asleep on Uni, my old stuffed unicorn, and the horrible sensation that there was a hole in my world.

There's this band I like called Nature vs. Nurture. They're amazing, and I think it's crazy that almost nobody knows about them. Lexi and I got to see them at a small club in San Jose last year, and they played a song called "Party No More" that I completely fell in love with. I made Lexi listen to it about a hundred times on the ride home.

There's a line in that song that goes, *The world keeps making all its spins, but every spin's been tilted since you left.*

Which was exactly what that morning felt like. The world was still spinning. Only without Daadee in it, it was off-balance. Wrong. Sure, she'd been in India for the last five years of my life, but she'd still always been *there*. There to listen when I called or hear me play the piano over the phone.

Everything in my life was changing, and it didn't feel like anything was changing the way it was supposed to.

I started crying again.

I wondered if Taj, my little brother, was crying in the next room over. Maybe not. He'd only been seven when Daadee left, and he wasn't as close to her as I was. Then I wondered why American culture doesn't allow boys to cry as freely and openly as girls. Which led me to wonder if maybe I should major in sociology at UCLA to figure that out. And then that brought me to UCLA and all the not-sleeping I'd been doing lately.

Yes, this is how my mind works.

My phone buzzed. I picked it up, fully intending to ignore whoever was texting me on WhatsApp at the butt crack of dawn. Until I saw who it was: Anandi.

I want to go to the ashram, her text said. Will you go with me? I want to find what she left us.

What was she talking about? Go visit the ashram? Now? I started typing as fast as I could.

Do you know what Daadee was talking about? She hasn't been to that ashram in like over forty years.

It was a few minutes before Anandi's answer came back.

She went back a year or so ago with a group of other people, just to visit. She told me she left behind some things that "belonged" there, but she never said anything about us finding them. Until last night. Then she kept talking about how she'd realized you and I needed what she'd left there, only she couldn't remember exactly what she left or where it was. So weird. She didn't say anything to you about this stuff before last night either?

No way, I texted back.

Yeah, I figured. I don't know if she changed her mind about the stuff staying there or the meds were just messing with her or what.

So do you think there's even anything there? I asked.

I do, Anandi answered a few moments later. And I want to go. This summer. I want to find what she left there. Even if she was out of it last night, I think she meant what she said. And before she got sick, she always talked about how you and I should go to the ashram someday. She'd want us to visit the ashram together. I know she would.

I studied the text and sighed. Of course a part of me wanted to visit the ashram that had clearly meant so much to my grandmother. Of course a part of me wanted to find whatever objects she had left behind for me and my cousin—assuming there was still anything at the ashram for us to find. And maybe that was the case, if she'd only left those things behind a year ago.

But visiting an ashram wasn't exactly part of my life plan. I had graduation to get through, summer jobs to apply for. A college to start attending in the fall.

Even if I couldn't figure out exactly where my life plan was taking me, it was a *plan*. And I always followed my plans—no matter what. I liked plans. They kept my mind from going in too many directions at the same time. They'd gotten me one of the highest GPAs in my class year after year. They'd get me through UCLA.

Plans were good. I needed to follow my plan.

Of course I want to go, I texted back. But no way I can right now.

The phone was silent for a long time, so I found my bathrobe and slippers and pulled my long, thick brown curls into a pony-tail. I was about to head downstairs for breakfast when my eyes stopped on something sitting on my dresser.

It was a necklace. Not one I wore very often, because I liked to save it for special occasions. It was just a thin gold chain, and people never even noticed when I wore it. Still, it was my favorite necklace, because Daadee had given it to me right before she left for India. It had been a gift from Daada, my grandfather.

I walked across the room and picked up the necklace, clutch-ing it in my hand. I was staring at it when the phone buzzed again.

The important things can always be done, my phone read.

My eyes filled with tears. That was something Daadee always used to tell me and Taj when we were young. When we claimed we didn't have time to do our homework or help her with din-ner or spend time with our parents, she would smile and put her hands on her hips and then tell us that. It worked every time. Somehow it always made sense when she said it.

Anandi definitely fought dirty—not that I cared right then. Because she was right.

I raced down the stairs still clutching the necklace in one hand, freaking out the dog and almost going ass-up over a soccer ball Taj had left on the stairs. Still, when I got to the kitchen, I was filled with determination.

"I'm going to India!" I announced to the room.

Dad looked up from his phone, where I was sure he was already e-mailing relatives about things like funeral plans. "In your bathrobe?" he asked.

"No." I pulled the robe closed and tied it, sliding the necklace into my pocket so I could grab onto it again if I needed to during this conversation. "Daadee wants me to go to the ashram she visited when she was young. So Anandi and I want to go. This summer."

Maybe demanding that I go to India so quickly was a bit much. But as I clutched the necklace briefly again, I was sure of one thing: if Anandi and I didn't visit the ashram as soon as we graduated, we'd never go. College would start and life would get busy and Daadee's words would fade away until we'd all but forgotten them. And then whatever she'd left behind would be forgotten, too.

I couldn't let that happen.

Dad set the phone down just as the refrigerator door closed to reveal Mom standing behind it. "Excuse me?" she said.

Her eyes were red-rimmed, and I felt sort of bad for springing this all on them so quickly after Mom had just lost her mother. But I was doing this *for* Daadee, right? Aren't you allowed to mess with your parents' peace of mind if it's for the sake of your grandmother's final wishes?

"Last night," I told them, "Daadee told me she wants me and Anandi to go to the ashram where she went all those years ago. She left something for us there."

"You want to go live in an ashram?" Dad glanced across the room at Mom. "Ray-Ray, you get mad when you have to spend an hour in a waiting room that doesn't have free Wi-Fi."

Oh, yeah. I'd forgotten that you weren't supposed to use technology in most ashrams.

Huh.

Mom cleared her throat. "Raya, hon," she said. "I love that you want to honor my mother's last requests. But Daadee was very ill last night when you talked to her. I doubt she meant much of what she was saying. And asking you and Anandi to go to India and live like hermits ... well, even for a few weeks, that's a tall order. Plus, I'm sure she didn't mean right away. She probably meant she'd like you to go after college, or something. You have plenty of time."

"No," I said, shaking my head back and forth like I was in first grade. "We need to go now—I'm sure of it. Otherwise we never will. I know it. Anandi wants to go right away, too. It makes sense! We have to find what she left us, and I don't want to go to UCLA anyway, and—"

I thought Dad was going to do a flying leap out of his chair. "You're not going to UCLA?" He said it like I'd just told him I was considering joining a band and tattooing the guitarist's name across my face.

"It's not that I don't want to go. Well, maybe it is. I don't know." I shuffled over to the table and tied my robe tighter before sitting down. Mom came over and placed a glass of orange juice in front of me. "I haven't slept, like, more than two hours since I got my acceptance letter. I can't even explain why. I know this was always what I said I wanted. I think I still do. I just..."

I didn't know how to explain it.

They waited.

I finally settled for, "I just don't know what I want to *do,* you know? With my life. What if I pick the wrong thing? What if I end up disappointing everyone?"

Mom laid her hand over mine. "Raya," she said softly, "as long as you do your best, you could never disappoint us."

I frowned. I knew that in theory, but there were so many days when it was hard to believe it. My parents had worked so hard for everything they had—all to give me and Taj the best lives possible. How could they not want to see us live out that potential? "It isn't like I don't *want* to go," I told my mother. "It's a great school. But ever since I got my acceptance letter, something's felt off. It's all Lexi's fault," I added, trying to lighten the mood. "She asked me why I was studying English. And I kind of couldn't answer her."

"This would be Lexi's fault," Dad grumbled. We both knew he didn't mean it. Lexi spent more time at our house than she did at her own.

"So just change to prelaw or business," Dad said, aiming his pointer finger at me the way he loves to do. "Major in one of those and you can do anything with it. I'm telling you."

He was probably right. But at the same time, I was 100 percent sure he was wrong.

They just didn't get it, and they probably never would. Neither of them had ever felt this way—I was sure of it. Dad went from growing up in a one-bedroom apartment in Los Angeles to being a super successful hedge fund manager. Mom went from being the only brown kid in her elementary school to running the legal department for a big nonprofit. They were two of the most driven and focused people I knew, and I doubted either of them had ever wasted a second lying awake at night wondering what to study in college. Finally I said, "It feels like going to the ashram is what I'm *supposed* to do. Just give me a month, okay? One month. Thirty days to see why this place meant so much to Daadee. That's all I'm asking."

They were both quiet for a while after that. Mom kept wiping the corners of her eyes, and Dad was frowning and studying me like we'd never seen each other or something. I clenched my fists underneath the table, slightly terrified that they were going to say no. What if Anandi went to the ashram without me? I couldn't imagine getting a text with the pictures of whatever she found there, knowing she'd walked the same paths Daadee had walked and touched things Daadee had left behind for us, all while I sat in the comfort of my bedroom half a world away.

"I never thought you should major in English anyway," Dad finally mumbled.

I let out a nervous laugh as my heart began to race. "Does that mean I can go?" I asked cautiously.

Dad sighed. "Couldn't you have waited until your midthirties to have an existential crisis? At least then you'd be out of the house."

I didn't know what an existential crisis was, but I sure wasn't going to admit it.

"We'll talk to your cousins." Mom stood up and kissed me on the top of the head, quickly, like she was already getting ready to say good-bye. She tilted up my chin so she could look me in the eye. "I always wanted to take a pilgrimage to an ashram like my mother, but I never got the chance. To be honest, I'm tempted to go with you, but with the cases I have coming up..." She just frowned and shook her head. "Between taking time off for the funeral and everything else, there's just no way. But if you want to do this, love, we'll support you. Just as I know Daadee would have." Her eyes grew watery again.

Dad did groan then. "You know I can't say no to anything when your mom gets teary like that. You sure you want to do this?" I nodded again. "Okay, we'll look into it. But," he added, "no more than a month! You will be back in this house in time to pack for orientation, whether you've 'found yourself' by then or not. And only if your cousin is going. I'm not sending you to some remote religious monastery by yourself. You'll end up in a cult eating nothing but kale."

I darted around the table to hug him. "Thank you, thank you! And don't worry so much—this is what Daadee wants me to do. It's the best way to honor her memory—I'm sure of it. Plus, kale's gross."

"What's going on?" Taj came into the kitchen, looking puffy-eyed and tired.

I should have known that even preteen dorkiness wouldn't outweigh Daadee's loss. Poor Taj. I ran over and hugged him.

"I'm going to live in India!" I told him.

"Oh." He frowned. "Really? But it's so hot there, and the food sucks. Hey, can I have your room?"

Typical Taj. I was pretty sure Mom couldn't decide whether to cry or strangle him. In the end, she cried and hugged us both.

Then Dad joined in, and soon the only things missing were our matching UCLA sweatshirts.

"I'll have to find us all some Rishi Kanva ashram shirts," I muttered into my mother's bathrobe as she smothered me. Mom squeezed me tighter and laughed. "I think Daadee would love that," she whispered in my ear.

I reached into my pocket and squeezed the necklace one more time. *I hope so,* I thought.

Later that night I lay in bed, waiting for the usual insomnia to hold me hostage. Only it didn't. Within minutes of shutting off my light, I could feel myself drifting off, and I knew right away I wasn't going to be able to keep my eyes open.

The thought of visiting the ashram didn't leave me feeling terrified and unsettled the way thinking about college had. The exact opposite, in fact. The idea of going to visit Daadee's ashram left me feeling more relaxed and sure of myself than I ever had before. I was more afraid to go to UCLA than I was to travel to a strange ashram in a country I had only visited once.

Because no one expected anything from me there.

two

HOMESICKNESS AND HELLISH PLANE RIDES

I'd been to India five years earlier, so I knew my trip to the ashram was going to be exhausting, confusing, and lots of other adjectives that made me so anxious I almost stopped sleeping again in the weeks leading up to the trip. Luckily my planning side kicked in hard-core, and a month before my trip Lexi was complaining about the "learn Hindi in the car" app I made her listen to on the way to school.

Whatever. I believe it's important to always know how to ask someone where a bathroom is. Even if lots of Indians also speak English.

Still, despite my Hindi phrase practice and my hours spent researching on TripAdvisor, I had a hard time letting go of my parents when they finally dropped me off at the airport.

"I'll be fine," I told my father as he squeezed basically all the air out of my lungs. Because I would be, right?

"I'll call you when I get there," I told my mother. Because the international plan that I had upgraded to *had* to work. If not, I was possibly going to flip out upon landing in Delhi.

"We love you," Mom told me, and she didn't even bother to try wiping away all the tears streaming down her face.

"You come home the minute you want to," my father said as he hugged me again. My gigantic bear of a father wasn't actually crying, but I swear I heard a quiver in his voice.

And then I—however hesitantly—stepped away from them and through the sliding doors of the San Francisco airport. I grabbed hold of a luggage rack next to me and waited for a moment while some near-crippling anxiety passed through me.

I can do this, right? I texted Lexi.

YES! she sent back immediately, because Lexi never went more than two minutes without looking at her phone. I believe in you, Rayers.

That was what I needed to hear. I headed for check-in.

So the adventure began. And the beginning of it was exactly as terrible as I'd expected it to be.

My parents had driven me all the way to San Francisco because I'd have fewer layovers than if I flew out of San Jose, but the flying time itself was still insane. It started with eleven hours overnight to Frankfurt, Germany, and then seven and half hours more to New Delhi.

Not much sleep happened for me on that trip. My insomnia during the first flight had little to do with college acceptance letters hanging over my head and more to do with the little kid sitting next to me who kept trying to climb all over my lap while screaming that she wanted her mom. *You and me both, kid.*

By the time we got to Frankfurt, I was so exhausted and homesick I almost texted my parents and asked them to buy me a flight back home from Germany. Only a quick check of my Instagram feed, and a picture Lexi had posted there, changed my mind.

It was a picture of the two of us someone had taken at our graduation. We were in our caps and gowns with our diplomas in hand.

MY BEST GIRL, THE ONLY ONE I WILL EVER TRULY LOVE, LEFT FOR INDIA TODAY. MISS YOU SO MUCH, @RAYA_ LISTON. LOVE YOU MORE THAN LIFE! HAVE THE MOST AMAZING ADVENTURE!

I smiled the most giant dorky smile the world had ever seen and then quickly ducked my head so my fellow passengers wouldn't think I was weird. I could do this. Lexi believed in me. So did my parents, underneath all those tears, or they never would have sent me. I could do this.

I decided to find some food that was typically German to really embrace my international travel. Three bites in, I remembered how much I hated sauerkraut and went off to find the nearest Starbucks.

Oh, well. The thought counted, right?

By the time we landed in Delhi, I was ready to *drop*. I'd slept about four hours out of the last thirty-six, and I think I was actually swerving back and forth as I walked off the plane.

At first glance, Terminal 3 in the Delhi airport looked kinda like the San Francisco airport: people everywhere, lots of shouting and talking and crying, terrible carpet with ugly patterning, and signs everywhere. Plus the signs were even in English *and* Hindi. Hindi might be the official language of India, but English was the official language of business here. So it wasn't even like there was a language barrier to make me feel totally out of place and wanting to run home.

The problem was all the details were wrong. The music playing in the background was some kind of Bollywood tune I didn't recognize. Shouts of *"namaste!"* ("hello" in Hindi), *"chalo!"* ("let's go"), and plenty of words and phrases I didn't know in all different languages echoed around me. Jeans and T-shirts were interspersed with saris and head coverings, the temperature seemed much higher than any American airport would ever allow, and the crowds around me were bigger and more congested than I was used to. I even felt thrown off by how *not* out of place I was. My dad is biracial and my mom is 100 percent Indian, so I don't always look like everyone else around me—especially at my majority-white school. But in this airport, I hardly stood out at all. That should have been comforting, but somehow it just left me feeling antsy and out of sorts.

Someone jostled me, and I looked up to see a family walking past. Mom, Dad, two kids. I gripped the phone in my hand a little harder and clutched the strap of my backpack. What if I lost one of them? My backpack had my passport in it, and I didn't even know *what* I would do without my phone. My parents were eight thousand miles away—I was totally on my own if something went wrong. I watched the family move toward the walkway, laughing and talking, and I felt my throat tighten. Was I seriously about to start crying in the middle of an airport?

Just then my phone vibrated, and I looked down to see a new notification: WELCOME TO INDIA, my service provider announced. Instantly I felt my whole body relax. International phone plans for the win. I immediately called my mother.

"Raya?" She answered on the first ring.

"I just landed in Delhi," I said. It was all I could manage to get out.

Luckily my mother is the most amazing woman alive, and she immediately understood. "You know what to do now, Ray-Ray. You've been in this airport before. Take the walkway to immigration check. Then Anandi will meet you at baggage claim. No trouble at all." Her voice was soothing, calm, and held nothing but confidence in me.

I took a deep breath, and some of the anxiety began to funnel out of my body.

"That's what I'm going to do," I told Mom. "Find Anandi. I love you, Mom. Dad and Taj, too. So much."

"We love you, too, baby. And we're so proud of you."

I can do this. I can do this. My mother said I could. And she was right at least 80 percent of the time.

I hung up the phone and quickly texted Anandi that I'd arrived. Then I opened up Instagram and looked again at the picture Lexi had posted. I took a deep breath, grabbed the handle of my carry-on, and started walking.

By the time I got onto the moving walkway that went toward the immigration check at the center of the terminal, I was mesmerized by everything around me. It was like the whole airport was an amalgamation of Indian culture mixed up with American details. I'd go by a sign entirely in Hindi for some kind of store I'd never heard of before, and then I'd go by a Pepsi machine.

I might have taken a picture of the Pepsi machine. Just because.

"*Kaise ho tum,* beautiful?" some dude called out to me. Thanks to all the time I'd spent with my language app, I knew that was Hindi for "How are you?" Either that or I had no idea what I was talking about and the dude had just said something to me in Punjabi. There are a lot of languages and dialects spoken in India.

I ignored the guy and quickly turned to face the other direction. I got a lot of that, unfortunately, but I guessed most girls did. It was one of the many reasons why I spent my life in jeans and T-shirts, much to my mom's disappointment. She was a bit of a fashionista, Priya Liston was.

At some point in my life, I developed this weird love for T-shirts printed with corny slogans. I've always liked puns and wordplay and stuff like that, and when I was ten, Lexi gave me a shirt that said JENIUS on it. I thought it was hilarious, and since then I've sort of collected shirts like that. The one I was wearing now said, WITHOUT MUSIC, LIFE WOULD B, and then the music symbol for "flat."

My piano teacher had given it to me. Adults had always gotten my sense of humor better than most people who were actually my age. Well, except Lexi. Lexi got me.

I was obsessing over how hard it would be for me to find Anandi and looking at my phone every ten seconds for a message, when I looked up and realized I was missing something *amazing*. The entire top of the wall over the immigration check area was like nothing I'd ever seen before: hundreds of golden bowls lined every single inch, and between the bowls were eight or ten giant bronze hands with flowers on the palm. The fingers were in various positions, but I didn't know what they meant. I definitely didn't remember these from the last time I was in India.

I couldn't stop staring at the wall as I waited in the immigration line, and suddenly being in India didn't feel nearly as terrifying as it had when I'd stepped out of the jet bridge. I swiped open my phone to take some pictures of the hands and found several new texts.

From Anandi: See you sooooooon!!!!!!

From my dad: Love you, baby. Try not to talk to anyone with kale. Ha-ha, Dad.

From Lexi: Well r you there?

I sent the laughing-so-hard-I'm-crying emoji to Dad. Then I sent a quick text back to Lexi. Just landed in Delhi!! Msg me now while you still can . . . on my way to the tech-free ashram soon! Don't forget to keep up the blog! I added at the end. Lexi guest posted on my blog a lot anyway, since we listened to mostly the same stuff and went to a lot of concerts together. She'd agreed to keep it going while I was *without access to normal human civilization,* as she'd put it. I couldn't abandon all 316 of my most loyal followers just because I'd decided to give up computers for a month.

Never. Def listening to the new Refrainers album tonight.

Meanie. She knew I'd been waiting for that album for months. Oh, well. It would still be there—hopefully on vinyl—when I got back to the United States.

The immigration line wasn't all that long—our plane must have landed at a lucky time—so I finished the immigration check more quickly than I'd expected to. Then I followed the crowd of people in front of me through a set of large doors and into the baggage claim area.

"Raya!"

Out of nowhere, 130 pounds (give or take) of pure energy came flying into me, crashing us both to the ground. I sat up and found my cousin Anandi next to me, beaming.

"*Namaste!* I can't believe you're finally here! We have so much to talk about. I have to know everything that's happened in America in the last five years. Don't leave anything out! And I got an earbud splitter so we can listen to music together on the train to the ashram. I love your shirt, by the way! I'm so glad you still like music. I was worried you might not anymore, and then what would we do on the long train ride? Oh, I don't know how I'm going to get through all those weeks in the ashram without my iPhone!"

"Hey, Anandi," I said. She blew her bangs off her face and grinned back. Anandi looked a lot like me, except she was much shorter with higher cheekbones and hair that was much straighter than mine. She also definitely had energy to spare. I had somehow forgotten how insanely exuberant Anandi could be about everything. It was one of the reasons why she and I had gotten along so well when we were twelve. She'd immediately reminded me of Lexi. I'm a little more reserved than either of them are, and I'd always thought Lexi and I balanced each other out. Hopefully Anandi and I would do the same for each other on this trip.

She stood and put out a hand to help me up. "This is the best. I'm so glad that you wanted to go to Daadee's ashram with me. I can't wait to see it. Can you? Oh, this is Shray." She gestured to a short guy, probably a little older than us, wearing glasses and a highly serious expression. He didn't even look up at us as he typed on his phone. "Hello," he said as he stared at the screen.

"Uh, hi," I told him. "Who's Shray?" I whispered to Anandi.

"He's interning in Dad's law firm. He's going to travel with us to the ashram."

"Is he from that part of India or something?" Anandi hadn't mentioned anything about us having a guide when we'd messaged back and forth about our trip plans.

"No, of course not! He's from Varanasi, too. But we couldn't possibly take this trip by ourselves; it's too dangerous. My parents wanted to take us, but I convinced them that you and I needed to do this ourselves." She beamed. "So they sent Shray."

Anandi and I had decided, for reasons that had totally made sense at the time, to make this trip way more complicated than it actually needed to be. We could have met at the Chandigarh airport, which is fairly close to where the Rishi Kanva ashram is. But I was going to have to fly through Delhi no matter what, and there's a special train route up through the Himalaya Mountains that's famous—people call it the Toy Train—that Anandi had always wanted to take. She'd told me about it when we started our trip planning, and she seemed so excited about it that we decided to just meet in Delhi and take the ten- or eleven-hour train ride up to the Himalayas. At the time it had seemed like an excellent idea. Now I was slightly regretting adding an eleven-hour train ride onto a plane trip that was going to live as one of the worst in my memory.

And it looked like we were taking that train trip with a strange chaperone who never looked up from his phone. Still, it *was* kind of nice that Anandi had talked her parents into letting us do this without them. In so many ways, this trip felt like my first real step by myself into the world.

I gave Anandi a sudden hug. "I'm really glad you're here," I told her.

She didn't seem surprised at all—she just hugged me back. "Me too." She slid her arm through my elbow. "Let's go, okay? Shray, are you ready?"

He nodded, still not looking up from his phone. And I thought Lexi had serious iPhone multitasking skills.

"Dad booked us a hotel here for a night so you can sleep before we catch the train. Shray will be with us, of course. Dad got him the room next to us. Are you tired? I bet you're tired. Mum says that your family slept for almost twenty hours when you first arrived the last time you visited."

I had no problem believing that.

Anandi led me through the airport, basically keeping me upright. Let's hear it for cousins. She barely even blinked when I tripped over someone's shoe and nearly ate shit on the overcrowded carousel.

Shray stood behind us at baggage claim, typing the whole time, while Anandi and I waited for my suitcase. "I'm just so happy you're here," she said. "The minute Daadee told me she'd left things behind at the ashram for us to find, I knew I needed to visit. But it felt wrong to go without you. She talked about you all the time these last few months."

I tamped down the jealousy building in my stomach again. There was no point in being angry at Anandi just because she got to spend the last few years of my grandmother's life with her and I didn't.

"Anandi?" I said hesitantly. "Was it nice? The cremation ceremony?"

Daadee's body had been burned at the sacred Ganges River, near Varanasi, where our family has lived for generations. But Taj and I didn't get to go. We would have missed too much school, and between graduation requirements constantly getting in my face and Taj's bazillion soccer tournaments, we ended up staying behind while Mom traveled to India to say good-bye to Daadee and pray she had achieved moksha—the end of the birth-death cycle. I hadn't been there to say good-bye. And Anandi had.

Anandi nodded, and her eyes looked watery for a moment. "It was perfect, Raya. Exactly what she would have wanted. I just know she found moksha."

My eyes felt watery, too.

Neither of us said anything for a long few minutes after that. Eventually the bags came up, and I felt strongly justified for demanding Mom let me buy the giant suitcase shaped like a ladybug. It was super easy to spot.

Anandi led us toward the sliding doors of the Delhi airport, with Shray still engrossed in whatever he was doing on his phone.

Then we stepped outside, and I started to wonder why I'd

ever thought it was a good idea to leave the comfort of my parents' house and travel across the world.

Car horns were going off everywhere, people were shouting for taxis and bustling around, and someone on a bullhorn was making the same frantic announcement over and over in Hindi. All that confusion was set up against a backdrop of large, flashing billboards that were mostly in English, and all the humidity, heat, and smog I'd started to feel moments earlier was suddenly encasing me, wrapping around me like a blanket that felt as though it could suffocate me at any moment.

Shray, who seemed not at all bothered by anything about this scene, snapped his head up from his phone. "I'll get a taxi," he said calmly, and then jumped into the fray of cars and waving hands until a large cab—which was honking loudly the whole time—pulled over next to us.

I can't lie: I felt instant relief as we settled into the air-conditioned taxi, away from the smog and insane heat, and drove out of the chaos of the Delhi airport. Anandi pulled out her phone, and I thought about texting my parents or Lexi or Taj, but I couldn't seem to look away from the sights around me. I might have visited India before, but I'd been a lot younger then. In some ways I felt like I was seeing it all again for the first time.

It took me a few moments to get used to the sensation of being on the left-hand side of the road—for a second I almost yelled at the driver that he was in the wrong lane—but once I got over that, it was easy just to get lost in taking in the world around me. It was shaping up to be a very cool drive. Until the traffic. Just. Stopped. And then for a long time we moved at approximately two miles an hour. I hadn't felt more at home since my plane had landed: that part of the drive reminded me a lot of when Mom and Dad took Taj and me to LA.

The hotel where we were staying was just on the outskirts of downtown Delhi, and the closer we got to the heart of the city, the more interesting the scenery became. Soon there were mopeds everywhere, and people crossing the streets whether or not there was a car directly in front of them. More and more bicycles and rickshaws appeared alongside the tiny cars that were all around us. A lot of the cars were parked in strange patterns all over the sides of the streets, and I texted Lexi a picture with the caption: Looks like one of your parking jobs.

Our driver spent the whole trip on his phone, talking loudly to someone in what mostly seemed to be English—his accent was thick—but occasionally he veered into Hindi and a third language I didn't recognize. He never once seemed concerned about the traffic and bicycles and people cutting him off and swerving around other cars in front of him.

He definitely reminded me of some taxi drivers in LA. Maybe taxi drivers are just badasses everywhere.

I studied the beautifully curved and intricate Devanagari text on billboards and storefronts, trying to see how many Hindi words I could recognize from my app sessions. It wasn't many, but I was proud to pick out two of three. I'd always loved watching Daadee write to her friends in Hindi—when I was little, I'd thought Devanagari was the most beautiful alphabet I'd ever seen. *Much prettier than this one,* I used to tell her, gesturing to the Latin alphabet as I did my homework in English.

Daadee. I wished so badly she were in the cab with me, seeing all these sights with me. So much of what I saw reminded me of her. Even the storefronts and buildings, interspersed with teal and orange and purple and every other color imaginable, reminded me of the saris she used to wear—all of them in beautiful satin and shades so loud and noticeable I remembered being embarrassed by her at a volleyball game. *Can't she just dress like everyone else?* I'd asked my mother.

Do you want Daadee to be like all the other grandparents? she'd replied.

The answer was simple: of course I didn't. After that, I never let myself be anything but proud of Daadee's saris. I watched closely for people in outfits that reminded me of hers, and I saw several of them in between all the business suits and jeans and sweaters and blouses.

"Here." The driver stopped talking on his phone long enough to announce our arrival at the hotel, and I realized I was slightly sad that our long ride was over. At least there was a bed in my near future.

At that point I didn't even know how many hours I'd been awake—I just knew it was far too many. We walked into the room, and I immediately passed out on the bed without even taking off my shoes.

I dreamed that Daadee and I were walking through the streets of Delhi together. She wore a long green-and-orange sari, and I wore my T-shirt that says LIFE BEGINS AT THE END OF YOUR COMFORT ZONE.

three

∞

FREAKY HEIGHTS AND FORTUITOUS MEETINGS

I woke up nearly fourteen hours later to Anandi dancing around the room with a towel over her hair, singing something that sounded vaguely familiar.

"Good, you're awake." She smiled at me as I sat up and tried to figure out why my head felt like a giant bowl of oatmeal. "Our train leaves soon. I was worried I was going to have to wake you up."

After I got over the shock of sleeping for so long, I took a very hot shower. I knew the Rishi Kanva ashram had indoor plumbing, but I also knew it was in a very, very old building. If this was going to be my last good shower for over a month, I was going to enjoy it.

At least I knew for sure the ashram had flushing toilets—that had been one of the first things I'd researched when Anandi and I were making our plans to visit the ashram. A lot of the toilets in India are squat toilets. Those are exactly what they sound like, and they are not my favorite thing in the world. I'd practically danced around the room when I learned the ashram's plumbing had been majorly renovated a few decades ago.

I did my best to shake off my jet lag while I got ready and Anandi talked. Mostly at me, because I was still way too groggy to join in.

"I'm so excited for this train trip. I've heard basically the whole ride is on the side of the mountain cliffs. I can't wait! I've always wanted to see the views of the Himalayas from this train."

Her excitement was contagious. My trepidation about spending eleven more hours traveling started to melt away. This was going to be *fun*.

After both Anandi and I made calls to our parents, during which I staved off at least 60 percent of my homesickness and spent five minutes reminding Taj that the 13.5-hour time difference meant it was already the next day in India, we found Shray waiting outside our room to take us to breakfast.

He was on his phone, of course. I wondered if he'd even looked up from it while he shaved that morning.

The café smelled like turmeric, cumin, and cinnamon—the spices tickled my nose and brought back memories of cooking with Daadee. I took in a deep breath and hoped that the ashram held more memories of my grandmother. I missed her so much.

After a breakfast of coffee and *dosa*s, which are like thin pan-cakes made of lentils, Shray escorted us to the train station.

The poverty in India wasn't quite as hidden at the train sta-tion as it had been in the airport. When Shray went to get our train tickets, two young boys dressed in dirty clothes that were way too small for them rushed up to me and Anandi. "Auntie, auntie, money, *krpya?*" one of them begged. I had some change from breakfast, so I tried to grab some rupees out of my bag, but Anandi slapped my hand. "Don't encourage them," she hissed at me. "You, go bother someone else!" Anandi shooed the boys away like they were flies, and they quickly disappeared into the crowd around us.

"What the hell, Anandi? Why can't we help them?" I asked. "They look like they need it."

"No, no." Anandi shook her head. "People here, they find cute little kids like that and force them to beg. It's like their job. If we encourage it, we only encourage the adults to continue the abuse."

I guess that made logical sense, but it seemed pretty harsh. My heart ached for the two kids, and I felt a righteous desire to help all the kids I saw begging, while at the same time feeling totally useless and small.

I zipped up my bag and gripped it tight. No one on the plat-form looked particularly suspicious—they were basically just a bunch of people standing around with suitcases—but my mom had reminded me that morning to be wary of pickpockets.

Shray came back with our tickets, but I still felt nervous. What if we were robbed? What if someone tried to grab one of us? I didn't think the six kickboxing classes I'd taken were going to be enough to destroy any would-be foe.

Not to mention that Shray *still* spent the entirety of our time on the platform just staring at this phone. "What does he do on that thing?" I asked Anandi at one point. "Stalk his fake girl-friend on Insta?"

Anandi rolled her eyes. "He doesn't want to be here with us. He's just trying to suck up to Dad."

"All he's doing is sucking up to whoever invented text messaging." *Wait.* Who had invented text messaging? Was it the same person who had invented the cell phone? Weren't cell phones actually really huge when they were invented? What had it been like to carry one of those around?

I thought about googling a picture of the first cell phone, but then I remembered I wasn't going to have Google as a lifeline anymore in just a few short hours. I guess I should start learning to live without it.

Finally the train showed up. Anandi's parents had gone all out and booked us a first-class car, which was air-conditioned and felt super luxurious compared with what I'd been expecting. I decided to enjoy it while it lasted. In Kalka, we'd be transfer-ring to the *Himalayan Queen*, the so-called Toy Train Anandi was excited about. It was called the Toy Train because it had to be super small to travel on the thin tracks in the mountains, and

TripAdvisor reviewers were not shy about sharing how hot and crowded the train got—but apparently the one-hundred-plus tunnels it went through made it worth it.

I'd been hoping to get a little more sleep on the trip to Kalka, but Anandi had other plans.

"I have all the Jonas Brothers' songs ready to go on my phone," she informed me as soon as the train pulled out of the station. "So we can listen to them over and over and—"

"The Jonas Brothers?" I interrupted.

"Of course. I've been listening to them ever since your last trip when you played me their songs on your phone. I've been obsessing basically nonstop over Nick Jonas's solo album." She sighed dreamily. "Someday I'll meet Nick Jonas."

That statement left me slightly speechless. Sure, back in middle school Lexi and I had listened to the Jonas Brothers constantly, and I'd probably made Anandi listen to lots of their stuff back then. But I'd left Nick Jonas in a cloud of music snobbery years ago when Lexi's brother first played us an Arcade Fire album on Spotify. We never looked back, and my phone was filled with artists like Car Seat Headrest and Lana Del Rey now.

Great. I'd turned my Indian cousin into an American time capsule of myself from middle school. I grabbed an earbud from her and pasted on a smile.

I did end up falling asleep for most of the trip to Kalka. Then we transferred to the *Himalayan Queen,* and from there on out I forgot all about either the Jonas Brothers or sleep. Because that train, and that train ride, were almost too crazy to be real.

Allow me to share Raya's Rules of Himalayan Train Travel:

Rule #1: If the train was made any time after 1950, you're probably not in the Himalayas.

Rule #2: If tunnels don't appear around every single corner, you're probably not in the Himalayas.

Rule #3: If you aren't staring down over a massive but beautiful cliff, waiting for the train to finally rattle off the tracks and crash down the side of a mountain, thus leading to your fiery death, you're probably not in the Himalayas.

Rule #4: If you're not staring out at the most gorgeous display of overpoweringly tall mountains you've ever seen in your life, you're probably not in the Himalayas.

Rule #5: If the train isn't full of random people fighting for seats and yelling at each other, you're probably not in Car 3A on train 61, traveling from Kalka to Shimla.

Rule #6: Don't eat the food at the train stops.

Actually that last one was definitely *not* my rule. It was Shray's, growled at us in between typing on his phone and barking into it about how he'd be back in the office just as soon as he got away from this "wretched cesspool of a trip," as he put it.

"He's a little high-strung," Anandi whispered to me while he growled. But she agreed with him on rule #6, sadly. I say *sadly* because the smells coming out of those vendors' food carts were heavenly.

We arrived at the infamous Barog station just as we finished eating our sad packed lunch. "I want to get out and look around, Shray," Anandi informed him. He rolled his eyes, just to remind us what a supreme annoyance we were, and then led us off the train.

I'd spent all of our ride on the *Himalayan Queen* feeling like I was moving upward into a different world. The Himalayas were nothing like southern India. Here the temperatures were much cooler, the climate seemed to change every few miles, and nothing about the scenery looked anything like either Delhi or Varanasi, the two places in India where I'd spent the most time.

And Barog was definitely like no place in India I'd ever been.

It was almost junglelike it was so bright green. Plants and trees lined every side of the tracks, except for the bright blue-and-white triangular-shaped buildings that lined up in rows to form the station area. The famous tunnel didn't seem all that impressive to me—it was just another tunnel, and we'd already gone through more of those than I could count. But I also knew what had happened to the man who had originally designed this tunnel. He was a British engineer named Barog, and he tried to dig the tunnel from opposite sides. When the two tunnels didn't end up meeting in the middle, the British government was furious. Barog eventually got the place named after him, but he also killed himself. Just knowing that someone ended their life over this particular tunnel gave it an almost haunted, eerie quality.

Behind us, we could see cliffs and mountains in the near distance, the same ones that had become so much a part of the view that they'd almost started to feel normal and not completely amazing and beyond-belief impressive. I took a few more pictures of them to add to the fifty billion I'd already taken. I still had a signal, so I made a collage and posted it to Instagram. #NoFilter.

Somehow I was feeling more comfortable in this uniquely bizarre train station than I ever had in Delhi. Maybe it was the enormous mountains still hovering over us, which made everyone and everything seem so very tiny. We were standing at what felt like the edge of the world, in a place that could be a gateway to anything.

"I've always wanted to see this place." Anandi gazed at the tunnel reverently.

"It's insane." I shook my head. "I can't believe someone killed themselves over that tunnel. Over a mistake."

Anandi frowned and stared out at the tunnel lining the front of our view. "Sometimes mistakes are costly," she said quietly.

I was so surprised by how serious she sounded that I accidentally tripped on a loose rock and almost took Shray down.

He looked up from his phone just in time to catch me and put me upright, and then he immediately went back to typing.

Weirdo.

The train whistle sounded just then, and we climbed back aboard, where Shray immediately immersed himself in his stalking project (maybe) and Anandi pulled up Nick Jonas's first solo album.

"Uh, Anandi," I said weakly, "listen. You should know that I don't listen to that kind of music as much as I used to. I've kind of gotten into some…other bands."

Anandi looked skeptical. "What kind of music could ever be as good as this? Demi Lovato? Justin Bieber?"

I didn't have the heart to tell her that one of my favorite bands was called Bieber Is Not Real Music. "Oh, you know. Just different bands. I'll play some for you sometime."

Anandi shrugged. "Sure, that sounds good. All music is good music."

"Yeah, I think so, too." It felt good to at least have a love of music in common with my cousin, even if we were now worlds apart in terms of the exact concerts we wanted to see. "If only I loved it enough to want to make it for the rest of my life or something," I murmured.

"What do you mean?" Anandi asked as she untangled her earbuds, looking intrigued.

I shrugged. "Nothing, I guess. I've just been wondering if maybe I picked the wrong thing to study. You know, next year.

At college. There's no way I would actually study music, though. I'm not *that* into it."

Anandi laughed, but the sound was almost harsh. "Seriously? You're so lucky you have a choice. That your parents aren't making you study what they did. Law is the only thing I'll ever get to study, just like my father." There was a definite bitterness to her voice.

"You're going to be a barrister, too?" Barristers are what they call lawyers in India. I realized it had never occurred to me to ask Anandi what she was going to major in next year.

Anandi smiled thinly. "That's what we do in my family. All of us. You know that—your mother even kept up the tradition in America. I start studying at BHU in the fall." I'd heard my mother talk about law schools enough to know she meant Banaras Hindu University, the top law college in Varanasi. She finished untangling her earbuds from her splitter and her whole demeanor immediately changed, her smile perking and her eyes lightening. "There we go. Want to listen with me?"

I took the earbuds from her and didn't ask any more questions about her burgeoning law career. But I was starting to think there was more to my cousin than just a happy Nick Jonas–lover.

People got on and off the train in Barog, and the new crowd we traveled with after that was mostly composed of kids in school uniforms who sang together in a mix of Hindi and English (Anandi called it Hinglish) and screamed loudly every time we went through a tunnel. I was all set to be overwhelmed, but there was something so innocent, fun, and distracting about them that by the third tunnel, they had most of the car screaming with them.

Well, except Shray.

We got to Shimla just as it was getting dark. It was built right into the Himalayan hills and weirdly reminded me of San Francisco, only a lot more crowded. "What's up with the buildings?" I asked. Lots of them didn't look like anything I'd seen in India.

"They were made to look like the buildings in England," Anandi told me. "So the British people in India could pretend they were actually in Britain when they vacationed here." Oh, yeah. This was where the British had come to escape the heat when they occupied the country.

I wondered what it was like to live in a place where so many things around you were a reminder of the people who'd held you down and tried to destroy your ancestors. Dad's family was originally from Georgia, and when we'd visited them once, we'd driven past a Robert E. Lee High School. Dad and his second cousin had talked for a long time about how terrible it was that the school district wouldn't change the name—that they made so many black kids go to a school named after a guy who fought to defend slavery. I'd been really young at the time and hadn't cared much about what they were saying. But now I wondered: how would I have felt if I'd ever had to go to that high school?

The taxi ride from Shimla to the ashram took about forty minutes on some of the narrowest, steepest roads I'd ever seen.

"You're from America?" the driver asked when I squealed as we went around a particularly sharp and terrifying curve.

"Yeah," I answered in between gasps.

"Here we say, when you ride in Himachal Pradesh: 'Good horn, good brake, good luck!'" He laughed hysterically at his own joke.

Himachal Pradesh was the state where the ashram was located. Shimla was its capital. If all roads in the area were like this, I vowed never to leave the ashram until the day it was time to go home.

Anandi bumped my shoulder and went back to listening to Nick Jonas. Clearly near-death experiences didn't faze her much.

In an effort to avoid thinking about crashing into an oncoming car, I tried to entertain myself by sending my parents and Lexi pictures I'd taken on our train ride whenever the car wound its way into cell service.

How high up are you?! Is that SAFE? Dad sent back.

Prolly not, I replied. If I die, take care of Uni.

Not funny, Raya, he answered just before I lost service again.

"The Rishi Kanva ashram," the driver announced as he pulled into a long driveway. I quickly put my phone away.

The car followed the curves of a swerving driveway, the moon showing off the trees lining each side, until we pulled up in front of a building.

And then I thought I understood why Daadee had traveled so far to visit this particular ashram.

Things I had learned about the Rishi Kanva ashram during my research, which I had definitely not overdone, no matter what Lexi said:

1. It was built in the early 1900s by some Indian royal with a lot of money who'd gotten super into religion.

2. The guy was also obsessed with the study of architecture, so the ashram had been inspired by *a lot* of different buildings—everything from the local building style to the ancient Mughal Empire, to Portuguese and British styles. One website called the place "a hodgepodge of the world."

3. The building had been renovated several times over the years, mostly because the ashram had a faithful following of people who loved it. It had a pool and updated plumbing and all that. But the ashram tried to keep its historical appearance intact.

Things I didn't know about the Rishi Kanva ashram until I finally saw it:

1. Pictures on the internet *did not* do it justice.

2. It was everything and nothing I'd expected it to be.

Lights from the walkway glanced off the two large square towers at the far right and left corner of the building, which were capped by enormous triangular-shaped roofs—actually, they kind of looked like an upside-down shrug emoji. The front of the building was brown brick with white shutters lined up neatly across it, but the sides of each tower were painted a bright shade of yellow with blue-and-white designs trimming the windows. The tower windows were made of stained glass, but in the dark I couldn't tell if they were patterned or just colored in. It was so bright and beautiful—why, I wondered, were the houses in America so boring? Maybe I could convince Dad to paint our house purple.

I walked a few feet to my right to get a better view, and I spotted numerous smaller buildings of every size and shape popping up and down behind it, almost like an entire small village had been joined together in one giant house.

"Wow." Anandi sounded even more reverent than she had in Barog.

Shray looked unimpressed.

I pulled out my phone and sent my parents and Lexi a group text of the best picture I could get with the limited light. Isn't it GORGEOUS?! No wonder Daadee loved it here. Just arrived. About to go inside. From here on out, all communication must come through actual mail. LIKE WITH STAMPS, LEXI. Better get some.

I had no idea what time it was in California just then, but Lexi texted back in seconds.

What's a stamp? she replied. Kidding! Heart u so much Rayers. That place is amazing!

It's beautiful! Be careful! Have fun! We love you! If you get sick, drink lots of fluids! I didn't have to even look at the sender to see who that text came from.

"Do you think we'll find it?" Anandi whispered to me. "Whatever Daadee sent us here to find?"

"I don't know," I answered. "I hope so."

She grabbed my hand. Together we walked up the wide steps to the large wooden door of the Rishi Kanva ashram, where Anandi rang the bell.

Then the door of the ashram opened. And standing there was the most gorgeous guy I'd ever seen.

four

GREAT HALLS AND GORGEOUS GUYS

A re you here to chant?" he asked.

"Excuse me?" I replied.

"Chanting. They love to do that here. Is that what you're here for?"

I had no idea how to respond to that. Partly because I had no clue what he was talking about and partly because I was completely distracted by how good-looking he was.

I mean, this was gorgeousness no other guy my age had ever possessed. Guys my age had always been long and lanky or stocky and short. But he was the perfect combination: tall but not too tall, fit but not covered in muscle. He had high cheekbones and skin so perfectly smooth that Lexi would have been begging to know what moisturizer he used. His hair was just long enough to drift around his neck and over his forehead and into his eyes. *And oh, his eyes.* His eyes were the deepest and most intense golden color I'd ever seen.

I couldn't figure out why Anandi wasn't giving him the same deer-in-headlights look I had to be wearing. Then again, she'd already gifted her heart to Nick Jonas.

"Uh, we're here to stay? You know, at the ashram?" I think I might have actually stuttered.

"I see." He shook his head sadly. "Hide your iPhones while you can," he whispered to us.

"Kiran, what are you doing?" A woman wearing a long magenta robe rushed up to stand next to him.

"Just welcoming our new guests, Vanya." He grinned at her.

"Well, I wish you'd stop; you're terrible at it." She smiled back, making it clear she wasn't completely serious.

"My heart, Vanya!" Kiran clasped at his chest as though she'd fatally wounded him.

"Shoo," she told him. "You'll miss dinner."

He ambled away from the door, but not before leaning back to grin at me and Anandi. "I wasn't kidding about the iPhones."

Anandi giggled, I stared, and the gorgeous guy disappeared from the doorway. Unfortunately.

I hadn't been around many guys I found hot (Lexi said I was the pickiest person she'd ever met), and I certainly wasn't used to my stomach turning upside down around them. If my stomach *was* turning upside down, it was probably not in a good way.

It was probably because Everett Jones, the biggest player on the planet, was trying to look down my shirt in science class.

"What was he talking about?" Anandi asked Vanya.

"Oh, that's just Kiran." Vanya sighed, still smiling. "He's a guest at the ashram as well. Not very…dedicated to our practices, I suppose you might say. Are you Anandi and Raya? We've been expecting you! *Namaste!*"

"We are! We're so excited to be here." Anandi reached out to shake hands with Vanya, and I found myself wondering if everyone at the ashram had to wear a magenta robe like hers while they were visiting. Kiran had just been wearing jeans and a green polo shirt, but I was getting the impression he wasn't a poster boy for ashram life.

I hoped the robes weren't a deal breaker. I was excited to follow in my grandmother's footsteps, but I was already having visions of my waist tie coming loose in the middle of prayer or something.

"I'll be returning to the train station, then," said a voice behind us. I turned around to say good-bye to Shray and was shocked to discover he had *actually put his phone away.*

"Thank you for escorting us, Shray," Anandi said politely. "I'll be sure to tell Dad how…helpful you were."

"Yes, we'll greatly miss your strong and helpful presence," I added. Anandi snorted.

"Fine. Good-bye." Shray headed back to the taxi like his life depended on getting away from us.

"When we get out of here, I'm totally following him just to figure out who he's been stalking," I murmured to Anandi.

She snorted. "I bet it's Darsha, Dad's accounts manager. Boobs for days," she added.

For a minute I was lost in thought, trying to imagine Shray looking up from his phone long enough to actually have a conversation with a girl. Then Vanya swung the door of the Rishi Kanva ashram open the rest of the way, and suddenly I forgot the outside world even existed.

Walking into the Rishi Kanva ashram was like walking inside a painting. Every inch of the front hallway—all the walls, the ceiling—was covered in color. The entire entryway was a giant mural, filled with pictures of people dancing while gods rose above them, pictures of trees and sky and light and darkness and everything in between. And between the images was a swirl of intricate patterns.

No one was allowed to take pictures inside the ashram, so there hadn't been any images on the internet to prepare me. The only people who even knew this beautiful art existed were people who had stayed here.

People like Daadee. And now me.

Daadee had seen this entryway once. Probably stared at it in amazement the same way Anandi and I were now.

Vanya laughed. "I've been here so long I sometimes forget to appreciate these walls. It's nice to bring in our new arrivals and be reminded of how special this place is. How different."

It definitely was different. And not just because the front hall was done up like the Sistine Chapel. The other immediate difference I noticed was the *quiet*. Having spent the majority of my life in school hallways and concert venues and living in a house with my exceptionally loud brother, quiet was something I usually had to hide in my bedroom to achieve. But the front hallway of the ashram resonated with a strange solitude that seemed to take over every inch, even though I could see people moving around inside. They just seemed to do it without making a sound.

"Are you ready to see the ashram?" Vanya asked. I nodded eagerly.

"Take off your shoes, Raya," she whispered to me. *Whoops.* I'd read that somewhere—no shoes in ashrams. I quickly slipped off my sneakers.

The front hall led into a large common area with colorful stained glass in almost every window and huge wooden beams arching across the ceiling. Those parts of the room looked maybe European (I wasn't sure), but the golden designs and tapestries lining the windows and doors were definitely Indian. The large tiles on the floor were all in primary colors—red, yellow, blue. *Kaleidoscope* seemed like it described both the inside and outside of the building. If *kaleidoscope* also meant "amazingly excellent and gorgeous."

"I'm sure you know that much of the ashram has been renovated over time," Vanya told us. "But the details you see—the glass and the beams—are all original to the building." She smiled proudly.

From the common area, Vanya took us to the great hall, where morning and evening prayers took place. The great hall looked almost exactly like the front entryway, with every piece of wall space filled with pictures and patterns, except that it was also filled with statues of Hindu gods and goddesses. I recognized Sarasvati, the goddess of learning and music, from the sitar she was holding. She'd been my favorite since I was a little kid. At age seven I'd thought a guitar-playing goddess was pretty cool.

Actually, I still did.

We walked down a long hallway, my socked feet barely making a sound on the tile—huh, maybe that was the ashram's secret—and into our bedroom. Which, as bedrooms go, was definitely acceptable.

The tile floor was covered with a large Persian rug in green and brown patterns. Our two twin beds both had quilts on them, and they looked handmade. Part of the ceiling was raised and painted with a blue floral pattern. There was a statue of another god in the corner of the room, but I couldn't remember which one he was.

It definitely wasn't the way I'd decorate my bedroom at home, but the place had a homey, relaxing feel. This was for sure a room I could live in for a month.

"I'll see you in the dining room shortly," Vanya told us, and then left us to unpack.

"Wow." I flopped onto a bed. "We're so lucky this is the ashram Daadee stayed in. They don't all look like this, do they?"

"Hell, no!" Anandi snorted. "Some of them don't even have running water. Living without a shower is supposed to be part of the religious experience or something. Yeah, we got lucky." She fell back onto the other bed and squealed. "I can't believe we're here!" she cried excitedly.

Mostly I was with her. The Rishi Kanva ashram had more than lived up to my expectations so far, and I couldn't wait to stand in that hall with everyone else for the first time and start searching for whatever understanding it was Daadee had found here. And I couldn't wait to find the things she had left behind for me and Anandi.

But at the same time, a small part of me felt like I did the first time my parents dropped me off at summer camp. As beautiful and comfortable as this room was, it wasn't mine. For a moment, as I looked around, all I could think about were Uni and my father's homemade pizza and all the concerts I was about to miss seeing with Lexi. Damn, I even missed Taj.

I checked my phone right away and saw what I'd been expecting to see: no Wi-Fi, and the 4G service I'd had just outside the front door of the ashram had mysteriously disappeared.

Hide your iPhones while you can, I thought.

"Knock, knock!" A British accent sounded loudly through our half open doorway. Anandi jumped off the bed and pushed the door the rest of the way open, and standing there was a well-dressed woman with dirty-blond hair and sparkly blue eyes. "Hi, I just wanted to introduce myself," she said. "I'm Devin. I stay across the hall."

"Happy to meet you!" Anandi held out her hand. "I'm Anandi, and this is my cousin Raya."

"Oh, my gosh, you're actually Indian, aren't you? I'm so excited to share a hall with some!"

I immediately knew Anandi and I were both thinking the same thing: *Did she just say that?*

"Oh, crap," Devin added, suddenly scrunching up her perfectly made-up face. "That was terribly racist, wasn't it? My friend Kate is always telling me, 'Devin, just think before you talk,' but then the words just come out anyway. Anyhow, I didn't mean anything by it. It's just that most of the people in this hall are boring vanilla, like me. There are so many Aussies here; I mean, I guess it makes sense since they're so close."

"Actually, I'm American," I told her. "And my heritage is only half Indian."

Devin brushed it aside. "Oh, well, you know what I meant."

I rolled my eyes—people were always trying to decipher my ethnicity like I was some kind of mystery series on Netflix. Unfortunately, I knew Devin's type. Like this girl Billie from my school. Billie walked around talking about how she protested injustice all the time and how she was going to help "eradicate racism" or whatever. Then one day I saw her hanging out with her friends, who were talking about how great it was that this neighborhood where we all got coffee sometimes was changing and getting too expensive for "those dangerous people." Billie just nodded along the whole time.

So yeah. But maybe Devin would prove me wrong. Stranger things, blah blah blah.

Devin walked us down to dinner and basically gave us a good portion of her life story along the way. She was from Sussex, and her father was some kind of lord. She was a recovering addict. ("Alcohol, of course, not pills. Pills are so *obvi* now, don't you think?") She liked ashram life but thought the people there were boring. ("So many of them are just old, darlings, and I know I'm considered old at thirty-two, but these people are an *old* thirty-two. I'm so thrilled to have some youth around me again!")

Anandi finally managed to get in some basic questions we'd forgotten to ask Vanya. Like about the magenta robes, which it turned out were optional. Thank goodness. Devin said she only wore hers if she was trying to impress someone who seemed particularly spiritual.

"But really, wear whatever you like. Like I was saying, so many of the people who stay here are white anyway," she went on. "Can I touch your hair? How lovely for you." Devin reached up and patted my curls, and I immediately jerked away. "Shit, was that terribly rude again?" she asked.

Okay. So it wasn't looking like Devin was going to prove me wrong.

The dining room looked a lot like the common area but was

divided into two spaces: one for silent eating and a separate place for people who wanted to talk during their meal. Devin led us to a table in the area where we could talk. Right away I knew that if I'd been starting to feel homesick and out of place in my room at the ashram, the dining hall *was not* going to help.

For one thing, Anandi, Devin, and I ended up sitting totally by ourselves. Devin waved at multiple people as they came in, but most of them clearly pretended not to see her or waved and then quickly sat somewhere else. I was not shocked.

Devin and Anandi discussed random things, like the ashram's daily schedule, while I figured out what food my stomach could handle. The ashram had enough westerners staying there that they served both food for the locals and some toned-down versions for those of us who weren't quite as used to having our tongues burned off. As much as I like Indian food, I figured I'd ease myself into things with the less spicy stuff. I had some lentil soup, which was excellent, and some vegetable *momo*s, which I'd had before and always reminded me of dumplings. The ashram served only vegetarian dishes, but that wasn't going to be a problem for me. My mother was a vegetarian—she'd even been vegan for a few years at one point—and Taj and I mostly were, too. My father refused to give up his burgers, though.

Since we weren't sitting in the silent eating area, I could hear snatches of people's conversations. They were almost all in English, thank goodness for me, but I also heard a few words of

Hindi here and there. For a while I tried to figure out how many Hindi words I could understand, but eventually I got bored with that and switched to people-watching.

It did not suck. At the table across from us, an older Indian couple was eating silently. They never said a word to each other, and I wondered if they had taken some sort of vow of silence. Was that a thing here? Meanwhile a young Indian guy kept running back and forth to the food table to refill their plates and glasses.

Huh. Could you hire some kind of special wait service at the ashram? I wondered how rich you had to be to do that.

That wasn't the strangest scene I saw, though. This little kid, about five, who was wearing filthy shorts that were too small for him and a T-shirt that had at least twenty holes in it, went silently through the food line, stopping to bow in front of every dish. He was the only little kid in the dining hall, but he just maneuvered his way through people as if he belonged there, eventually ending up at a table near ours.

I watched as he set his food down on the table and turned to the woman sitting next to him.

And then the weirdest thing happened.

He reached up and grabbed this woman's cheeks between his tiny hands, got up on his knees on the bench so they were eye level with each other, and *stared* at her. Straight in the eyes.

She didn't seem to think there was anything strange about this, and everyone in the room except me just kept eating their food and talking, like a kindergartner hadn't just taken some adult's face hostage so he could have a staring contest with her.

Then all of the sudden he nodded, let go of her face, and sat down, and both of them went back to eating their food.

Like there wasn't anything unusual at all about what had just gone down.

I was starting to get tired by that point—my jet lag was getting its second wind—and I didn't have the energy to ask Devin what the hell *that* was all about. I figured I'd find out tomorrow. I was about to tell Anandi that I was heading back to our room when *he* walked in.

The gorgeous guy.

He sauntered in through the heavy wooden door and stopped suddenly, like he wanted to take everything in before he joined the rest of us. His eyes slowly worked through the room, traveling across every face and every plate of food. Until they stopped.

On me.

Neither of us blinked as he stared at me and I stared back. His mouth slowly wound its way into a half smile that was laced with humor and mystery and a mischievousness I knew I'd never had.

My own mouth turned upward in a smile, and I actually found myself *shivering* slightly. Lexi was never going to believe that looking at some random dude across a room had actually made me *shiver*.

We stared at each other for a few long moments, like neither one of us wanted to look away first. Then someone called across the room, and I turned to see where the noise had come from. When I glanced back, he'd moved across the room to the food line.

The "spell" or whatever it was had been broken. But that shiver still hovered somewhere in my bones.

five

∞

SANSKRIT AND SECRET STATUES

Prior to my time at the ashram, I had not gotten up at four thirty very often. I'd definitely gone to *bed* at four thirty after a great show or party or a long TV marathon with Lexi, but I'd never actually woken up before the sun voluntarily.

But at the Rishi Kanva ashram, the day started at 4:30 a.m. Anandi had mentioned it to me while we were doing trip planning, but I hadn't thought much about it, because who wants to think about having to get up at 4:30 a.m.?

Then our alarm went off the next morning, and not thinking about it wasn't much of an option anymore.

I reached over to make the alarm clock stop chirping at us and realized I didn't know what to hit. I'd always used my phone as my alarm. How did these things even work?

"Good morning!" Anandi popped out of bed like some kind of jack-in-the-box and immediately leaned over to press a button on the alarm clock. It stopped shouting at us, and I breathed a sigh of relief. "Our first morning prayers. Aren't you so excited?"

I glanced out the window, where everything was dark. As it should be. Because it was *fucking four thirty in the morning*.

"Of course," I told her, yawning. "But how are you so *awake* already? It's like the middle of the night."

"I like waking up early," she said earnestly. "I'm going to shower. Make sure you don't fall back to sleep!"

She pranced into the bathroom, and then I had to wake up because the pipes immediately started to wail like someone had attacked them. We'd learned last night that the plumbing at the Rishi Kanva ashram, while modernized, sounded like it was stuck somewhere in the 1920s.

It took a few minutes, but eventually I managed to pull myself out of bed. I was trying to sort through the cotton in my head to figure out where my shampoo was when a disheveled-looking Devin appeared at the doorway. Frowning.

"You get used to a lot of things here," she informed me. "You never get used to this."

I figured she was probably right, but as I showered and changed into jeans and a T-shirt (plain purple—we were going to be praying, after all, and I wasn't sure if people appreciated reading witty T-shirts while praying), the fact that it was the middle of the night felt less and less important. I was about to take part in my first morning ritual at an ashram.

The ashram where Daadee had once prayed.

By five thirty, we were all in the great hall. People just sort of gathered in bunches, silently, all of us waiting. Eventually a bald man in a magenta robe appeared at the front of the room. He started singing in Sanskrit, while a woman with short hair next to him sat down to play some kind of instrument.

I didn't understand most of what he was singing, but the sounds were beautiful, the words repetitive, and the music serene and calming.

When he switched to a new chant, everyone began repeating after him.

The process repeated over and over again, and by the third time or so, I was actually able to keep up and even say the words somewhat correctly—or at least I think I was. I knew this part of the morning ceremony was called *kirtan*. The vibrations in the room from the chanting were so strong they seemed to move through the room with a life of their own; I could almost feel them with my hands. It was like nothing I had ever heard or experienced. Next to me, Anandi had closed her eyes and was focused totally on the chants, murmuring them over and over again while she pressed her hands together in front of her heart. I knew Anandi's family was pretty devoted; I remember when we brought Daadee back to India, they had a small shrine in their home where we prayed. My family doesn't really practice back home—most of my knowledge and experiences came from Daadee.

Devin, who was standing on the other side of me? Yeah, not the same reaction. She looked like she'd fallen asleep standing up. Drool was pooling on her plumped lips and her hair flapped across her forehead like Donald Trump's. At least her honesty was endearing: there was no way I was going to admit to anyone in that room how tired I was by falling asleep. I couldn't help but smile when I glanced over at her.

I followed Anandi's lead, pushing my own hands together and closing my eyes to let the music and words wash over me. At first it felt almost impossible to shut off the normally endless weirdness that cycles through my head. *What's going to happen after this? What's that instrument? I wonder if any bands I like ever use that instrument....It's the most beautiful sound. They should. It would fit perfectly into the Populists' new album....*

But eventually, even my nonstop thoughts were no match for the lulling of the chanting crowd. I actually let myself relax and just listen and respond to the energy that filled me.

It was amazing. I actually felt calm and at peace in a way I never really had before. It was a completely new, yet somehow familiar, experience. And just like that it stopped.

My eyes snapped open, and I realized about half the people in the room had moved. Everyone seemed to want to be closer to the front, where the musician had been.

Then a woman appeared, dressed in a magenta robe and

looking...well, *together.* That's the best way I can describe it. She just had this air about her like she knew exactly why she was where she was and exactly what she needed to do next. She was short, not even five feet tall, but she managed to walk like she was the most important person in the room. Everyone bowed their head slightly as she came through and stepped behind a curtain there.

"That's Guru Baba," Devin told us, leaning over. *Oh.* That made sense, then. The guru was supposed to be like the master of knowledge in an ashram.

Or something like that. I doubt anyone actually calls them Master of Knowledge. Though come to think of it, the Master of Knowledge would make an excellent band name.

"Are we going to have to talk to her?" I whispered back, suddenly panicked. Don't get me wrong—I wanted to talk to the guru. *Eventually.* But I'd just barely learned to chant, and I wasn't even sure which gods were represented in half the statues in the room. What if she expected me to know stuff? Worse yet, what if she saw right through me?

"Raya." Anandi shook her head. "No one just automatically meets the guru. She has to choose you to be part of her audience. I mean, she'd probably want to meet with Nick Jonas right away if he came here. But you're definitely not Nick Jonas." I relaxed and let out the breath I was holding.

Sure enough, Guru Baba invited a select group of people who had been lining up to join her behind a curtain.

Then the rest of us participated in prayer. It felt sort of similar to the chanting, actually, just without the music—the bald man would say something in Sanskrit, and the rest of us would repeat after him. I liked the chanting with the music better, but the prayer also helped calm my ever-running brain. I didn't understand everything he was saying, but I knew a lot of it was in reference to the gods who were sitting around us. There was definitely a reference to Brahma and something else about Vishnu.

I knew not every Hindu ashram had the same rituals or way of doing things. Still, now that I was standing in the middle of one, I was gladder than ever that I'd grown up in a house with Daadee. Thanks to her, I understood a decent amount of what was going on around me. Daadee had been very religious and super dedicated to Hinduism, and I'd spent a lot of my childhood listening to her teach me about various Hindu practices and who the gods and goddesses are. She loved to tell me stories from the *Bhagavad Gita*, which is an important book of Hindu scripture. Once in a while when she'd travel to the nearest Hindu temple, which was over seventy miles from San Jose, she'd even take me with her.

She'd sort of been my only connection to religion, actually. My dad had given up on being a Baptist before I was born, and the only time we went to a Baptist church was when we visited his family. My mom was never very into Hinduism, even though she'd obviously been raised with it. *I've made my own decisions about religion,* she used to tell me and Taj. *Dad and I will let the two of you make your own decisions as well.*

If it hadn't been for Daadee, I also might have felt completely disconnected from my Indian heritage. Mom decided not to teach me and Taj Hindi, even though she spoke it. That used to drive Daadee crazy.

We finally finished prayers, and after that came meditation.

Meditation was actually the part of the morning I had the most practice with. Priya Liston might have given up on her Hindu practices, but she sure loved her yoga classes. I went to yoga with her a lot, and the hardest pose for me, always, was *savasana,* where you're just supposed to lie quietly in silence and let go of all thoughts and feelings. I usually made it all of three minutes before I started worrying about my next math test or thinking about the concert I wanted to go to or trying to remember when my next soccer practice was coming up or wondering why anyone would ever want to eat an Almond Joy bar.

Lately, I'd been spending most of those lost *savasana*s obsessing about what I was going to do with my life.

But if I was going to master the art of completely shutting my brain off and "embrace the soul that exists between the thoughts," as my mom liked to say, it had to be now. I was in an ashram. Daadee's ashram, damn it. I had self-discovery to accomplish. I hadn't come all the way to India to fail at nonthinking.

I sat in lotus position and tried to force myself not to think. I might have made it four minutes.

The thinking started innocently enough: *Look! You're doing it! You're not thinking!*

No! I responded to my inner self. *Stop! That was thinking!*

It doesn't count, my inner self insisted. *Anyway, you turned off some thinking during the chanting.*

Oh, yeah. Yeah, that was good. Speaking of chanting, I wonder why that guy from last night hates chanting so much?

Good question. Haven't stopped thinking about him, huh?

Meditation stood no chance after that. My mind latched on to one thing: Kiran.

I wish I knew exactly why his face kept circling back in my brain or why I'd felt that strange connection to him when we'd locked eyes the night before. I'd never been the type of person to believe in love at first sight—that was all Lexi. Whenever she claimed some girl she'd just met was the one for her (which she did, like, every three days), I'd be the first to tell her it was all hormones. You didn't fall for someone just by looking at them. That wasn't actually a thing. So there had to be some other reason why I couldn't get Kiran out of my head. Maybe it was just the fact that he was completely and utterly gorgeous—hormones, like I always told Lexi. Maybe it had something to do with being in this place, which was so new and different from everything I was used to.

At least I didn't have too much time to dwell on Kiran just then. The person who had led the chanting and meditation called us from our meditative stances as the guru emerged from behind the curtain. Each person who stepped from the curtain brought their hands to their hearts in prayer position and bowed briefly in front of her before going back to their seat. The guru returned the gesture to each one of them.

Someone brought out a large, old-fashioned-looking lamp with a brightly lit flame in the center. This, I knew from Daadee, signaled the beginning of *arti,* the prayer ceremony that would close our morning together. Everyone in the room began to sing as the person swung the lamp in a circle in front of a statue and then moved to circle it in front of the guru and those of us in the audience. They each cupped their hand over the flame and then raised their palm to touch it against their forehead. I remembered Daadee telling me that this ritual was thought to transfer a deity's power to the person in prayer.

It was a short part of the overall morning, probably less than four minutes. But it was lovely and peaceful and one of my favorite pieces of the whole experience. My least favorite piece had definitely been meditation. Once again, I had managed to suck at nonthinking.

Oh, well. There was always tomorrow.

I closed my eyes briefly as the ceremony ended, and the guru dismissed us to our daily activities. When I opened them again, I was looking at a statue I hadn't noticed before: a statue of Bharat, a major figure in Hindu mythology.

A memory jolted through my brain.

"Anandi," I practically shouted, tugging at her sleeve. "That statue, isn't that Bharat? Daadee used to have one just like it on her bedside table, remember?"

Her eyes grew wide. "She'd touch it every night before she went to bed."

We both rushed over to the statue, leaving Devin yawning and bleary-eyed with confusion behind us. "Where are you going?" she mumbled.

Anandi and I examined every inch of the three-foot-tall statue, but no part of it gave any hint as to where our grand-mother might have hidden any random items. I sighed, suddenly grouchy and annoyed that I'd been sure we'd find something from Daadee the moment we started looking. "Nothing," I mum-bled. "Never mind. It's not like we were going to find Daadee's stuff in the very first place we looked anyway."

"It's a good idea, though, looking near a statue of Bharat. I wonder if there are any others here." Anandi frowned and tilted up the statue to look underneath it.

"Were you looking for something?" Vanya, the woman who had let us into the ashram the day before, appeared next to us.

I had no idea how to explain this bizarre scavenger hunt Anandi and I had just started. Luckily, my cousin took over. "Our grandmother had a statue of Bharat that meant a lot to her. We think she might have left something behind for us in the ashram. We were hoping this statue might give us some kind of clue...or something like that," Anandi trailed off.

I half expected the woman to laugh us out of the ashram, but she just nodded. "Well, Bharat is quite important to the Hindu faith. There are statues of him all over the property and this entire area. You have many more places to look."

Then she winked and walked away. And just like that, whatever grouchy cloud had begun to settle over me lifted again.

"Bharat," I told Anandi. "We've gotta find more Bharats."

six

BHARAT-HUNTING AND BIG MEETINGS

We ate while Devin reminded us of the rest of the day's schedule. As ridiculous as her comments were ("Would it be possible to have you show me how to tie a sari I bought in town? I'm dying to wear it for the Indian costume party my friends are throwing me when I get home"), it was helpful to have her around. At least she knew the deets on everyone staying and working there and had the daily routine down, even if she had slept through most of the morning part.

"So you'll do service for a few hours after morning rituals," she reminded us. "I work in the garden. The packets in your room will tell you where you've been assigned. We all do some kind of service. Keep the ashram running and all that. I was assigned sweeping and mopping duty—can't tell you how quickly I had *that* changed. Devin needs fresh air to stay up and running—and this mani has never touched a mop."

Anandi and I grinned slightly at each other from around our cups of tea.

"Anyhoo, then there's lunch, and then free time in the afternoon. Some people do more service within the village here or swim in the outdoor pool or river, but I usually nap. How the hell else are we supposed to get up at four thirty every day? After that, dinner. Then we all sit together for a quick *satsang,* which is where the guru gives a short talk or we all discuss a topic together. Then bed, thank Christ."

"Did you just say 'thank Christ' in an ashram?" I asked.

She waved her hand at me. "Like it matters."

I was assigned to food prep. I left Anandi in the great hall to scrub and dust all those gorgeous paintings and statues while I went to find the kitchen, where an Indian woman wearing the infamous magenta robe was pouring carrots into a pot.

"You must be Raya, our newest addition! You'll be doing vegetable prep with Samaira. Come, I'll introduce you. She can tell you what needs to be done."

I followed her through the rattle and banging of pots and pans to a small table next to a window. It looked out over the pool area, and the girl sitting there was also Indian. She was a little younger than me, maybe fifteen or sixteen, with long, straight hair and absolutely no facial expression whatsoever. Completely blank.

"Samaira, this is Raya. Raya, Samaira. Oh, and I'm Saanvi," she added for me. "I'll let you two get on with it." Then she disappeared.

I eased myself into a chair. *"Namaste,"* I said to Samaira. "What are we doing today?"

"Namaste. Peeling and chopping potatoes." Her voice was soft and calm and heavily accented as she handed me a peeler and a knife, and then dumped a bunch of potatoes in front of me. Then she went back to peeling.

"So. How long have you been here?" I asked.

Samaira shrugged. "Some months." She never looked up from her potatoes.

Okay. That wasn't a very effusive answer. Had I landed in service with another Shray? At least Samaira wasn't actively glaring at me and everything around us.

I tried again. "Do you like it here?"

"It's fine." She said it so quietly I could barely hear her.

Homegirl was clearly not into conversation. We *were* in an ashram—maybe she was there for silence and peace. I decided to stop bugging her and focus on the potatoes.

Good thing Anandi liked talking to me. Twenty minutes into peeling, I was bored stiff by her silence, and I would have taken a long discussion over which Jonas Brothers album had the most artistic merit over this silent treatment *any* day.

Eventually I started staring outside while I worked through potato after potato. The courtyard right outside our window was gorgeous, and I hadn't been able to see any of it the night before. It was enormous and lined on all four sides by the walls of different ashram buildings. The pool stood in the center, with raised garden beds and benches taking up almost every other inch of space. Two of the building walls I could see were the same brown color as the front of the ashram, but the other two were a bright-orange color that reminded me more of the buildings I was used to seeing in India. Across the garden was a large covered patio with stacked firewood and a table holding a bunch of shiny golden pots. I started to ask Samaira what they were, but I stopped myself just in time. I wasn't about to annoy people who wanted their space to be all extroverted with me.

People started coming out to clean the pool and work in the garden beds. I didn't see Devin, but that didn't surprise me. I was willing to bet she napped through a lot of her service. The older couple from dinner were working together as they cleaned and swept the deck area where all the pool chairs were. The man who had been bringing food to them kept following the woman around, and it looked like he was trying to take the broom out of her hands. Only she wasn't having it.

Was he offering to do her service for her? When she didn't want him to?

When the guy made another grab for the broom and she leaned too far away from him, he tripped, almost falling backward into the pool behind him. I couldn't help it. I started laughing.

"It happens every day," a soft voice said. I looked across the table and saw Samaira smiling.

"He almost falls in the pool every day? You'd think he'd ask for a different service."

She smiled. "Not the falling part. His assignment is not pool service. Each day he finishes his own service and then goes out to the pool to beg that woman and her husband to let him help them."

"Why?" I asked incredulously. What was wrong with this guy?

Samaira shrugged. "They are old Indian royalty from an ancient family. People say he wants to be part of their social circle. That he is trying to gain an invitation to their home."

"Kiss ass," I murmured.

Samaira just smiled. Not a very big smile. But maybe it was something.

We went back to peeling potatoes and I decided to try again with the whole conversation thing. "So you've been here a few months?" I asked Samaira.

"Yes," she told me. "It was weird, at first. All the prayer, the schedule. But you get used to it. Now I like the predictability of it. The stability."

I thought about the calm I'd felt during the chants and *arti*.

"If you have questions," she added, "you can ask me. I remember what it was like. To be new here. To be confused."

And she probably wouldn't answer with all of Devin's

accidentally insulting side comments. Excellent. "I do have one, actually," I told her. "What's with the little kid who ate dinner with us last night? The one who grabbed that woman's face?"

She nodded. "That's Vihaan. He lives in the village, I guess, but I've never seen his family. He comes here for dinner a lot, and no one refuses him a meal. Sometimes he plays football after dinner."

"What's with the face thing?" I asked her. "Why does he do that?"

"I doubt anyone's ever asked." She frowned. "Come to think of it, I've never heard him talk."

Weird. So far this ashram had a kid who mysteriously grabbed people's faces, a boy I couldn't get out of my head, and a bunch of stuff my grandmother had hidden in some place that I was determined to find.

Even though I was destined to spend the next thirty days peeling potatoes and meditating, I was starting to think life in this ashram wasn't going to be boring.

After lunch Anandi and I geared up to play detective. "Gotta find Bharat statues," she said as we finished some delicious *peda. Peda*'s almost like this supersoft cookie—sooooo sweet and sooooo doughy and sooooo good. I'd had three.

"For sure," I agreed. "Where should we look first?"

"Vanya said the statues would be all over the property. Maybe outside? I kind of want to look around anyway. Can you take the area by the pool and I'll take the part of the property near the river?"

"Sounds good." Anandi disappeared, and I went back to the ashram entryway to find my sneakers. Where I might or might not have stopped to stare at one of the ceiling paintings for, like, ten minutes trying to figure out which gods and goddesses were in it.

Eventually I made my way outside. I followed a path Vanya showed me out of the west side of the courtyard and down to a rocky path that weaved its way alongside a small, bubbling river, which marked the boundary of the ashram property. Pretty soon I started seeing what Vanya had been talking about: randomly placed statues of Hindu deities near the steps of the path. Most were small, less than two feet tall. I found another one of Sarasvati, and one of Ganapati, who removes obstacles. I stopped to pray there. Maybe he could remove all the obstacles between me and my grandmother's forgotten objects. Eventually I started doing searches of all the statues, just in case something helpful popped up.

I was in the middle of trying to figure out if there was something inside a Vishnu statue when I heard a voice behind me.

"You know, I hear you can feel up statues in the great hall just as well as you can out here."

If I hadn't been sitting down on the ground, I probably would've jumped a foot in the air. I'm easily startled. I looked up, and standing next to me was Kiran.

"Hi?" I said. Only it came out like a question for some reason.

"So? Why are you treating that statue like he needs to buy you dinner?"

I burst out laughing. "Funny," I told him.

"Thank you. Seriously, what are you doing?" Kiran sat down next to me.

I blushed, suddenly not sure how ready I was to tell a very random—and hot—stranger about this bizarre quest I was on. Especially a stranger I was having so many weird feels for. "I'm looking for something," I finally said.

"Something you lost."

"No. Something…someone left for me here."

He nodded and waited for me to go on.

And waited.

Eventually I broke. "My grandmother was in this ashram a long time ago. She told me and my cousin she left some things here for us to find when she came back to visit last year. She used to love a statue she had of Bharat, so we thought maybe she hid the stuff around a Bharat statue. I couldn't find one, but I figured…"

"That you'd paw at poor Vishnu instead." He smirked at me.

"Ha-ha-ha. But yes."

We both smiled.

"So," I said, "you're Kiran?"

"I am. And I hear you're Raya."

"Yup."

"It's good to meet you again, Raya." He dropped back on his

elbows and smiled up at me. "Sorry I didn't see you this morning. I'm not into getting up while it's still dark outside."

"Yeah, I sort of got the impression you're not much for the morning rituals. Especially the chanting."

He wrinkled his nose. "I hate the chanting. Every damn morning at the crack of dawn, all those people making all that noise." He sighed. "I've started wearing earplugs *and* sleeping with a pillow over my head. It helps."

"Why are you here?" I asked him, laughing. "Isn't chanting, like, half the ashram experience? Maybe you should actually try joining in."

"Let's just say I'm not here for the typical ashram experience." He picked up a rock and tried to skim it across the water. It didn't even make one hop over the surface before it crashed against the current and fell in. "I'm trying to improve my rock-skimming game," he added, grinning. "And I heard beautiful girls hang out here sometimes."

I definitely blushed.

"Actually," Kiran continued, "I'm not here by my own choice."

"Really," I said drily. "I never would have guessed. So, tell me. How do you end up in an ashram against your will?"

He plucked a piece of grass from the ground and began chewing on one end of it. "My parents think they're important people. I mean, they *are* important people in Delhi, I guess, just not as important as they want to be. Anyway, I made a video about my school. It was…satirical. Just a joke. Only my parents hated it. And they really hated it once I put it on Twitter."

"You're here because you made a video and put it on Twitter?"

"And Instagram."

"That must have been some video."

"Oh, it was," he agreed. "Actually, even the headmaster liked it. But my parents sure didn't. I'm here to restore the family image, or some bullshit like that. What about you?"

I found myself answering him before I even thought about what I was going to say. "Like I said, my grandmother came to this ashram when she was young," I told him. "She died recently."

His eyes softened, and *gawd damn,* they were even more gorgeous when that happened. "So you're here to honor her memory, then? Or just to find what she left here? And she just randomly left things attached to statues around the property for you to find?"

"Something like that." I grinned at him and wondered what it would feel like to brush the hair off his forehead. That wouldn't be breaking the ashram's chastity vows, right? "Mostly to honor her memory. And then, like I said, she told me and my cousin she'd left some things on the ashram property she wanted us to find. Only she was pretty sick by that point, and she couldn't give us any details about where the stuff *is.* Longest I've ever traveled for a scavenger hunt," I added, making him laugh. "But also..." I shook my head. "I've been...trying to figure some things out. I guess I thought coming here might help." I shrugged, wondering exactly how stupid that sounded.

"Oh, no, you're one of *those.*" He rolled his eyes.

"What's that supposed to mean?" I wanted to sound angry, but I couldn't manage to fit that tone into my voice.

"One of those true believers who hope they're going to find answers or discoveries by chanting every morning." He smirked.

I looked away from him, at the water rushing in front of him. "Yeah," I told him. "That is what I'm hoping for."

We were both quiet for a moment, and I thought about walking away. Sure, he was beyond beautiful, and even sweet in his own cynical way, but our attitudes were clearly miles apart. Plus, something about him made me feel almost embarrassed, like I needed his approval—which wasn't a feeling I had very often with guys my age. It was foreign and uncomfortable.

But also exciting. Definitely exciting.

"How long do you plan to be here?" he finally asked.

"One month, exactly. I have orientation at UCLA later in the summer." And there was no way Malachi Liston was going to stand for me arriving late for orientation.

"UCLA." He nodded. "I figured you were American. UCLA is near USC, isn't it? I'd love to study there someday. They have an awesome film school."

"You want to be a filmmaker?" That explained his scandalous Twitter behavior.

"I *am* a filmmaker," he told me. "Or at least I will be again once my parents decide I'm reformed enough to leave this place." He sighed. "I can't wait. Although I have to say, this afternoon is definitely making me wonder if the rest of my stay won't be so bad." He stared at me while I stared back, and a slow grin spread across his face.

I was blushing again. Where had this guy come from?

Well, Delhi, apparently. Or possibly heaven. Maybe Swarga Loka, since we were in a Hindu ashram.

"What is it you want to study at UCLA?" Kiran asked. "Aside from detective work."

I didn't answer right away, and eventually Kiran nodded.

"Oh," he said softly. "That's what you're trying to figure out. Makes sense."

That surprised me. How quickly, how easily, he understood.

Kiran stood up and began brushing off his jeans. He was wearing a plain polo shirt that matched his eyes but seemed way too subdued for his personality. I wondered if dressing like that was part of his "sentence" here at the ashram. "I have to go take care of something," he informed me. "But I'll see you again, Raya." Then he smiled at me one last time before he walked away.

I searched the property for more Bharat statues after he left, but I couldn't really focus. All I could think about was Kiran. His eyes when they softened. His laugh. I'd never met someone who controlled my thoughts like this. Was this love? Was I turning into Lexi?

I wondered what it would be like to kiss him. I'd been kissed before, but never by someone who looked at me the way Kiran did.

This was *crazy*. I was in an *ashram*. People in ashrams were chaste—no sex, no kissing, no nothing. Not even married couples could get any action. If Daadee was watching this, she had to be so disappointed in me.

But that didn't stop me from thinking about Kiran all through the rest of my failed statue hunt. Or through dinner, when I met up with Anandi, who hadn't found anything, either. Or the first three hours I was supposed to be sleeping that night.

I was failing at ashram life in all the most important ways. And for the first time in my life, failing didn't feel anything but good.

seven
∞

COWS AND CO-PILOTS

My second full day at the ashram was nearly as busy and confusing as the first had been. And sadly, it also began at 4:30 a.m.

When the alarm went off at that ridiculous hour, my first thought was how much I hated getting up while it was still dark out. My second thought was that I'd only been at the ashram for a day and I was already back to being an insomniac.

Anandi bounded out of bed chirping out a cheery "good morning" before she dashed into the shower, calling out something about not being able to wait for morning prayers. I, on the other hand, glared at the shrieking alarm clock for exactly four minutes before I finally worked up the energy to reach over and smack it into silence. Then I moved on to glaring at everything else in the room while I tried to force my poor, exhausted body out of bed.

I hadn't gotten to sleep until almost midnight, and it was all because my mind wouldn't stop wandering around every single aspect of my conversation with Kiran. Every time his face passed through my brain again, I felt this weird giddiness. Guys never made me feel anywhere close to giddy. Ever. Not even Ed Ulster, who had been a pretty decent kisser.

Anandi and I met up with Devin in the hallway, where she was blinking blearily. "Not a damn stitch of coffee in this place, either," she informed us sadly.

I hadn't been missing lattes all that much, but I still nodded sympathetically. Anandi, bless her obnoxious morning-person heart, was already halfway down the hall ahead of us.

I started *kirtan*—"chanting time"—solidly determined in my quest to focus entirely on my spirituality and self-discovery. And just like the day before, it wasn't a total disaster. There was something about the instrument playing during *kirtan*, something about the vibrations that I looked forward to, that calmed and comforted me. As they continuously echoed throughout the room, I was able to relax into it all and just focus on the words coming from my mouth and echoing around me.

Meditation, though? Not so successful.

It started out okay. I focused on my breathing, on emptying myself of thoughts, and I worked hard to put up doors in my mind every time it tried to wander elsewhere. I was all set to start doing some serious mental congratulations for my improvement in focus...and then disaster.

I was doing my best to focus on nothingness when something rattled in the room. Just like that, my focus was all over. *What was rattling? Could breakfast be ready? Maybe that was a breakfast cart! Would Kiran be at breakfast? No. I wasn't focusing on Kiran; I was focusing on nonthinking! I could think about Kiran later. Maybe. Probably I shouldn't, but maybe I could. Time to go back to nonthinking. Except maybe if Kiran was at breakfast I'd just say hi to him?*

Yeah. It all sort of spiraled from there.

By the time we got to breakfast, I was totally confused and more tired than ever. All I wanted was a nap.

"Raya!" Anandi hurried over from the tea cart to our table with cups for both of us. I hope she'd gotten me something with some caffeine in it. "You'll never guess who I just heard is at the ashram!"

"Nick Jonas," I joked.

But Anandi just beamed. "Close," she said. "Pilot McRae!"

That name sounded familiar, but I couldn't quite place it. I must have looked confused, because Anandi gasped. "You don't know who that is?" she demanded. You would have thought from her facial expression that I'd just told her I didn't know who Kim K. was.

"Sorry?" I said. "I mean, the name sounds familiar, but..."

"He used to be on the Disney Channel! He starred in *Ghosts and Lockers*! He knows Nick Jonas!"

Oh, that's where I'd heard of him. *Ghosts and Lockers* had been a popular TV show when I was in middle school. It was about two dead kids haunting their old school's hallways. Lexi and I had watched it all the time.

"That's cool," I told Anandi. "But you know, Nick Jonas isn't on the Disney Channel anymore, and Pilot probably hasn't been on it in years, either. Plus if he's here, I bet he wants some privacy. He won't want tons of people bugging him about—"

"I can't wait to ask him about Nick!" Anandi interrupted me. "I want to know all about what he's like and whether Nick's going to make any more movies...."

Poor Pilot. My cousin was an excellent human being, but I had my doubts this guy was going to be able to focus his time at the ashram on anything but the Jonas Brothers if she had her way.

I grabbed some kind of spicy potato patty for breakfast and worked on getting my head into the day. Devin and Anandi helped not at all by talking incessantly.

In between Anandi going on and on about how excited she was that she was going to meet Pilot McRae and wondering where he could possibly be, Devin wouldn't stop going on and on about the man she'd apparently fallen in love with the night before. At *satsang*, which is this time after dinner where you're supposed to engage with others in discussions about spirituality and self-improvement and stuff like that. Not troll for dates.

Like I was anyone to talk these days.

"He's perfection," she cooed into her tea. "He's a video game designer, but I heard him telling someone else that he has a gambling addiction. Isn't that just too amazing? I simply had to chat him up after the guru was done speaking. We're both addicts, I said. We have *so* much in common. I told him that I just know there is so much we can learn from each other!"

Anandi and I snuck each other a prize-winning side glance after that statement.

Unfortunately for Devin, I had a feeling her Mr. Right didn't feel the planets aligning around their relationship to the same extent she did. When he finally came into the dining hall for breakfast, Devin immediately stood up, calling out, "John, John! Over here!" His face went dead white and he fled the room out a side door without even trying to be slick.

"Must not have seen me." Devin seemed unfazed as she sat back down.

"Guess not," Anandi said without a hint of sarcasm. Until she winked at me.

Food prep started the same way it had the day before: in complete silence. Samaira worked through her pile of potatoes as though I weren't even in the room after giving me a quick head bob when I sat down. I thought about trying to pull her into conversation again, but I didn't want to bug her. I figured I'd try to practice some basic meditation skills while I peeled some potatoes. Clearly I still had plenty of work to do in that area.

Except that four minutes into my "meditation" I was already thinking about Kiran.

By the time I'd let my mind wander again over his laugh, his eyes, his hair, and his grin, I started to think about Daadee. She probably would be so disappointed I was using her beloved ashram like it was some kind of hookup app. Especially when I'd come here with so many goals of my own, and those goals definitely didn't include breaking the ashram's chastity rules.

Daadee, if thinking about Kiran is so wrong, why doesn't it feel that way?

I was still mulling that question over when the royal couple appeared in our window. It wasn't long before their wannabe servant was trailing behind them.

Unfortunately for my personal entertainment, he did not almost eat shit into the pool again. He did, however, nearly get into a fight with the woman over the broom she was holding when he tried to take it away from her.

A slight giggle from across the table brought my eyes off the couple and their minion. "Every single day," Samaira told me, and it was impossible to miss the laughter in her eyes. I studied it, trying to figure her out. Why she was so silent all the time. Why she refused to even speak to me until people were making fools out of themselves in front of us.

I was still studying her—trying not to be too obvi, of course; I didn't want to make things completely weird—when her mouth reshaped itself into a scowl.

I looked back out the window, half expecting to see some kind of horrible sight there.

Nope. It was only Devin.

Clearly she wasn't giving up on the idea that she and John the video game designer were meant to be. He was standing in the garden, trying to do something with a tomato plant, while she whirled around him, talking nonstop and gesticulating wildly.

Poor guy. His face sure wasn't white anymore. Now he looked redder than the tomato in front of him.

"What's wrong?" I asked. "Do you know him?"

She shook her head. "No. But that woman has said very rude things to me. My first night here she asked if I was here because of a drug problem. You know, because I'm skinny. Then she told me she had a therapist who could help with my eating disorder."

Sadly, that sounded exactly like Devin. I couldn't blame Samaira for glaring out the window at her. "She's actually not that bad," I said quickly. "I mean, she is. She won't stop asking me if she can touch my hair because she thinks it's so weirdly exotic or something. But she doesn't actually mean any harm, if that makes sense. She just doesn't really think before she speaks." I frowned as I realized I wasn't exactly doing the best job of defending my kinda-sorta friend. If I could even call Devin my friend. "I mean, take what's happening out there right now. She's super into that guy, and I don't think she's even realized that he's not into her, not at all. She's just kind of...oblivious."

We watched together while Devin continued to circle Video Game Dude, talking incessantly as his face got redder and redder. Eventually he finished whatever he was doing to the tomato plant and rushed off, but not quickly enough. Devin was right behind him.

"See?" I said to Samaira. "She just doesn't notice stuff that most people notice."

Samaira looked perplexed. "But how can someone not even notice when they're saying or doing something terrible to another person?"

I shrugged. "Lots of world leaders do it every day." I thought about all the time I had spent *not* correcting Devin's faux pas, even the more horrific ones. "And maybe we don't call people out on it enough."

Samaira frowned. "I feel bad for the man in the tomato patch."

"John, the video game designer," I informed her.

"He designs video games?" She looked super intrigued.

"You like to play video games?" I blurted it out without even trying to hide the shock I laced through the statement.

She leveled a cool gaze at me. "Why wouldn't I? I'm excellent at video games."

Oops. Good job, Raya. Way to make assumptions. Looked like Devin wasn't the only one who could say terrible things to another person without realizing it. "Sorry," I said quickly. "I think it's cool that you play video games; I wish I was good at them," I added.

It was looking like Samaira and I were back to giving each other the silent treatment, and this time it was all my fault. Until

Samaira said, "Maybe he should design a game where one person has to escape another's crush."

I glanced up fast and saw a hint of a smile on her face. "Great premise," I told her. "There could be levels. Like the first level is you just work together in an office or go to school together or something, but the hardest level is you live together. In an ashram. And you can never leave."

Samaira's smile grew. "You have to hunt for escapes."

"And powers like invisibility."

"You earn points for bad dates."

We spent the next hour or so planning our game, and I don't think it would sell too badly if it ever hit the market.

I went into the common area for lunch hoping to catch a glimpse (or more) of Kiran. No such luck. But I did find yet another person being held socially hostage by one of my friends in the ashram.

Anandi had finally found Pilot McRae.

I discovered them sitting together in the dining hall at the table where Anandi, Devin, and I usually ate. Pilot was trying to eat his lunch while Anandi chucked question after question at him.

"What's he like on set? I mean, is he as sweet and funny as he seems? And does he really collect baseball cards? What do you think about his solo career?"

To Pilot's credit, he didn't even look pained by Anandi's

rapid-fire interrogation techniques. More like bemused. "I mean, I haven't seen him in years," he told Anandi. "But Nick was a great guy back then, so I'm sure he still is. And yeah, he was really into baseball. I wasn't surprised his solo career took off. He's crazy talented."

"Raya, you're here!" Anandi finally looked away from Pilot long enough to notice me. "Look, I found Pilot! He was getting his food when I came into the dining hall, so of course I had to talk to him right away about Nick."

I grinned. Of course she did.

"Pilot, this is my cousin, Raya."

Pilot held out his hand. "Nice to meet you, Cousin Raya."

"Nice to meet you, Nick Jonas's Friend Pilot."

He laughed as I sat down. "You're not Indian?" he asked. "That sure sounded like an American accent."

"It is. My mother's family is Indian, but I was born and raised outside San Jose."

"Cool. I'm from Atlanta. You look like you might be the only other black person in this place," Pilot drawled.

"I'm half. A few of my cousins on my dad's side live in Atlanta, actually," I replied.

"This is going to be the best lunch!" Anandi squealed. "I'm going to get my food. Raya, should I get you anything?"

"No thanks. I'll go up in a minute." I smiled gratefully at Anandi as she left the table in a cloud of excitement.

"She's got great energy," said Pilot.

"She does. It's really nice of you to answer all her questions. I know she seems sort of Nick Jonas…"

"Obsessed?" He laughed. "It's totally cool. Fans are how we get paid to do what we love, you know? I'm happy to have a meal with someone who appreciates Nick's and my work."

I shrugged. "Just be warned that it might not be one meal. The last time I visited India, when we were twelve, I played some Jonas Brothers music for Anandi. Apparently I created some kind of monster."

"So this is all your fault." Pilot shook his head at me jokingly. "It's cool, I swear. Would it be nice to have some down time away from fans while I'm working on myself here? Absolutely. But like I said, it's the job. And without people like your cousin, there is no job."

Wow. I had to admire his Zen attitude.

I got up to find food and almost lost my tray when Anandi crashed into me by the tea cart. "Can you believe it?" she whispered loudly in my ear. "He's here! He's really here! Someone who actually *knows* Nick Jonas. It's amazing. Your thoughts really do become reality, just like the guru was saying at *satsang* last night." She squealed and then dropped her tray onto the counter long enough to give me a hug. "Thank you so much for making this trip with me, Raya!"

"Sure," I called after her as she picked up her tray and rushed back to the table. I decided not to remind her that Pilot had already told us he hadn't seen Nick Jonas in years and that her exact thoughts were not turning into reality. I didn't want to yuck her yum, so I let that one go.

"So, are you going to launch a music career, too?" Anandi asked as soon as we sat down. "I still remember that song the two of you sang to fund-raise for war victims. You had some amazing harmonies. You even hit a high G, didn't you?"

Pilot blinked dark-brown eyes in surprise. "Wow, you know your notes. Do you sing or play?"

For just a moment, Anandi's face clouded, and I was reminded of how she'd looked when she'd told me that *mistakes can be costly* next to the tunnel in Barog. But in just a few seconds, her facial expression rewrote itself with her usual customary smile. "Nope. But I'm surprised you haven't made an album! Did you ever talk to Nick about touring with him?"

The rest of lunch followed almost that exact same pattern: Anandi asking question after question, Pilot barely getting in his answers, me squeezing in words wherever I could, Anandi squealing. Devin never showed up to add to the mini chaos, though, which was probably just as well. I figured she was chasing Video Game Dude around somewhere.

"Hey, this has been great," Pilot said as he got up to clear his tray. "Thanks for eating with me, ladies, but I gotta run. I'm doing volunteer service for that little school across the river in the local village this afternoon."

"You are?" Anandi's eyes widened. "That sounds like so much fun!"

Panic dashed across Pilot's poker face. I decided to throw the poor guy a bone.

"Anandi, I'm so sorry," I said. "I actually already told Vanya I'd help out at the school, and they only needed one more volunteer. I thought doing a little service within the local community would be interesting. I can tell her I changed my mind if you want."

"No, of course not!" To the credit of my cousin's amazing resiliency, she didn't even look disappointed. "You should absolutely do the service. Pilot and I can always talk more at dinner and *satsang*."

She beamed, and Pilot mostly hid his pained expression. Mostly.

"You didn't really sign up for service at the school, did you?" Pilot asked as we left the dining hall.

"Nope, but I'm about to."

He let out a deep breath. "Thanks. I owe you. She's nice, she really is. It's just..."

"I totally get it," I told him, because I did. If there was one thing I understood, it was wanting the Rishi Kanva ashram to be a place for self-discovery. Even if the interruption of my self-discovery wasn't exactly something I was running away from.

Not that I'd had the chance to run from that interruption lately. Kiran never showed up for lunch. I wondered if Daadee was trying to send me some kind of sign.

I dashed my signature across the bottom of the community-service sign-up sheet and then walked along the river with Pilot to the footbridge that would take us to the town's school. I have to admit, it was nice to be hanging out with another person at the ashram I felt so comfortable with so quickly. Like when we stepped into the village and saw cows wandering around a terrace right outside what was probably someone's house, it was nice to have someone laugh when I said, "What even is this place?"

"It's crazy, isn't it?" said Pilot. "Sometimes I think about my relatives and friends who'll never step foot outside Georgia. Like my granddad. Man won't get on a plane. He'll never see a place where some people consider cows holy."

"Or where there are statues of giant hands in airports," I added.

He shook his head. "Just goes to show that normal is all relative, you know?"

I considered some of my classmates back in California, the ones who thought Lexi and I were completely abnormal because we'd rather listen to Coldplay than Travis Scott. "Yeah," I said. "It sure is."

We started our walk into the village, and I wondered if I would ever get over the pure amazingness that was the foothills of the Himalayas. The mountains were some of the largest I'd ever seen; the only thing that came close might have been the Rocky Mountains in Colorado my parents had taken me and

Taj to see once. These mountains loomed large above the village and the ashram, almost as though they were standing guard over them. Trees lined the few roads that made up the main area of the village—mostly evergreens, but definitely some others I couldn't name or had never seen before. This village was small and pretty far from the tourist towns in the area, so I wasn't surprised to see very few cars or people along the paved streets. The buildings we walked past varied in size, shape, and even color, but most of them looked as though they could have used a good remodeling. Still, they were brightly painted, in blues and greens and yellows, and that combined with all the laundry hanging on lines attached to windows made the whole place feel warm and homey.

"So what's the deal with this school?" I asked Pilot as we passed a series of small shops selling everything from saris to soda. "Are we organizing books or reading to kids or something?" Pilot was carrying a stack of books with him that he'd told me had been donated by patrons of the ashram.

"First of all, I don't want you to get the wrong idea about public schools in Himachal Pradesh," he told me. "Just like in America, all the schools here are different."

That didn't sound ominous at all. "What do you mean?" I asked.

"Some of them are doing amazingly well. The government here prides itself on offering some of the best public education in India. But in the smaller villages, like this one, sometimes schools fall between the cracks. You'll see, okay? Just keep an open mind."

Okay. I could do that.

The school was a small building at the opposite end of town. Soft-pink paint was peeling off the walls outside. Pilot opened the door to reveal one large space with a gravel floor, bright yellow walls, and a series of benches spread throughout the room. A group of kids—the girls were all wearing pink and the boys were wearing blue, so I guess that's a thing here in India, too— around five or six years old were sitting on some of them while a woman wearing a bright-red sari held up a chalkboard with both Hindi and English words on it. The setup definitely didn't look as modern as I knew plenty of other schools in India were, but it didn't look all that bad, either.

Then I glanced to the other side of the room, and I got a better idea of what Pilot had meant when he said, "Keep an open mind."

Another group of kids sat hunched over chalkboards at the back of the room. They were probably between seven and eleven years old, but some of them looked older. They seemed to be struggling through some multiplication problems on chalkboards together, but no teacher was helping them out.

It made sense that some of those kids would be practicing basic multiplication, but that math should have been way too easy for the older ones.

"Where are the other rooms?" I whispered to Pilot. "And the

other teachers? And all the other...stuff?" I glanced around. The room had a few cabinets and bookshelves, but not half as many as there were in the schools I'd been in my whole life. "Is this it? This is the whole school?"

"Yeah." Pilot nodded. "It's a small village, and there's a teacher shortage here."

Jeez. I tried to imagine going to school in the same room for years and years on end, sitting on a wooden bench to do all my work.

"Pilot!" A little boy from the multiplication group, maybe around nine years old, dropped his chalkboard and waved at us excitedly. "*Namaste!* Did you bring us more English books?" he asked.

Their teacher glanced over, and her face lit up when she saw us. "Ah, Pilot! You have found more books for us! *Dhanyavad.*" She walked over to us, beaming. Pilot kissed her on the cheek.

"This is my friend Raya. Raya, this is Khatri. She's the teacher here."

"It is lovely to meet you," she said, still beaming. "Would you like to read with the children today? They have been practicing reading Hindi this week and could use more help with their English. Or perhaps help them with their figures? That group is in the middle of their math lesson."

"Absolutely." Pilot stepped into the older crowd of kids, and a bunch of the students immediately stood to gather around him and clamor for the new books.

For a few minutes, I just looked around the room, trying to figure out what to do next. The students not gathered around Pilot were all still engrossed in their math work, and I didn't want to bother them.

Finally I started walking around the back of the room, looking over the shoulders of the students slaving away at their chalkboards. Most of the ones who hadn't run to Pilot were the older students in the room, probably around Taj's age or a little younger. I'd been watching one of them try to work out a double-digit multiplication problem when she glanced over her shoulder at me.

"Can you help?" she asked. "I don't understand this."

"Uh, sure," I said. I'd been doing problems like that since the third or fourth grade. But this girl definitely looked older than that—maybe even sixth grade.

I walked her through the steps, and eventually she was able to solve one of the board problems on her own. "Thank you so much!" she said, grinning widely when she got her third problem right in a row.

"Sure," I told her. The other students around me were still engrossed in their math, and Pilot and the teacher were both working with small groups of kids in different parts of the room, so I figured I might as well stay where I was. "Hey, do you want to read a book?" I walked over to the pile Pilot had left on a bench and pulled out one that looked like it would be right for someone her age.

Her face fell. "I won't be able to read that," she told me sadly. "My English reading isn't that good yet."

I knew all the kids in Himachal Pradesh learned both Hindi and English at school, but Khatri had said they should practice their English. "Do you want me to read it to you?" I asked. That would still be good practice, right? I'd basically learned to read just by listening to my parents and Daadee read to me every night before bed while I followed along.

Her eyes lit up. "Yes!"

We settled on a bench together. "What's your name?" I asked.

"Pihu," she said, her facial expression ringing with a brightness that only Anandi could have rivaled. "I wish I could read this book myself. It looks interesting." She pointed to the one I'd picked out, which had a dog and a boy on the cover. I was guessing the dog probably died at the end.

"Can any of your classmates read it to you?" I asked.

"Not most of them. They can only read those kinds of books, too." She pointed again to the picture book Pilot was holding.

I hoped her reading in Hindi was farther along. That book should have been way below her reading level.

Still, it was hard to worry about any of that once I started reading out loud to Pihu. She was into that book hard-core from the first sentence, gasping whenever a character did something surprising and clinging to me and squealing when there was any kind of suspense. I couldn't help but giggle along with her whenever she laughed at something silly a character did.

She sighed with happiness when we reached the end of a chapter. Just then Khatri clapped her hands from the front of the room. "Students!" she called. "That is the end of lessons for today. I will see you tomorrow."

"No!" Pihu pouted. "Will you be back tomorrow?" she asked me.

"Maybe not tomorrow," I told her. "But I'll be back. Soon."

"Tomorrow!" she urged. "I want to read more!" Then she wrapped her arms around me before I even realized what she was doing. "Come back tomorrow!" she called again as she raced to follow her classmates out of the room.

Then Pilot and I helped Khatri stack the new books he'd brought onto a bookshelf with some others. At least the pile was a little bigger now.

Pilot and I were both quiet as we walked through the village toward the footbridge. "Well?" he finally asked. "What did you think?"

"I don't know what to think." I shrugged. "If lots of the schools in Himachal Pradesh are doing so well, why is Pihu still working on basic multiplication?"

Pilot frowned. "I don't completely get it, either, but from what Vanya's told me, the Indian public education system is in a big state of transition. I mean, you know it wasn't long ago that millions of Indian kids didn't even get to go to school, right?" I nodded slowly. I knew that vaguely. Knew that the unspoken caste system in India meant people in lower classes didn't always have access to things like education. "Well, the government finally decided to fix that. They passed something called the Right to Education Act in 2009. And this area has done a pretty good job of trying to get great public education access for all. But I guess it's just hard to reach everyone."

I supposed that made sense.

"There's a teacher shortage here," Pilot went on. "Like I told you. And some of the more remote villages like this one are still waiting for basic things like school buildings. What makes it all even worse is that when the public schools aren't very good, the parents who can afford to will send their kids to private schools. So lots of the public schools are losing all their students anyway." He sighed. "So it's the parents with no money or with no transportation to get their kids to a better school who have to settle for whatever school is nearby. In a lot of ways the whole situation isn't actually that different from the education problems in America."

I was about to argue with him that American education was *nothing* like this—and then I realized he was probably right. The high school I'd gone to in San Jose was public, but it was also one of the best schools in the country. Even so, Taj's soccer teams played plenty of school teams not that far away from us that didn't even have halfway decent uniforms. The only difference between Taj's team and the other ones was that those kids' parents couldn't afford to live in our district.

I wondered why I'd never thought much about that before.

Most of the time, going to school felt like a chore more than anything else, definitely not a privilege. Sure, I'd always known abstractly that I was lucky to live where I did and go to a high school that had laptops for every student and music classes and good sports teams. But I never thought much about the fact that a decent education was something some people just *got* while others didn't.

"What was your high school like?" I asked Pilot hesitantly.

He looked far away but answered. "I'm a black gay guy from a black neighborhood in Atlanta. I'll let you guess." He kicked a rock in front of us. "That's why I like to help out at schools whenever and wherever I can. I do it in LA, too. I've got a lot now, and sometimes I feel guilty about that, but guilt doesn't solve anything. You know?"

My dad said that a lot. He'd grown up in one of the poorer neighborhoods in LA, and he almost never talked about the schools he'd gone to. Then again, I never asked him much about it, either.

"You going to come back with me tomorrow?" Pilot asked.

Pihu's face lit up my thoughts. "Definitely."

"Cool. It's become one of my favorite parts of the day here. Makes me happy to be alive. Makes me feel better about the times I haven't always done what I should have." Pilot's face clouded over.

He didn't say any more than that, and I didn't ask what he was talking about. I found it hard to believe that too many skeletons were hiding in Pilot's closet, though. He was an ex–Disney Channel star. But I'd also spent enough time on Instagram to know that celebrities aren't perfect.

We were almost back to the ashram when I realized something. "Hey," I asked. "Why wasn't Vihaan there? Doesn't he go to school?"

Pilot frowned. "You know what? I don't think I've ever seen him there."

Interesting.

We separated by the garden. Pilot wanted to go for a swim and I had Bharat statues to look for. Anandi and I had agreed that she'd keep searching the east side of the courtyard that afternoon while I looked for statues along the river. I'd already covered the ashram side, so I used the small footbridge to cross the river and start looking on the other side. *Daadee,* I wondered, *are we ever going to find what you sent us here to look for?*

I didn't have very long to wonder before someone pulled me behind a tree.

eight

LIES AND LUST

"You scared the shit out of me," I gasped as I dropped my hands to my knees and tried to catch my breath. But I couldn't help smiling when I looked at the person standing next to me.

Kiran. Because of course it was.

"What's going on?" I asked.

"Just kidnapping you," he said. Charm was basically radiating from his sexy smile—until it faltered ever so slightly.

"Too much?" he asked quietly. "Seriously, I just wanted to talk to you." He stepped back from me.

"Uh, yeah, a little. Couldn't you just wave me over like a normal person?" I joked as my lungs finally caught up with the rest of me.

He shrugged. "I like memorable entrances."

"Typical movie guy." I shook my head, but I knew the grin on my face matched his.

"So," I finally asked, "why the kidnapping?"

He actually looked a little nervous. "I think I may have found something you'll want to see."

My ears perked up. "What? What did you find?"

"Trust." Kiran turned and started walking up the riverbank.

"Seriously, what did you find?" I called as I rushed to catch up with him.

"You're looking for a statue. At least you were yesterday."

"So? You already knew that. Will you slow down, already?"

"Guess you'll just have to try harder to keep up," he teased. "Because I think I found some statues you'll want to see."

"Can't you just tell me where they are instead of making me run after you?" I asked as I finally caught up with him. Wherever we were going. "Okay, you really do like drama."

"Maybe just a little." And then, no lie, he actually *winked* at me. "Anyway, I was doing some wandering out here yesterday—"

"Probably when the rest of us were in rituals or service," I murmured.

"Probably. And I found a small statue garden in a grove of trees."

"And it has a statue of Bharat?" Now I couldn't even contain my excitement. "No way!"

"Yeah." Kiran grinned at me. "I hoped you'd be this excited."

I didn't even bother to try to contain my excitement for the rest of our walk. Why would I? He'd found another Bharat statue! Anandi and I hadn't managed to find another one on the whole property. This *had* to be the one.

It had to be. Because if we weren't supposed to start looking with Bharat, I had no idea where we were supposed to start.

Kiran led us farther and farther up the river, until I was pretty sure we weren't even on the ashram property anymore. Just as I was about to ask if he was leading me to some kind of serial-killer death, he made a sharp turn and took us into a grove of trees.

Hidden there, under the branches and streaming moments of sunlight, were seven small marble statues.

"No way," I breathed.

"Way." Kiran pointed to the statue in the center of the grove. "And there's Bharat."

"Look, an ashram-resistor who knows his statues." I rushed over to the statue and picked it up, looking for anything that might be stuck to it or inside it. But it was thick and solid, and I couldn't imagine how anything Daadee had attached to it would still be there, even if she'd only put it there a year ago. "I don't understand," I whispered, frustrated.

"What exactly are you looking for? Do you know?" Kiran knelt down next to me.

"Nope, not at all. She said we'd know when we found it."

Kiran nodded and studied the statue for a minute. Then he

frowned, patted the ground where the statue had been sitting, and started digging.

Oh, yeah. That made sense. I joined him.

We dug together in silence for a while before my hand bumped into something hard. "I can't believe it," I whispered. We both began frantically pawing at the dirt until we'd moved enough off it to reveal a small, plain wooden box.

I tugged it out quickly. Kiran sat back on his heels, smiling.

"Okay, you don't have to look so smug," I teased.

"Just basking in my brilliance. When I saw this garden, I thought right away that it might be what you were looking for."

Something occurred to me. "You weren't out looking for a statue you could show me, were you?"

Kiran was the picture of innocence. "I don't know what you're talking about." But the red high in his cheekbones gave him away.

I leaned over and kissed him gently on one of those cheekbones. Another shiver, similar to the one I'd felt the first night we had locked eyes in the ashram's dining area, ran gently through me. "Thank you," I whispered.

"Thank me by opening it." He nodded at the box.

I undid the latches on the front of it and flipped it open. Inside were two pictures. They were older, and fraying at the edges, but I immediately recognized at least one person in them: Daadee.

"It's her," I whispered, running my hand gently over one of them. "My grandmother."

There she was, looking bright and cheery and entirely different from how she'd looked when I'd known her—yet exactly the same. Her smile was the same. Her eyes were the same.

In the first one, she was standing with a large group of women. I recognized the background—it had been taken right in front of the ashram's gate. She was alone in the second, standing in front of a group of trees and the outline of some kind of large box. I had no idea where that one had been taken.

"Why would she bury pictures?" Kiran asked.

"I'm not sure," I murmured. "But I'm going to find out. Thank you so much for finding this. For looking for it. I can't believe you did this for me. Why did you?" I stopped quickly, suddenly not sure I wanted to hear his answer.

Kiran looked away. "I started to think," he said, "that maybe I didn't leave you with the best impression yesterday. You know, when I was saying all those things about people who come to ashrams. I wanted to make up for that."

This boy was full of surprises. "You were honest. Honest is always good." I meant it, too. I was glad Kiran hadn't tried to spin me some far-fetched tale of how much he loved the ashram and how much he hoped to accomplish there just because he thought it might make me fall for him or something.

"I was." His nose wrinkled slightly as he spoke, just as it had the day before, and I told myself it wasn't completely adorable *at all*. "But I also sort of shit on what *you're* trying to do here, and that's not okay. If there's one thing a filmmaker knows, it's not to overshadow the protagonist's plotline."

I rolled my eyes. "Please."

"What?" He pasted on a textbook-innocent grin that he quickly let fade away. "Really, though. I am sorry if I belittled what you're trying to do here. Sometimes I forget that not everyone thinks this place is as insane as I do."

I stared at him, waiting for his own words to finally sink in. When they did, his eyes widened.

"Uh...sorry," he said, blushing. "I could keep trying?"

I burst out laughing. "I can't wait to show these to Anandi," I said as I placed the pictures gently back into the box. "My cousin," I added, in case Kiran didn't know. He nodded, and I figured he'd known that all along. Just like he seemed to know everything that went on in this place.

"So are you happy you found what she left for you?" he asked as he settled down comfortably between two statues, one of Shiva and one I didn't recognize.

My heart sank as I realized something. "I don't think this is what she was talking about." I sighed as I set the box down next to me. "I mean, I think she wanted us to find this. But I think there's more. She wouldn't have sent me halfway around the world for a few pictures."

"But there aren't any more statues of Bharat at the ashram. At least, I'm pretty sure there aren't." Kiran looked concerned. For me, I realized.

"Yeah, I think you're right about that." I moved to sit down next to him as I gently patted the mysterious statue. "But this is a start. Daadee never did anything without a reason. We'll find what we're supposed to. Now that we have this, I'm sure of it."

Kiran nodded and sat back on his elbows, staring up at the bright sky and the sunlight streaming into the grove. The statues were glinting and shining in the moments of sunlight that danced through the trees, and I knew why Daadee had loved this place so much. Why she would have left things behind here that clearly mattered to her. I only wished I knew what else I was supposed to find.

"I still can't believe you," I said, shaking my head as I looked at Kiran. "I can't believe you found this place."

He shrugged. "You'd be amazed what a person can accomplish when they're not doing any of the things they're supposed to."

Good point. "What do you do all day?" I asked. "While the rest of us are in *arti* or at *satsang* or service..."

"Honestly? I spend a lot of time planning for all the films I'm going to make when I finally get out of here."

The words *get out of here* seemed to brand themselves onto my brain. I tried to imagine how I'd feel about the Rishi Kanva ashram if I'd been sent here against my will. If my parents had woken up one day and announced that I was going to be locked up in what was essentially a monastery for months.

No texting with Lexi. No concerts. No going out to eat with friends. No Instagram trolling. And none of it by my own choice. No wonder Kiran had attitude about the ashram.

"I'm sorry you hate it here so much," I told Kiran softly.

He glanced over at me, and a hint of appreciation moved across his face. "Thanks," he said. "But you know what? Things are starting to look up."

I blushed. Hard. Damn cheeks.

"What kind of movies do you want to make?" I asked. Anything to make both of us not notice that my face was not its usual shade of brown.

"Mostly comedies," he told me. "I like making people laugh."

"Like Bollywood stuff?" I tried to imagine Kiran directing people through dance routines while they sang at the top of their lungs.

"No way," he answered, looking horrified. "I sort of hate that everyone in the world seems to think Indian films either have to be filled with musical numbers or depressing docs on how poverty-stricken and horrible all our lives are."

I tried my best to look like I hadn't sobbed my way through all one hundred and twenty minutes of *Lion*. Best. Movie. Ever.

"So what kind of comedies, then? Like *SNL* stuff or dark comedy?"

"More traditional comedy. I love being able to sneak a joke into a scene when an audience isn't expecting it.... That's the best part of making movies for me. Finding ways to use things like camera angles and light and surprise to create something that makes people smile."

The passion that emanated from him as he talked about what

he liked to create . . . it's hard to describe how impressive it was. It was exactly what I was hoping to find in the ashram: a passion like that for *something*. Anything.

"It's too bad you're sort of cut off from it right now," I told him. And wow, did I mean it. I might have needed the ashram to help me figure out where I was going, but Kiran? He clearly didn't need to be at the Rishi Kanva. He needed to be out in the world somewhere, making his movies.

"I do what I can. He reached into the pocket of his jeans and pulled out an iPhone.

My eyes widened. "You're not supposed to have that!" Then again, you also weren't supposed to skip prayers, *kirtan*, *satsang*, and basically every other part of ashram life. Or half wish you were making out with a guy in an ashram statue garden. Or ashram-adjacent. I still wasn't sure where we were.

"I've been sneak-charging it at night while my roommate is sleeping. I mean, it's not like there's Wi-Fi or a signal I can get onto unless I'm willing to walk way into town. But it's got a video camera, and that's all I need. C'mere, I'll show you." He moved close to me until our knees were almost touching.

He pulled up his camera app and hit Play on a video. The screen quickly filled with images I could tell were shot by this river, only they didn't look like the river I knew. He'd managed to do something with the camera, with focus and perspective, to make it look as though sunlight was climbing through tree limbs and into the fast-running water.

"Wow," I breathed.

"This place does have some good landscapes." He sighed. "The things I could do with a tripod. Not to mention all my other equipment."

The video footage ended, and I shook my head. "You're full of surprises, Kiran."

"Kiran Parashar," he said abruptly.

"Huh?"

"That's my last name. We've hunted down tiny statues together. You've seen my contraband iPhone. I figured it was time you knew exactly who I am." He said it as though I should have known who he was all along.

"And I'm Raya Liston," I answered.

He grinned, but it wasn't the same charming grin he'd first worn when he'd pulled me from behind that tree. It was softer, gentler, somehow. More genuine.

"I know," he told me.

Of course he did.

He slipped the phone back into his pocket. "There, I just showed you one of my secrets. Tell me one of yours."

I lay back across the grass. "Not much else to tell. You already know I'm going to UCLA in the fall."

"Are you?" he asked, his quiet voice filled with curiosity. "You sounded like you weren't too sure about that."

I frowned into the sun. "Oh, I'm going," I said. "Whether I'm ready or not. And what else would I do instead? I've always

121

wanted to go to a good college. That's what you're supposed to do after high school."

"Oh. Well, we're all supposed to do a lot of things, aren't we?"

I closed my eyes against a glint of sunlight and his ever-present smile. Truth.

Kiran and I stayed by the river until almost dinnertime, but the conversation was lighter after that. We talked about simple things, like families and favorite foods. I learned he was an only child and kind of a freak for cheese. I told him about Taj and I somehow let it slip that I'd once eaten six hot dogs in one sitting.

Eventually it was time to go back to the ashram. When we reached the area where the river met the back gardens, Kiran gave me a short bow. Anyone else probably would have looked ridiculous trying to pull that movement off, but not Kiran. He actually managed to make it look regal.

"That," he told me, "was a lovely afternoon."

And he was right. It had been a lovely afternoon. An important afternoon. We'd found a piece of my grandmother together. "Yeah," I agreed softly. "Thank you again for helping me."

He nodded. "Anytime, Raya." And then, almost before I noticed what he was doing, he leaned over and brushed his lips across my cheek. Then he disappeared into the gardens.

I moved my fingers over my cheek, feeling the ghostly tingle his lips had left there.

My stomach growled, and I decided it was time to stop thinking so hard and go find dinner.

Anandi was already sitting in the dining hall when I raced in and threw the box on the table. "You'll never believe what I found!" I told her breathlessly.

She popped the dirty box open curiously, and immediately her eyes widened. "Oh, wow," she whispered. "Where were these? Did you find another Bharat statue?"

"Um, well, kind of. I mean, someone showed me where one was," I said quickly. "The box was buried underneath it. Anyway, I don't think this is the only thing Daadee wanted us to find, but it's a start!"

"Yeah, it is." Anandi looked as reverent as I probably had earlier as she pulled the photos out gently and studied them. She frowned. "You think she left us more than this?"

"I mean, I can't be sure. But yeah, I do."

"Well." Anandi grinned. "We're going to find out." Her expression was so intense that I didn't dare laugh.

We started eating, with Anandi glancing around every few minutes to look for Pilot. But he never showed up in the dining hall.

"Sorry," I told her. "I haven't seen him since we left the school." Poor Anandi. First I'd stolen Pilot away for most of the afternoon, and now he'd gone AWOL and disrupted her plans to interrogate him over our meal. Not that I blamed him.

"Anandi?" I dropped my forkful of *saag* and rice and tried to figure out how to break it to my supersweet cousin that she might have terrified a man accustomed to being followed by paparazzi into a hunger strike. "Here's the thing. Pilot thinks you're really nice, and he loves his fans and all, but..."

"But he wants me to leave him alone?" Anandi sent me a crooked smile.

"I think he wants to step away from the acting world while he's here," I said, super fast, like I was trying to rip off a Band-Aid. "You know? Get some real mental clarity. Not think about LA or Nick Jonas or movie sets or anything like that."

"Oh." Anandi frowned. Deeply. "I guess that makes sense. So do you think it's okay if I just ask him one or two more questions tonight after *satsang?*"

I sucked in a deep breath and tried to figure out how to answer that.

"Kidding!" Anandi held up her hand and laughed. "Your face, Raya. That was hilarious. But I get it—I do. I'll try not to bug him so much. I promise."

I let out the breath I'd been holding.

"You won't believe the day I've just had!" Devin crashed into the chair next to me and began fanning her face with a napkin. "John has the most impossible schedule; it's been dead hard getting two minutes alone with him. Did you know he actually meditates for two hours before dinner? I'd be bored off my ass, but I do love a man with dedication and commitment."

I let another deep breath right out again. I was fairly certain I didn't have it in me to crush *two* people's dreams in one dinner. Anandi and I were in the middle of sharing a no-you-tell-her glance when Devin loudly exclaimed, "Who is that adorable young man who can't stop staring over here?"

Happy to move the subject onto absolutely anything other than John the video game guy, I quickly followed her gaze across the room...straight to Kiran.

He was sitting at a long table in the corner of the room with a group of people who seemed to span every possible age range and nationality. I only recognized one of them: Vihaan, the mysterious little boy of face-grabbing fame, who was sitting at the other end of the table.

Before I could look away, my eyes caught Kiran's. He winked, again, and smiled slightly at me—so slightly that I couldn't be sure I hadn't imagined the whole thing.

"He winked at you, Raya!" Anandi squealed.

So apparently I hadn't imagined it.

"Isn't that the guy who opened the door when we got here?" she went on. "The one who kept talking about chanting? Do you know him, Raya?"

"What a hottie," Devin added. "Too bad he's so young; he almost gives John a run for his money. Raya, love, tell us how that picture of youthful masculinity has come to be winking at you from across dining halls."

I was just about to tell them everything—the river, the statue garden, the iPhone films, all of it. But as I pulled my gaze away from Kiran, it traveled somewhere else: Vihaan. We stared at each other for a long moment, his eyes like magnets that locked onto mine and kept me glued to his serious, studious expression.

Until he nodded and looked away. And then I made a choice.

"I've never talked to him before," I said. Okay, lied. Blatantly. "Not since the day we got here."

The weirdest part was that I couldn't have explained, for the life of me, why I was lying to them. Why I suddenly wanted Kiran to be a secret I kept for myself. Anandi and Devin wouldn't have cared. Devin seemed to think the ashram was some kind of dating website, and Anandi wasn't exactly the judgmental type. But something kept me from being honest with them.

"Looks like someone's got herself an admirer, then," Devin said. "Ah, young love."

"Not love," I quickly corrected her. "No love in an ashram. All chastity here, remember?"

Devin snorted. "Darling, it's been my experience that chastity has little to do with love."

Interesting point.

I spent the next morning failing horribly at meditation.

I know—meditation isn't exactly supposed to be a competitive sport. But I'm just not very good at being *bad* at things. Lexi, who goes through life looking for fun first and success later, is baffled by this. *It's not like your parents would be pissed you actually got a B-minus in a class,* she told me once. *So why don't you cut yourself a break?*

Logically, I always knew she was right. No one was going to ground me if my GPA dropped to a 3.7. But I also knew how proud my parents were of my good grades and my volleyball trophies and my piano awards. I knew how hard they'd both worked to make sure Taj and I had more opportunities than they'd had. I just didn't want to squander any of that. Didn't want either of them to ever feel like I didn't appreciate it. And plus I had this weird idea that maybe mastering meditation would help me figure out what I was doing with my life or whatever.

Maybe it would even help me find whatever else Daadee had left behind at the ashram.

So I went into morning rituals determined to focus on clearing my mind. And as per usual, *kirtan* went okay. Something about all that chanting kept me grounded and focused in a way I just couldn't achieve when silence descended over the room.

But then we got to the meditation portion of the morning, and once again, I found myself losing every piece of focus I had. And thinking.

There's probably not much mystery as to what—or who—I was thinking about.

Within a few minutes of the beginning of meditation, my mind had moved completely to Kiran Land. As always, he had been conspicuously absent during the ashram's morning rituals. I doubted his eyes had seen 4:30 a.m. once since he'd arrived. Would he ever take part in any of this? I wondered. Ever try to feel the magic that happened when a group of people worked to bring a set of words to life in a room together?

Probably not. But then again, I had a feeling Kiran already saw plenty of magic in the world—likely in places where I would never spot it.

Anyway, most of my morning meditation went something like this:

Quiet your thoughts, embrace stillness. . . .

I wonder if Kiran will be around this afternoon?

Stop thinking about him! Stillness!

Okay, stillness. You know what's amazing? The way the right side of his lip curls up when he smiles.

You're not supposed to be thinking about that right now.

Yeah, sure, stillness. Maybe later Kiran will want to be still with me. . . .

By the time we got to *arti* and closed our morning together, I was definitely not in a place of contemplative focus. Not at all. Actually, all I could think about was the look on Kiran's face when he'd shown me that statue garden.

I was a little frustrated with myself, and Anandi and Devin eventually stopped trying to engage my grumpy ass in conversation over breakfast. Samaira didn't show up for service, so I spent some long hours peeling potatoes and wondering if I'd ever come out of a meditation feeling like I'd gotten anything out of it at all.

I didn't bother going to the dining hall for lunch; I wasn't really in the mood for Anandi's cheer or Devin's nonexistent love life. Instead, I just grabbed some soup and took it out to the pool. Once I finished eating, I just sat there, looking out over the gardens and water in front of me. Thinking too much. As always. About pictures and the guy who found them. Failed meditations and where I was supposed to look next for whatever else Daadee had left behind.

"You look like all the hardships of living in perfect contentment are finally getting to you," a wry voice said next to me. I squinted up and saw Pilot standing there.

I gestured to the pool, which was a perfect shade of blue, in front of me. "Yeah, it's a hard life."

Pilot laughed. "I'm going back to the school. Wanna come? Tell Dr. McRae all your troubles?"

I took his hand.

"So what's up?" he asked as we crossed the footbridge together. "Your cousin figure out how to sneak Nick's greatest hits into your room?"

I laughed. "They're all on her phone if she wanted to go rogue." An image of Kiran's "illegal" iPhone flashed through my mind. "Nah, Anandi's great. I guess I'm just...I dunno, questioning. Worrying. Are you good at meditating?" I blurted out.

Pilot looked startled. "Good at it? I don't think anyone's handing out prizes, Raya."

"I know that." I rolled my eyes. "I'm just...not so great at letting go. Shutting my mind down, I guess. I've only been here a few days and I'm already worried I won't get anything done that I came here to do because I can't even meditate right."

Pilot's face took on a more thoughtful expression as we padded up the streets toward the library. "I think maybe that's pretty normal for us westerners. It's not what we're trained to do—shut down and let go. Focus on stillness. My whole life's been centered on moving, doing, achieving. Meet one goal, then move on to the next."

That felt exactly right. "Yeah," I agreed. "Me too."

He shrugged. "So you see the irony, right? You're worried about not 'achieving' the perfect meditation and not meeting your goals because of it. You're trying to impose all our western shit on something that is definitely not western."

Whoa. I stopped walking and just stood there for a moment, staring at Pilot. "You're blowing my mind," I told him.

He laughed. "I'm gonna tell you to do something I'm terrible at doing: maybe just go with things for a few minutes. Stop worrying about whether you're getting it all right. Just be."

Huh. Was that what Kiran did? Was that why it was so easy for him to see light and color in places I never noticed it?

I shook my head. "You know something, Teen Award winner? You're very wise."

Pilot gave me a mock bow. "I appreciate that. Now, let's go read books to some kids and discuss something other than my life of past Disney Channel glory."

"Good idea," I said as we started walking again. "I still can't bring myself to tell Anandi that one of my favorite bands is named Bieber Is Not Real Music."

"Oh, they're great," Pilot said brightly, just before his face dropped back into a slight frown. "But I can see why you might not want to tell her that."

I squinted up at him, trying to imagine how someone this intelligent, this kind, had done something terrible enough that he thought he needed to do penance for it. Maybe someday I'd figure out how to ask him what *that* was all about.

Khatri was pumped to see us again, and within a few minutes I was sitting on the floor with Pihu and some of her classmates, listening to them read aloud.

"I want to try this page!" Pihu squealed excitedly when it was her turn in the circle. I frowned. We'd just hit a particularly hard part in the short book we were all reading together, and I knew enough about Pihu's English skills by that point to know she didn't understand most of those words yet. "I can read this one if you want to wait," I told Pihu gently.

"But I want to try!" Pihu answered brightly. "Some of the words are hard, but who cares if I get them wrong anyway? My dad says it's okay if I don't know things. Saying the words wrong first makes me learn how to say them right." Then she immediately launched into the first word, stumbling through the sounds until she figured them out.

Meanwhile, I sat back and wondered if an eleven-year-old had just nailed down exactly what I was doing wrong in life.

After I was done working with that group, Pihu and I read another chapter from the book we'd started together the day before. "I love this book so much," she sighed as we finished a page. "I can't wait until I can read it myself someday."

"You'll get there," I encouraged.

"I know." Pihu nodded seriously. "When reading is hard, especially in English, I just remind myself that once I couldn't even walk. I learned how to do that, and I'll learn how to do this, too."

Out of the mouths of babes, my dad would have said. But seriously. How had this girl gotten so wise? When she hugged me at the end of the school day, I gave her the hardest hug back that I could manage.

I was quiet on the walk back to the ashram, thinking about Pihu and Daadee and meditation and failure and life paths and a whole mess of things that made no sense separately or together. I didn't even notice who was standing next to the footbridge when Pilot and I got back to it.

"Hey, man." Pilot embraced Kiran in a bro hug. "Do you know Raya?"

"We've met." He smiled at me, always shyly. "Is she helping out at the school with you?"

"You know about the school?" I asked him.

"Only what Pilot's told me. We talk." He shrugged. "Gotta discuss film stuff when I can, and Pilot's the only one around here who's all that interested. He's gonna star in my first movie someday."

Pilot nodded. "You know it, man. So how'd you two meet?"

Kiran and I both looked at each other. I was trying to figure out how to put words together to describe whatever was going on between the two of us when Kiran answered. "I opened the door when she got here," he told Pilot, his eyes still glued to mine. "I was the one who let her in."

"Yeah," I agreed softly. "He did."

I suspected Pilot was trying very hard not to smirk at us. Then he gave us both a slightly awkward glance before abandoning us at the edge of the footbridge. "I'm gonna go grab a nap," he said. "Catch you guys later." He quickly disappeared.

"Subtle," I said drily.

Kiran laughed and grabbed my hand. "Sometimes subtle is overrated. Let's take a walk. I had an idea last night."

We walked along the river together, our fingers still lingering against each other's. "So what's your idea?" I asked.

Kiran frowned. "Stop," he suddenly ordered.

"Huh?" I repeated.

"That shot—you, with the river behind you. It's perfect. Just needs the right focus. Mind if I take some footage?"

I nodded stupidly.

"I wish I had my light meters," he murmured, circling me with his iPhone in his hand. "Good thing you're perfect enough to make up for that."

Perfect? What? Really? *Far from it*, I thought. But maybe Pihu was onto something where imperfections were concerned.

Kiran finished up whatever shots he was taking, and we ended up sitting next to the river, listening to the sound of the gurgling water while Kiran gently tossed rocks into it.

"Can I see?" I asked him, gesturing at the phone that was still in his hand.

"Of course." He pulled up the app and pushed Play on a video where I slowly brushed my hands through the water while the color and shape of the land moved around me. He'd done something to the speed and look of the video to make it appear as though I was the center of everything beautiful around me: like I was anchoring it or something.

"Oh, my God," I whispered. "How did you make me look like that?" I was 100 percent certain I had never looked like that in a video anyone else had ever taken of me.

He brushed a loose hair off my forehead. "Easy. I just high-lighted what's already there."

I didn't have any idea how to answer that. I stared at him for a long time while he looked back, studying some part of me. And I had a sudden feeling it might be a part I'd never seen before.

"You never told me your idea," I finally blurted out, anxious to break the tension that seemed to be building between us.

"Oh!" He grinned at me, and the entire landscape seemed to lighten even more with his smile. "I was thinking. You know how you said you thought there were more things your grand-mother left you here, but you're not sure where to look next?"

"Yeah."

"Well, I was thinking. We didn't really look at what was *behind* her in the pictures, did we? I mean, the first one was pretty obvious, but the second one..."

Oh, my God, he was right. "Kiran," I whispered. "You're a genius."

"What can I say? You bring out the best in me, Raya Liston."

nine

∞

The next morning, Anandi and I obsessively studied Daadee's second photo over breakfast.

"There's something there," she murmured. "Like a large box? And more statues, maybe? I can't tell."

I shook my head. "We haven't seen anything like that on the ashram property." By that point we'd walked most of place looking for statues of Bharat.

"I think we're going to have to ask some people for help with this one." Anandi handed me the picture. "Ask people during service today if they've ever seen this place before. I'll do the same thing tomorrow."

"Sounds good. We'll just keep detective-ing this ashram up."

Anandi laughed and rolled her eyes at me.

Devin, meanwhile, had decided it was time to take action, as she informed us over breakfast. "I just don't think John's a man who notices when someone's sending him signals," she complained to me and Anandi. "It's like he's oblivious to me."

I hesitated. "Devin," I finally said, "have you wondered if maybe John just isn't interested?"

Devin scoffed. "Don't be ridiculous. It's not as if the pickings are enormous here, and I'm clearly one of the few of us who's bothering with hair product. Except you two, of course," she added hastily.

So much for me trying to be real and honest.

"Maybe he's not interested in a relationship right now?" Anandi suggested gently. "I mean, he *is* in an ashram."

Devin scoffed. "What else are you supposed to do here all day?"

I wondered if Devin realized she was possibly wasting a lot of money on this whole ashram experience. Anandi and I didn't answer her.

Samaira was back at service and back to her vow of silence. She barely even nodded at me when I sat down. Luckily for me and my brain's neurons, which were desperate for stimulation three potatoes in, the older couple and their lackey were back.

The episode that day was a doozy. The husband and wife were definitely having some kind of fight. He kept pointing at her, and she was gesticulating so wildly I was a little worried her large magenta robe was going to fall off her thin frame. (That fear was still reason number one why I refused to wear one of the things.) The volunteer servant was standing off to the side, glancing rapidly back and forth like he was watching a tennis match and wasn't sure who to cheer for.

"I wonder what they're saying," I said to Samaira. "What do you think they could be fighting about?"

At first Samaira just stared out the window at the couple, frowning. After a few moments, I gave up on her ever answering me. I was peeling my third potato since asking the question when a soft voice said, "Maybe whether they should push their helper into the pool once and for all?"

Her answer was so unexpected I burst out laughing.

Saanvi glanced over from where she was stirring something at the stove, but when she saw us both smiling, she just waved and went back to what she was doing.

"Love it," I told Samaira. "I can just imagine it." The husband began shaking his hands over his head wildly, and I somehow managed to say in a baritone voice with a deep Indian accent, "We have no other choice; he is beneath our caste! He will never leave us alone otherwise!"

Samaira giggled. When the wife responded by crossing her arms across her chest and shaking her head, Samaira replaced whatever her real response was with, "I just don't think murder is the answer, husband."

I deepened my baritone. "We won't kill him. A simple coma will do, wife," I ad-libbed while the husband shook his own head in response.

Samaira laughed loudly.

We played out the rest of the scene in full. In our version, the argument ended with the wife admitting that she actually liked having a hot, young man follow her around all day and the husband storming away, shouting about how he could never compete with the younger man's perfect ab muscles. By the time they both went their separate ways, the wannabe servant looking completely unsure who to follow, I was laughing so hard my sides hurt. Actual tears were running down Samaira's face.

"This," she said, hiccupping, "is definitely the most fun I have had in months. You make me feel so normal, Raya."

Her words shocked me right out of the laughing fit I was in. "What?" I asked. "Why don't you feel normal?"

Just like that, Samaira's face was back to the stoic piece of ice I'd first seen when I walked in the room. "I have to go," she said quickly, and then disappeared before I could say anything else.

I spent lunch trying to figure out what Samaira had been talking about and whether she'd ever talk to me again. Probably not.

Pilot didn't eat lunch in the dining hall, so I met him on the footbridge for service at the school. Naturally, I showed him the picture and asked him if he knew anything about the background.

"Sorry, no," he said as he handed it back. "I've been here for a few weeks, and I've never seen that place before. But hey, at least you found a starting place. That's something. No offense, but I sort of thought you were crazy when you told me you were going on a treasure hunt for something your grandmother left here."

I sighed. "Yeah. Me too." I shrugged. "To be honest, we wouldn't have found anything at all so far without Kiran. He's the one who tracked down that statue garden."

"Ahh." Pilot wiggled his eyebrows suggestively.

"He seems like a good guy," I hedged, blushing. We walked past several homes, one with a cow hanging out happily in its front garden area, and I decided it was time for a subject change. "Sometimes it seems so random that a royal decided to build an ashram here, in this village," I said, thinking of the statues and the more-than-beautiful pool back at the ashram and what a contrast that entire scene was to the shabby buildings we were walking past.

"Yeah," Pilot said, "but don't forget that there are a lot of *really* nice villages and towns in this area of the country. Who knows if this village has always looked this way? Plus I sort of get the feeling that in India they're not too thrown off by seeing metaphorical stacks of money next to starving people. We're kind of the same in the US to a degree. I volunteer at this school in LA where a huge percentage of the kids have been homeless at least once in their lives. Just a few miles away, people are living in houses worth millions of dollars. Plus it's not like this village is all *that* poor. You've seen some of the shadier parts of Delhi, right?" I nodded. "Then you've seen how much worse it can get."

I thought about the children at the train station begging for money. That was probably the type of scene a lot of Americans envisioned when they thought of India, but Pilot's comment about the LA school made me think that America still had a long way to go when it came to taking care of its own. My parents hardly ever took Taj and me to the part of LA where my dad's from, even though a lot of his family still lived there. And when we did visit, we usually stayed in the nicer area, where there are plenty of ritzy hotels. My dad didn't even like us driving to his cousin's house after dark. *It's not safe*, he always told us. *I don't live here anymore. I don't know the systems.*

I remembered thinking during one trip how weird it must be to need to know "systems" just to survive. Especially if you were just a little kid without a dad and with a mom who worked two jobs, like my dad had been.

But most of the time I just forgot about all that and went about my life in the California hills. It seemed like India sort of operated on a similar system. Maybe just with a lot more poverty.

We arrived at the school and quickly got sucked into helping out with simple math problems and sentence deciphering. Eventually Pihu curled up with me in the corner to listen to me read more of our book.

"I can't wait to see how it ends," Pihu told me when Khatri called for the end of the school day. "Would it be bad if we just skipped ahead and looked at the last page?"

"That's cheating," I told her. "Don't worry. We'll get to the end soon." It was a short book, and we were already almost halfway through it.

"I hope so. But what if you have to go back to America soon?"

141

Her words tugged at my chest in a way I hadn't quite expected. "Don't worry. I'll be here a little longer," I assured her. "I still have to find something my grandmother left for me here." Maybe knowing I still had things to do in India would make Pihu feel better.

"What are you looking for?" she asked curiously.

"I'm not sure," I told her. "Something she left at the ashram for me and my cousin."

Pihu's eyes widened. "She left something behind for you? Like a treasure?"

"Maybe. We already found some pictures she left for us. We think she left us other things, too."

"Ooh, it's a mystery." Pihu sat up eagerly, and I laughed.

"Kind of. I'm hoping she left me something that will give me some...ideas."

"Ideas about what?"

"Ideas about what I want to be someday." It was amazing, how easy it was to articulate that thought to Pihu, when I could barely articulate the concept to myself most of the time.

"Oh." Pihu nodded. "I already know what I want to be. A teacher, just like Khatri. Just like you."

My cheeks warmed with pleasure, and for a long moment I almost couldn't speak. Pihu thought I was her teacher?

"Pihu, I'm not your teacher. I'm just a volunteer."

Pihu shrugged. "You teach me things. That means you're my teacher. I want to be just like that someday." She clutched our book to her chest. "Plus teachers get to read all the time. I want to read all the time."

I grinned. "I can definitely see you as a teacher, Pihu," I told her.

"Thank you," she said seriously. "And I bet you find the mystery treasure. Do you have any clues?"

I pulled out the picture Anandi had handed me that morning and showed it to Pihu. "We think it might be in this spot, but we're not sure where it is."

"Oh!" Pihu's entire smile, which already could have lit up a small city, grew three shades brighter. "I know where that is! My mother takes me there sometimes." She grabbed my hand and stood up, her small body taking me with her through sheer force of will. I followed her outside to the front of the school, where she pointed to a high hill just past the end of the street we were standing on. "It's up there!"

I said good-bye to Pihu and was on my way to that hill basically *a second* later. Only I didn't quite make it to the shrine without stopping. I was just passing the place where I usually turned to go back to the ashram when someone grabbed my arm.

"What?" I gasped as I bent over my knees, panting loudly. No wonder athletes trained at altitude. Usually I was a halfway decent runner. I looked up to see who had stopped me, even though I was fairly certain I already knew the answer.

Kiran grinned, and a dimple I somehow hadn't noticed before popped up in his left cheek. "In a hurry?"

"I found it!" I told him excitedly, pulling the picture from my pocket. "Pihu, one of the students, she knows where this is!" I pointed to the hill ahead of us, where my Daadee's treasure waited. I hoped.

Kiran's eyes widened. And then he started running, too.

We raced through the streets, past shopkeepers and pedestrians and cows that didn't seem bothered at all to have random people sprinting past them as though their lives depended on it. When we got to the hill, we finally had to slow down. The climb wasn't exactly a trek up Everest, but it was no joke.

"Do you think it will still be here?" I asked him as we quickly hiked the path. "Whatever it was she left us?"

"Yes," he answered without a trace of doubt.

"Why?" I asked, startled by his answer.

He shrugged. "I just know it will be. It feels like that's what's supposed to happen next for you."

I hoped he was right.

Just then, we came over the crest of the hill and saw it: a small wooden shrine, in the shape of a large box, surrounded by statues that were sitting among the trees. It looked exactly like the one in my grandmother's picture.

"Oh." I dropped to my knees and prayed. To my grandmother, and to all the gods she had worshipped with all her heart.

Kiran stood next to me, head bowed. When I finished and stood, he nodded at me. We both knew what came next.

We walked the periphery, examining the statues closely. Bharat was the fifth one we came to. Kiran easily lifted him out of the way, and we both began digging.

It was only a matter of minutes before we found the box.

Kiran reached it first and lifted it out reverently, almost as if he'd struck gold in that ground. He did the work of setting the dirt and statue back in place while I brushed off the worn pine box he'd removed. It looked exactly like the photo box we'd found, only larger.

When he was done putting the holy place we'd just disturbed back together, he shot me a brief grin. And then I opened the box.

Inside were two small journals. Each one said DIYA on it in large letters.

Daadee's first name.

"We found it," I whispered. "We found *them*." I flipped a few pages into both books. One was filled with poetry written in Hindi, and the other one was full of dated journal entries written in English. The first date looked to be from when Daadee would have been about my age. I ran my hand over the familiar handwriting—the loopy *H*s, the wide *A*s and *O*s. "I can't believe we found these."

He smiled. "I guess you were meant to find them."

"*We* were meant to find them," I corrected.

Kiran blushed. "I'm glad I could help. Plus, as you've pointed out, I don't do much all day. So I had the time to—"

Before he could finish his sentence, I leaned over and kissed him.

It wasn't a hard, sloppy kiss, like the ones I was used to giving and getting in movie theaters or outside school classrooms. It was soft and warm, like the perfect mountain summer day surrounding us; spicy and sweet, like the tea I drank every morning after service. It was everything I had never thought a kiss could be and everything I knew a kiss should be all at once.

Until we finally broke apart and I realized what I'd just done: I'd kissed Kiran. I'd kissed Kiran, and I'd definitely broken the ashram's chastity rule.

Or maybe I'd broken that rule the moment Kiran opened the door to the Rishi Kanva ashram.

"Wow," Kiran said, breathing hard.

"Yeah," I agreed. Suddenly everything about the moment felt overwhelming: the box, the kiss, the broken vow. I stood up fast. "I have to go," I said awkwardly, and then, before I could glance at Kiran's face and change my mind, I took off down the hill toward the ashram.

I could just imagine Lexi's response when I told her about this: *Way to kiss and run, Rayers!*

ten

∞

SATSANG AND SAUCY SECRETS

Anandi and I stood over the two journals, staring at them as though they were the Holy Grail. And for us, they might as well have been.

Or the Hindu version, at least. I wondered if there *was* a Hindu version of the Holy Grail. I was going to have to google that once I had access to modern technology again.

"I still can't believe you found them." Anandi ran her fingers gently over each book, shaking her head in awe. "I can't believe your student knew about that place in the picture."

I just nodded. I'd told her the story but conveniently left out the part about Kiran's help. Oh, and the part where I made out with him.

The whole thing reminded me of something Aunt Charlise,

my dad's sister, liked to say: *You plan, God laughs.* Only whose God exactly, and why the hell would he laugh at me *in a house of worship?*

"Have you read either one of them?" she asked. We were sitting on my bed in our room, where I'd rushed to find her as soon as I got back to the Rishi Kanva.

"No, not really. I just looked inside them. One's in Hindi, and it looks like it's full of poems. The other is her journal. That one's in English."

Which had surprised me, a little, but Anandi said Daadee's parents had both spoken English and that she'd learned English and a few other languages when she was very young. Seriously, why do American kids learn only one language?

I opened the journal and began reading aloud from the first entry there.

May 27

I have arrived at the Rishi Kanva ashram!

It is a strange sensation to be in this place after dreaming of it for so long. When I think of all the days I argued with Mother and Father about coming to this place...well, only Mother, really. Father has always been so supportive of my dreams, as unconventional as they may be. Mother remains determined to marry me off to Sanjay

Sadana so that I might spend my life in a state of perpetual boredom, propriety, and respectful indifference. She has clearly never noticed that the boy talks of nothing but accounting and I could never fall in love with him. Nor does she care.

All that hardly matters now, though. When Father left me at the ashram's doors this morning, he held my face in his hands and whispered, "Go become what you are meant to be." In that moment, I knew that I would accomplish this dream of mine.

I will become a guru.

Throughout my entire life, my love of Hinduism has spoken to me more strongly than anything—even more strongly than my family. I am never happier than when I am in the presence of peaceful knowing. Here, at the Rishi Kanva ashram, my entire being feels at peace. Centered.

My mother may not believe that women are meant to become gurus, but I hardly care. And thankfully, the people here do not, either. That is why I have traveled to this place, to this ashram. Not every ashram is so accepting of a woman who wishes to put faith as her highest life priority. I must see this journey through to the end. I know what I must dedicate my life to. I believe I have always known.

More than ever, I believe the Rishi Kanva ashram will help guide me on my path.

Holy Sarasvati. Daadee had wanted to become a *guru?*

"This doesn't make any sense."

I agreed wholeheartedly with Anandi on that one. I nodded.

"She married Daada."

I nodded again.

"They had kids right away. Her faith always meant a lot to her, but she never..." Anandi shook her head.

"She never said anything," I whispered. "I never had any idea she trained to be a guru." Except a part of me was screaming that this wasn't so strange at all. That the journal entry *did* make sense, when I really thought about what I knew of my grandmother: her intense love of her faith, her ability to read and study aspects of Hinduism for days at a time without a moment of boredom or disinterest. It wasn't crazy at all, really, that she'd wanted to be a guru.

What was more confusing was why she hadn't finished her training.

Anandi flipped open the book of poetry and began translating the first poem out loud for me—which I appreciated, since my knowledge of Hindi was still somewhere around the kindergarten level. The language in it was almost mysterious. Songlike, and filled with imagery that I wasn't completely sure I understood even though it sounded beautiful. Anandi sighed when she came to the end of it. "Wow. It says that was by Mahadevi Varma. I've heard of her, but I've never read any of her stuff. The one on the next page is by someone else.... I guess Daadee must have recorded all her favorite poetry in this book. Listen."

The next poem was just as beautiful as the first. But even as Anandi's face glossed over with happiness while she read, I realized I felt nothing like I had when I'd read the words in my grandmother's journal.

When Anandi closed the poetry book, she held on to it. I picked up the journal. Without even speaking to each other, we both knew which book belonged to which person.

Of course, I couldn't read one of them. But even if that hadn't been the case, I still think she would have held on to the book of poetry and I would have taken the journal.

"I want to read this slowly, if I can," I told Anandi. "Savor it. No more than a few entries a day...or something like that. I want to hold on to her for a while this time." I couldn't stand the thought of reaching the end of this journal and saying good-bye to my grandmother for a second time, and I was 100 percent sure that was how reaching the last page of Daadee's words would feel.

"Same," Anandi told me.

"I'll tell you everything I learn," I added.

"Me too. Of course."

We both opened our respective books again, and I reread that first entry once more, studying the handwriting and remembering the voice behind it. My grandmother had wanted to become a guru. Had traveled all the way to the ashram to make that happen. I wondered if even my mother knew that.

For now it will be our secret, Daadee, I promised my grandmother. *Only you and I and Anandi will know. Until I'm sure you want me to tell others.*

I read on in the journal, promising myself I would stop after a few entries. I had to make this time with Daadee last. I *had* to.

June 15

You will hardly believe what happened today, my journal. I met the most impertinent man! I was attempting to lead satsang in the great hall after dinner. The guru here has been most excited by my eagerness to accelerate my spiritual studies, and he kindly allowed me to direct the evening's discussion. I spent days planning the topic, and eventually settled on the story I love so greatly: that of Bharat's beginnings. Given the many, varied lessons that reside within that story, I was confident this topic would ensure a satsang filled with wonderful conversation.

Sadly, it did not.

Very shortly after we began the discussion, a man began questioning the importance of the story. He seemed to feel that Bharat's beginnings were not worth discussion, and he continually tried to steer the discussion toward a larger discussion of moksha—which made absolutely no sense, of course. I was infuriated, though I did my utter best not to show it.

Then he made things even worse! After *satsang* ended, as I walked back to my room, he followed me!

"I hope you didn't find my questions and observations too disruptive," he said, smiling widely at me. Smiling! How dare he!

"Of course not," I assured him. I wondered if gurus are expected to lie often; that would seem to be a strange contradiction. "Conversation like that is what *satsang* is for." More lying, of course. Inside I was seething.

He took my hand then and kissed it. Kissed it! Can you even imagine? In an ashram, no less, where chastity is paramount! I removed my hand as quickly as possible.

"I beg your pardon, of course," he told me. "I only meant to apologize if I have indeed offended you. I would never wish to offend a lady as lovely and interesting as you."

I could hardly believe what I was hearing! Then he was gone before I could even respond. I can't begin to imagine what I will say to him when I see him next!

I peeked up out of the journal, ready to laugh with Anandi about what I'd just read. But she was engrossed in Daadee's book of poetry, so I found myself contemplating the words on my own. *I met the most impertinent man....*

I smiled as I thought of Kiran at the ashram doorway, asking if we liked to chant.

And then I went back to the journal. *Just one more entry*, I promised myself.

June 30

My journal, you shouldn't even believe what has occurred since last I wrote. The strangest things have been afoot. The man I wrote of—the man of impertinence, the man of rude skill, the man who drove me to lies and nearly broke our promises of chastity—has become of great importance in my life.

It is astonishing, I know.

What happened is this: the day after he nearly destroyed my first satsang, he came to apologize again. He meant no harm, he insisted. He merely enjoyed a strong and thorough discussion. He seemed sincere, and I could hardly begrudge him that point. I, too, enjoy satsang to be a time of deep and meaningful conversation. So I agreed to have dinner with him.

So we did. And then lunch the next day. And then breakfast the day after that. Before I even knew what was happening, we were taking every meal together.

Lately I find that I hardly want to be apart from him. We attend satsang together, frequently walk to morning prayers together, and occasionally he even joins me in my service. I have learned a great deal about him. He is from Varanasi, and he is studying to become a barrister. He is spending some time at the ashram in hopes that it will clear his focus and give him the spiritual strength necessary for his upcoming career, which is sure to be a taxing one.

I find myself wishing I could spend every waking moment with him, even though I know to wish for such a thing is wrong. I have a path here, one I have always dreamed of fulfilling. I cannot let my plans to become a guru be derailed by whatever I feel for this man.

I know I should cease spending so much time with him, but I find doing so nearly impossible. Whenever he meets my eyes across a room, I immediately feel as though I cannot look away. As though our eyes will remain locked together until I go to him.

I pray every morning to find the separation I need, but thus far I have not found the strength to cut him from my days.

Tomorrow I will simply pray harder.

Wait—Daada had been a barrister. From Varanasi.

She wasn't talking about Daada, was she? No way. Why wouldn't Daadee have told me she met my grandfather in this ashram?

One thing was certain, though: Daadee had fallen for somebody here. Somebody who had clearly meant a great deal to her. And she'd struggled with whether to let that connection move forward.

For a few minutes, I couldn't even let go of the journal and sit up long enough to ask Anandi what she thought about this man. All I could do was clutch it to my chest while one scene played over and over in my mind: me kissing Kiran and then running away.

"Does your neck hurt or something?"

I jerked my head up and looked over at Anandi, who was frowning at me in concern instead of eating her dinner. *Oops.* So much for trying to keep myself from looking over at Kiran, who was sitting across the room.

"Uh, just a cramp," I told her. "Can I get you more tea?"

"You've already filled it twice," Anandi said, showing me her full cup. "The last time was, like, four minutes ago. Raya, you sure you're okay?"

"Obviously she's suffering from the same thing we all are." Devin groaned and rubbed her temples. "Sheer boredom. I can't believe I thought I'd find some kind of bloody enlightenment in this place. All I'm finding is a path straight to the loony bin. Do you know I haven't gotten off in *twenty-six days?*"

I swallowed. "Uh, isn't that kind of the idea of spending time in an ashram?" Never mind that I'd been making out with someone less than four hours earlier.

Devin groaned. "Fuck chastity. Fuck tea. Fuck this place."

"Things with John not going so well?" Anandi asked sympathetically.

She waved her hand dismissively. "Apparently he's keen to do this thing right. Keeps avoiding me, going on about all the ridiculous shit we do here like it actually matters. I'm beginning to think that one's a nonstarter."

"Uh, Devin," I said, trying to figure out exactly how to word what I was about to say, "not that Anandi and I don't love spending time with you, but why are you still here if you hate it so much?"

"Believe me, love, I nearly packed a bag just last night. But I told my friends I was doing sixty days in this hellhole, and they'll never let me live it down if I show up back in London before then."

I thought of Kiran. Some people were imprisoned here, while others, it seemed, imprisoned themselves. Anandi patted Devin's shoulder sympathetically.

After dinner Anandi and I started walking toward the great hall for *satsang*, but Devin didn't follow us. "I'm going back to the room for an early sleep," she said. "I can't listen to that woman patter on for one more night about our souls."

"Poor Devin," Anandi commented as she and I settled onto the floor of the hall for *satsang*. It was the same space where we did morning rituals, but it felt completely different, somehow, in the evening. The guru joined us on the floor and sat with us, rather than beckoning people behind a secret corner like she did in the morning. It had more of a meeting-space feel, and lots of times the conversation turned into a full discussion with most of the room getting involved. While the mornings felt serious and sacred, the evenings felt relaxed and communal. Still spiritual, but more like we were finding the spirit with each other. Almost like the coffee hour after the service at the church in LA where my aunts and uncles always took us.

"I know. Sixty days?" I shook my head. "I don't think she's gonna make it." I couldn't bring myself to tell Anandi that from a chastity perspective, I already hadn't.

Guru Baba joined us, and the chatter in the room quieted for a moment. "*Namaste*. Thanks for being with us this evening," she said, just like she had every evening that I'd attended the after-dinner *satsang*. *Satsang* literally meant "good company," and I liked that the guru always made it feel that these discussions were about the company of all of us, not just her company.

"Today," she said, "I'd like for us to consider the importance of others in our lives, and what they bring to our spiritual journey.

"Let's begin by focusing our thoughts on who the important people in our journeys are. Take a moment to clear your mind of all thoughts. Then simply ask yourself: who are the people in this life who bring me joy?"

This felt suspiciously like meditation, but who was I to refuse a guru? Plus wasn't I desperately trying to figure out how people (well, one person in particular) fit into my journey at the ashram? I closed my eyes.

I did my best to shut down the chattering in my head and focus on people. The people I loved. The people who brought me joy.

Pictures began flashing through my head.

My mother, of course. She was laughing at something, wearing a perfect outfit without a single hair out of place, as per usual. My father, looking slightly menacing with that hint of laughter behind his eyes. Taj, playing a video game. Daadee, humming while she cooked something spicy and delicious-smelling in our kitchen. Lexi, dancing next to me at a concert. Anandi, looking at Pilot with those puppy-dog eyes of hers that were so naive and endearing at the same time.

And then the picture that made my eyes fly wide open.

Kiran. Sitting next to me, a phone in his hand, showing me all the beauty he searched for in a day.

"People are a gift to this cycle in your life." The guru started speaking again, and I found myself clinging to her every word. "We learn in the ancient texts how all journeys are influenced by those who travel alongside us. We must embrace these fellow travelers. The joy they bring, as well as the disruption they often create. They are all sent as teachers."

Others in the room began asking questions. The discussion moved over into Brahman, which is basically how Hindus refer to the entire universe and everything in it; all the gods and goddesses in Hinduism—including Brahma, the creative force of Brahman—are just manifestations of Brahman. It was a pretty interesting discussion, actually, but I didn't participate. I just sat there, drinking in the guru's words.

I suspected they'd been true for Daadee. Maybe they could be for me, too.

By lunch the next day, I was still trying to figure out what to say to Kiran the next time I saw him. Assuming I ever saw him again. If some guy had kissed me and then run off, I'd...actually, I had no idea what I'd do. Because no one had ever done anything that weird or terrible to me.

I pushed my food around my plate while I wondered if Kiran would try to come find me that afternoon. At least no one at the table expected me to make conversation. Pilot and Anandi had somehow ended up in a deep discussion about the validity of the pop music genre.

"Don't you think music should have depth?" he asked her.

"Please. Only snobs say things like that," Anandi argued. "There's plenty of depth in pop music—especially in the vocals! Speaking of which, why haven't you done any singing projects since you left *Ghosts and Lockers*? That special episode where you did the Christmas carols was amazing. I can't believe you can hit some of those notes! And your vibrato on those long D notes..."

Now Pilot looked more suspicious than skeptical. "Are you sure you're not studying music?" he asked again. I'd been about to ask the same thing. As far as I knew, Anandi had never taken a music lesson in her life.

"Nope," Anandi said, but her cheer was more manufactured than I'd ever seen it. "I just like it. That's all. I swear. *Pop* music, specifically."

"Me too," Pilot told her. "I mean, not pop music." He smiled while Anandi glared. "But I do love music in general. I just don't want to make it the center of my career. I like acting too much."

"It's too bad. Maybe you could revolutionize the pop music genre if you tried. You know, finally give it some *depth*." Anandi smirked at him.

Pilot was still working on his comeback when I saw something flash next to me on its way to the ground. I leaned over to pick it up.

It was a piece of paper folded into a star pattern. I looked around, trying to figure out if someone had dropped it by accident. But whoever had lost it seemed to be long gone.

I tugged at the paper's fold until it opened into a square. In handwriting I didn't recognize, a short sentence read, *Meet me at the statue garden?*

"I have to go," I said, standing. "I'll be right back," I added when confusion wrote its way into Pilot's and Anandi's otherwise relaxed expressions. "And if I'm not, I'll see you at the school, okay?"

"Sure," Pilot responded easily. "I guess."

Anandi shot me a look that left me certain I was going to be answering a lot of questions later. After she answered a few of mine. I'd been taking piano lessons for ten years, and there was no way I knew exactly what notes my favorite singers were hitting in random songs.

It didn't take me long to find him. He was sitting on the ground, leaning back on some shrubbery, and staring up at the cloudless sky. It was a cooler day than others, but still warm, and the sun gave instant heat to everything it touched. I gave another silent shout-out to Daadee for picking this particular ashram to spend her months of study. Delhi was probably around ninety degrees or higher right now, but the area around the ashram tended to stay between the sixties and eighties during this time of year. Almost always perfect. And we were visiting before the monsoon season, so it hadn't even rained that much.

"You got my note," he said. "Imagine what our parents must have gone through before texting was invented."

I laughed and dropped to my knees. "You don't hate me?" I asked. "For taking off yesterday?"

"If I'm being honest, I would have preferred that you stuck around." He smiled softly at me. "But of course I don't hate you. I could never hate you, Raya Liston."

And then I knew what I wanted—no, needed—to say to him next. Daadee hadn't kept herself from the person she wanted to spend time with here, and I wasn't going to, either.

"When I kissed you yesterday," I told him, "I got freaked out because I was breaking the ashram rules and maybe ruining what I'm trying to do here. But I've been thinking: what if the rules are wrong? Maybe you're an important part of whatever it is I'm doing here. Maybe you're supposed to be, if that makes sense. And I think I want you to be. In fact, I *know* I want you to be. But you have to promise me that you won't stop me from finding what I'm looking for here."

"I thought you were looking for that journal?"

I glared at him, and he laughed. "You know what I mean."

He pressed his hand underneath my chin. "Raya, I know how important the ashram is to you. I would never want you to feel like you lost out on something because of me. If you tell me you don't want me to ever kiss you again, I promise I can do that. I'll fucking hate it, but I'll do it. For you." He paused. "I never want to be the reason why you give up anything."

That was exactly what I needed to hear him say. "Besides, I double-checked and this statue garden is definitely not on ashram grounds."

I wrapped my hand behind his neck and pulled him into me so I could kiss him again, his body warm and comfortable against mine. For a long moment, all I could concentrate on were the feelings of hope and calm that filled me, and my mind seemed to empty of every possible thought.

It felt better and more familiar than any meditation I'd ever attempted, and I was more certain than ever that Daadee would have approved of the choice I was making.

eleven

∞

PARABLES AND PROTEIN BARS

Four thirty the next morning came way too quickly, and my head felt like it was wrapped in cotton for most of prayers. Not much sleep had happened for me the night before. First I'd lain awake for almost an hour just thinking about Kiran and the time we'd spent together that day. Then I'd decided all that obsessing over a guy wasn't healthy and I should obsess about something else for a while. So I'd decided to read a few more of Daadee's journal entries, which ended up being a *huge* mistake. After that, I hadn't been able to fall asleep for another two hours. I couldn't stop thinking about what I'd read.

I showed the last entry I'd read to Anandi after our morning rituals, while we were on our way to breakfast.

July 5

I find myself spending a great deal of time studying the
story of Bharat lately. Particularly the story of his origin.
The story of his parents and their love.

   I have always enjoyed their story. The mystery
surrounding their meeting, the great lengths they took to
reunite despite all the odds that were stacked so greatly
against them. True love, I have always believed, is the height
of faith, and the story of Bharat's becoming defends this
idea more than ever.

   I think of this story now as I sit by my favorite shrine
up on the hill next to a man I have only begun to know
at my side. We continue to spend more and more time
together, and more and more I find myself wondering
precisely how interconnected our paths are intended to
be. But I find it strange that the gods would continue
to bind us together—our fates, unlike those of Bharat's
parents, are destined for separate ends. I have always
wanted to become a guru, and this is a dream I will
accomplish, regardless of what anyone else in my family
may say. And the man who sits beside me is promised to
another. His marriage date is set, his wife already chosen
for him.

He tells me he has never met her. I believe him. But he does not say he wishes to terminate the wedding. We both know our paths, and to deny them would be to deny everything that is our entire worlds.

"Some of the entries have been kind of boring—no offense to Daadee," I told Anandi. "Lots about what she was studying and why, the stories she wanted to discuss in *satsang,* all that kind of stuff. But check out this one! Do you seriously think she's talking about Daada? Was Daada promised to someone else before he married her?"

Anandi rolled her eyes and handed me back the book. "I told you yesterday when we talked about this, of course the guy is Daada," she said. "How many barristers from Varanasi does one person marry in a lifetime?"

Okay, good point. Especially if you weren't from Varanasi yourself, and Daadee hadn't been. "But I don't want it to be Daada. It can't be, Anandi. You know she probably gave up on being a guru for this guy, right? And Daada wasn't like that. He loved her—I remember how much he loved her. He never would have asked her to give up on her dreams for him."

Anandi squeezed my shoulders in a hug as we reached our usual table. "Look, you don't know that she gave up being a guru for the person in that journal—who is Daada, by the way."

I glared. "Maybe there's some whole other reason why she gave up on being a guru that we haven't even considered."

"Has the poetry book told you anything?" I asked. "About who he might have been?"

I could tell she had to stop herself from reminding me again that the person in the journal had to be my grandfather. "No. She doesn't comment on any of the poems. She just copied them there, like she wanted to remember them and reread them whenever she could. I see why. They're all perfectly her." Her voice and demeanor took on the drifty, blissful tone and look that usually only came over her when she discussed the Jonas Brothers' first single. "The way the words drift together, I can almost feel how they should be set to music. There's this one poem that I'd put in the key of E and add a bridge to it. Then I'd ..." All of a sudden she seemed to snap out of what she was saying. "Anyway, they don't really tell a story," she added abruptly.

"Sure," I murmured. After that, I was so busy wondering why Anandi got so sus every time we discussed musical theory that I forgot to ask her if she knew anything about Bharat's parents' story.

Samaira didn't show up for service again, which left me wondering if I'd driven her away forever somehow during that whole "normal" conversation. The kitchen was stuffy with the smell of turmeric and ginger, so I pushed up the window next to me and let a small breeze in while I worked on my pile of potatoes. I had reached a level of boredom where I was actually reciting

167

my multiplication tables in my head when an Australian accent floated in through the window.

"I dunno, love," said a male voice. "I just can't eat the food here. Disagrees with me, you know? All that spice!"

"You're not trying," a woman with a strong Hindi accent answered, sighing. "The food is much spicier in Mumbai, and we met there! So why do you insist on eating these terrible protein bars when you could be eating delicious, authentic Indian cuisine?"

I almost choked on my giggling as I craned my neck trying to see where the voices were coming from. It was a young couple, both sitting a few yards away from the window by the pool. She was wearing the ashram robe; he was wearing a T-shirt and khaki shorts. And carrying a box of protein bars.

"Honestly, darling? I was trying to impress you then. I spent most of that week in the bathroom."

I could barely stifle my laughter, and I looked up when I swore I heard someone laughing with me.

It was Samaira. Giggling lightly, potato peeler in hand. Just like nothing had ever happened.

"Poor man," she whispered. "It's like she wants their bathroom to smell terribly or something."

I burst out laughing, and after that, Samaira and I spent most of service trying to figure out which foods the Australian guy might be able to choke down and which ones should remain entirely off-limits for his bathroom's protection. We giggled a lot, and I never once asked her about her "normal" comment.

I was dying to know what she'd meant. But I had a feeling if I asked her now she'd disappear forever.

Pilot brought a whole stack of books with us to the school that day, so I gathered a bunch of the students on the rug and set them up to read out loud. By that point I basically knew who was up to which levels of reading difficulty, and I tried not to call on them to read in places where I knew the words would be too hard. Pihu, of course, completely dismissed me when I told her to wait to read a different section. "I want to try it," she told me and the other students eagerly. "I'll make a lot of mistakes, but that's okay. I don't mind."

And then she started reading. And she sure did make a lot of mistakes. But just as she'd said, she didn't care. Neither did anyone else.

Pilot and I were both quiet on the walk home. "They are such amazing kids," I said softly at one point.

Pilot nodded. "They make me feel like maybe I'm worth something."

The harshness of his comment left me stunned. "What the hell, Pilot? Why do you always say things like that? You're a great guy."

Pilot shook his head and stared off in the distance, at the hill where we'd found the shrine. The one my grandmother loved so much. "You don't know what I did, Raya. At least, I can't imagine that you do. If you did, there's no way you'd still be talking to me."

"Do most people know?"

"My fuck-up was all Twitter could talk about for at least a few weeks." Pilot laughed harshly. "Not that I didn't deserve it."

I couldn't imagine Pilot ever having done anything horrible enough for Twitter to take him down. "What happened?"

"You'll find out eventually. When you get home and have the internet again. No worries about that. Until then, if it's okay with you, I'd rather keep a few people around who don't know all my faults."

"Sure," I told him softly. I wasn't exactly in a place to go around suggesting everyone at the ashram spill their biggest secrets.

We arrived at the footbridge, where *my* secret appeared.

"Want to take a walk?" Kiran asked, holding his hand out for me.

Uh, *yes*. I tried not to blush like the smitten person I totally was when he took my hand, and Pilot rolled his eyes.

"You two have fun," he called out as we walked away. "Don't worry about me, all alone, just contemplating my singlehood over here...."

Kiran laughed.

We stayed by the side of the river, walking up toward the bottom of the foothills. The sun was bright, shining in through the trees and their necessary shade. It was a hot day. "How was your day of chanting?" Kiran asked me.

"I like chanting," I reminded him. "So it was good. So was

kitchen service. And Pilot and I just helped out at the school, which was fantastic. Overall, it's been a good day." I shook my head. "My grandmother's journal is getting stranger and stranger, though. This guy she was in love with? He was promised to someone else!"

Kiran shrugged. "Back then? Raya, I'd have been surprised if he wasn't. Even now it's not crazy for parents to try to set up their kids in India. My parents definitely have two or three people in mind for me when I leave here."

I scowled. "Not if I have anything to say about it," I murmured.

"Oh, really?" Kiran teased, pulling me into his arms and brushing a set of kisses down my neck that left me feeling shivery—again—and warm at the same time. "Planning to kick some fiancée ass, are you?"

"I'd totally take them," I growled lightly. Just before I moved my mouth down enough to meet his lips.

"You should come to the school with me sometime," I told Kiran when we finally detached our lips from each other's and sat down in the grass. "I'd love to introduce you to Pihu and the other students."

Kiran grimaced. "I don't mind helping out at the village library once in a while, but I don't know how you and Pilot can work in that school. I visited there with him once, and all it did was make me angry. As soon as I get home, I'm telling my parents to donate some money or something. I don't understand how the government let that happen—those kids are way too far

RACHEL ROY AND AVA DASH

behind. And they don't even have desks," he added, frustration ringing through his voice.

"I know," I said. I grabbed his hand. "That would be great, if your family could help them out. Those kids work so hard, and Khatri really is trying her best. But being there makes me so happy. Maybe you wouldn't have to be so upset about what's happening if you helped, too."

"I doubt it." He shrugged. "All I see when I go there is sadness."

Which explained why he avoided it. Kiran obviously thrived on finding beauty in corners of the world. It made sense that he would avoid ugliness. I squeezed his hand, wondering if there was any way I could ever get him to see the beauty I found in that school.

For a long time we just made out in the sun, our hands gently exploring each other's bodies. My clothes stayed put, but I liked it that way. For now.

I suddenly remembered what I'd never asked Anandi earlier that day. "Do you know anything about the story of where Bharat came from?" I asked. "About his parents? My grandmother said something in her journal about loving the story of how they met, but I'm not sure I know anything about them. I don't remember Daadee ever telling me about Bharat's mom and dad."

"Oh, that story." Kiran played lightly with a strand of my hair. "The famous story of Shakuntala and Dushyanta."

I sat up fast. "Wait, what did you say?"

Kiran sat up, too, looking confused. "Bharat's parents. Their story is a famous legend: the story of Shakuntala and Dushyanta."

I just stared at him. It was like I was frozen in place.

"What's wrong?" Kiran asked quickly, grabbing for my hand.

"My middle name…" I whispered. "My middle name is Shakuntala. I always knew my grandmother had chosen it, but I never bothered to ask her why. And now it turns out this epic Indian love story with my name in it was her favorite."

Kiran smoothed the hair back from my face and kissed the corner of my mouth. "Can't think of anyone more deserving."

Well. You can't not kiss a guy who's just said something like *that* to you. We went back to making out, obviously.

I was definitely going to have to learn more about Shakuntala's story if I wanted to learn more about my grandmother and her time at the ashram. But just then all I wanted to learn more about was the guy sitting next to me.

By the next afternoon, I was wondering if the ashram was missing something huge by encouraging chastity. Especially when a note, folded into the shape of a star, appeared on the floor next to me during lunch.

After you finish work at the school today, it said, *meet me by the footbridge.*

Who was I to ignore texting in its ancient form?

"You again?" I joked to Kiran as I arrived at the footbridge after school later. He was wearing a pink polo shirt, navy Dockers shorts, and black Ray-Bans. He looked like a Ralph Lauren ad, only hotter.

He grabbed my hand and gave me a light peck on the cheek while I glanced around, paranoid that someone might be watching.

"Don't worry," he told me. "I'm the only one from the ashram who was coming this way." He pulled me over the bridge to the other side of the river and said. "Now we're safe. How was saving the world?"

"Great. Pihu and I only have a few chapters left in that book we're reading. I still think the dog is gonna die."

"The dog always dies. It's like a rule." He flashed another smile at me. He looked really good in pink, and I couldn't help but feel slightly self-conscious. Maybe wearing my I LISTEN TO BANDS THAT DON'T EVEN EXIST YET T-shirt hadn't been such a great choice that morning.

"You're so beautiful," he told me, as if he were reading my mind. "I hope people tell you that all the time."

I blushed. *Hard.*

"So what's up?" I asked. "Why the note today? We almost always meet after school gets out anyway."

"I have something I want to show you."

He led me past our statue garden, away from both the ashram and the village, until we got to another footbridge I'd never seen. I followed him across a stream and through some trees.

"You sure you know where you're going?" I asked. We had

to be at least half a mile away from the ashram now, and there didn't seem to be anything around here. Where could he possibly be taking me?

"Yup. I promise. I found this place while I was doing some exploring a while ago—shot some footage here. I was thinking about it last night, and I realized you might like to see it." We walked another fifty yards or so, until we reached a long wooden fence.

Behind it were rows and rows of apple trees.

"What are these doing here?" I grabbed the fence, staring in awe at what was in front of me. I had no idea apple trees even grew in India.

"Some American guy who helped out with the Indian resistance—well, some people say he helped out, but other people say that story's blown out of proportion—brought apples over here with him. I guess they actually do well in the climate in this part of India. Now there are apple orchards all over the place here. They're actually a major crop in this state." He kissed me. "I thought it might remind you of home."

"Oh, Kiran. That's so sweet." I laughed. "You know, I've actually never been to an apple orchard. I think there are some south of San Jose, but my parents never took me there."

Kiran winced. "Oh, shit. Sometimes I forget how big America is. Sorry, Raya."

I hugged him hard. "Don't be sorry—I love that you brought me here. I love that you thought to show me this place." I pulled him more tightly against me, nuzzling my face into his neck. "I can't believe I didn't know apples were a major crop here. I did so much research! How did I miss that?"

Kiran just smiled and kissed me again.

I had him take a bunch of pictures of the orchard with his contraband iPhone, which he promised to send to me once I was no longer phoneless. Then he wanted to do some action shots of me walking in front of the apple trees. I felt like a model or something, following his directions to walk this way or that, to stare at a specific apple, all while he filmed. I'd never gotten the appeal of acting or modeling before, but just then it started to make sense. There was something weirdly empowering about knowing your actions, your whole demeanor, were driving how someone moved a camera and what they did with it.

After he finished filming me, we walked back to the statue garden together, where I could basically not keep my hands off him. That was possibly the most romantic date I'd ever had. He'd barely sat down next to the river before I was on him. My entire body felt like it was slowly catching fire, and all I wanted to do was to touch more of him, be closer to more of him.

Every sexual encounter I had ever had before that had been ridiculously awkward. Limbs everywhere, tongues in wrong places. And don't get me wrong—Kiran and I definitely didn't have it *all* together. Like when I moved to slide my hand under his shirt and almost tipped us both over. Or when he tried to snake his hand up my thigh and accidentally shoved my funny bone into the ground. But even when ridiculous moments like that happened, we just laughed together and moved on. Or he'd rub my funny bone for me, because that one did actually hurt. Before, I'd always felt like I had to pretend those sort of moments weren't crazy awkward and uncomfortable. With Kiran? They just weren't. Everything was just fun and natural, even when it shouldn't have been.

I'd done a decent amount with guys, and I didn't exactly consider myself inexperienced, but I was a virgin. Lexi and I both were. *Everything-but girls,* she jokingly called us. Lexi always claimed that she wanted her cherry popped in college. *With an older girl,* she said. *Someone who actually knows what the hell they're doing.*

And me? I wasn't sure exactly what I was waiting for. I just knew it wasn't lukewarm kissing and awkward tongue placement. But now, with Kiran's hand moving farther and farther up my thigh and my heart pounding a million miles an hour while strange and new sensations coursed through every part of my body, I wondered if this was what I'd been waiting for all along.

I was just considering pushing my hand even farther up Kiran's shirt when I heard a loud thrashing sound in the trees nearby. I jumped off Kiran as fast as I could, smoothing my hair while he pulled down his shirt.

Bulky footsteps came clomping near us, and a moment later someone moved through the trees and into the statue garden. It was the Australian Samaira and I had been watching the day before. "Excuse me," he said, his thick accent laced with anxiety, "but I've stashed some protein bars somewhere around here and I can't seem to find them. Could you possibly help me?"

Kiran's eyes widened. "You stashed *what?*" he asked.

I spent the next five minutes trying not to laugh while the poor Australian dude explained that his wife had forbidden him to eat anything that wasn't in the dining hall, so he figured he'd hide his protein bars just off the ashram grounds. "It was either that or starve, mates," he told us sadly. "And I saw the statues nearby here, thought I might use them as a landmark...."

I could practically see the movie script Kiran was writing in his head.

We'd been searching for the lost bars for about twenty minutes when suddenly a screaming Indian woman came raging into the clearing. "Looking for these?" she shouted, holding up a large brown box that read CHOCOLATE PEANUT MADNESS on the side. "Are you seriously going to hide food? Are you twelve? You think I don't know everything you do? How can you not even try to eat the food of the country you are in, *my country?*"

"Your country makes my IBS act up!" the Australian guy shouted back. Apparently he'd completely forgotten Kiran and I were there. Or he just had no problem announcing his digestive difficulties to the entire world.

"Maybe your bowels wouldn't irritate you so much if you'd try new things!" she shouted back.

I could tell Kiran was going to start howling with laughter, and I wasn't doing the best job of holding it back myself, so I grabbed his elbow and started tugging him to the path by the river. We'd barely made it out of the clearing before we both lost it.

"He...said...her culture...IBS..." Kiran was actually holding his sides, he was laughing so hard.

"Maybe his bowels wouldn't irritate him if..." Tears were running down my face.

"Wow." Kiran pulled in a deep breath. "That's definitely going into one of my films someday."

"I knew you were gonna say that," I told him as he reached out to take my hand.

"Of course you did."

twelve

LEGENDS AND LOSERS

July 8

I fear I am losing my purpose.

　　I am filled with guilt that I am not being true to my original intentions in visiting this ashram. The man I have taken to calling *meri jaan* when we are alone (it would not do to be caught calling someone "my darling" at an ashram) constantly reminds me that we have broken no rules in our time together, and he is correct in all technical ways. Our relationship is entirely aboveboard, and I intend to ensure it remains that way.

　　But in my heart, I know that my time here has never been truly dedicated to the study of my faith. It has never

been truly dedicated to an understanding of all things
Brahman, as I originally intended it to be.

No. My time in this ashram has, rather, become a study
of myself. A study of feelings I didn't know I was capable of
having for another human being.

Meri jaan becomes more and more dear to me—he
opens my heart in ways I never thought possible. He is the
first thing I see when I awaken in the morning, and the
last thing I see in my mind when I fall asleep at night.
As blinded as I may be by my passion for him, I am not so
blind as to misunderstand what that means.

Here in an ashram, where I came to find my way into
the spiritual world, I have traveled another path entirely. Is
he my test? Has he been put in my path to test me?

I can no longer say whether I am lost or found.

Holy shit.

I finished Daadee's journal entry while Anandi got dressed
for morning rituals. I rubbed the last bits of sleep from my eyes,
breathing hard, trying to further understand what all this meant.

"It can't be Daada," I insisted again to Anandi on our way to
morning rituals. "This guy has to be the reason why she gave
up on being a guru. And Daada just wouldn't have done that." I
thought again of my grandfather. The way he doted on Daadee,
bringing her tea and rubbing her feet every night. All he ever

wanted was to make her happy—he never would have asked her to give up something that mattered to her.

Anandi rolled her eyes. "Raya, you really have to get it out of your head that Daadee somehow fell in love with two barristers from Varanasi in her life. She didn't. She's talking about Daada, okay?"

I frowned at the tiled floor beneath us. "But this *doesn't make sense*. Daadee says in this entry that she feels like she's letting go of all her studies for this guy. I can't see her staying with someone who caused her to do that."

My stomach twisted as I said those words.

Anandi shrugged. "Maybe Daadee changed her mind. Maybe things changed around her. Daadee was *happy* with Daada—we both know that. I think..." She hesitated. "I think there's not much point in being upset about getting exactly what you want. Even if it's not what you first *thought* you wanted." She sighed. "After all, not everyone's lucky enough to get what they want, right?"

I was starting to think Anandi was the queen of thinly veiled wisdom.

We gathered for prayers in the great hall, and I watched as a line of people formed, all hoping for an audience with the guru. Sometimes she only invited one person behind her curtain, other days she invited several. Different people lined up each day, for the most part.

Anandi, Devin, and I had never ventured near that space.

I imagine Devin might have slept through any audience she had with Guru Baba, and Anandi seemed perfectly content with her spiritual practice as it was. Personally, I just couldn't imagine what I would say to the spiritual leader of an ashram where I'd already broken one of the most important guidelines.

I was sitting next to Anandi, taking deep breaths and preparing for a relaxing *kirtan*, when the guru appeared from behind her curtain.

And beckoned to me.

I was so surprised that at first I didn't even react. I just sat there, staring, trying to figure out who she could possibly be pointing at.

When she pointed her hand toward me and lifted it one more time, Anandi leaned over and whispered, "I think she wants to see you, Raya."

"But I'm not even in line!" I whispered back.

She shrugged. "She asks to see people in the audience all the time. Haven't you noticed?"

I hadn't, actually. So much for my excellent observational skills.

I stood up and began to slowly make my way across the hall toward the curtain. Nearby, Samaira caught my eye and gave me an encouraging nod.

You can do this, I told myself. What did I possibly have to be nervous about? Unless she'd figured out I was making out with the ashram's bad boy and was calling me up to kick me out of the Rishi Kanva.

My stomach clenched as I reached the curtain and stepped behind it.

The guru's space was small, just a few pillows and cushions scattered across the floor. They were neat and colorful, just like the tapestries surrounding us. "You are Raya," the guru said, smiling.

"Yes?" It came out like a question.

"I am Guru Baba, as you know." She grasped my hands firmly in hers. "I have been looking forward to speaking with you alone, Raya."

The sounds of *kirtan* began to fill the room on the other side of the curtain from us, and I suddenly felt slightly trapped. There was no getting out now. This woman and I were clearly about to have a conversation, whether I wanted to or not.

"Sit, sit." Guru Baba gestured at the pillows, and I sort of half fell onto a bright-purple one. It was as soft as it looked.

She sat down across from me on a bright-green pillow, folding her knees until she was cross-legged. "Tell me about your time at the ashram thus far, Raya."

Which part? The part where I like chanting a lot or the part where I've been making out with Kiran in a statue garden? "It's been... an adjustment," I finally said. "But I'm enjoying it. My grandmother once stayed at this ashram. It feels good to be connected with her."

The guru just nodded, like maybe she'd known that all along. But I didn't see how she could have.

"I believe you are in the midst of an important discovery, Raya," she said. "One that may require guidance."

She stopped talking. How was I supposed to answer that? Exactly what journey was she talking about? Was she talking about the big discovery I was hoping to make—and if so, what did she possibly know about me and my purpose? She definitely couldn't be talking about Kiran. I wasn't exactly about to tell her that I might be finally on my way to discovering what a good orgasm felt like.

"Well," I said, "I did find something. It took some time, but I found it eventually." Damn, I was babbling. "It's an old journal my grandmother kept when she was living here. I've learned some things from it already. Like where my middle name comes from." *And other things,* I added silently.

"Hmmm." She pursed her fingers together. "And where is that?"

I frowned. "Shakuntala is my middle name. My grandmother chose it because she loved the myth of Shakuntala. But I don't actually know the story. Not yet," I added hastily.

The guru smiled. "Then I believe that time is now. I know that story well," she told me. "Would you like to hear it?"

That time is now. I nodded.

The guru collected her hands on her lap. "If I tell you this story," she said, "you must promise me you will see it through Shakuntala's eyes, Raya."

I wasn't sure exactly what she meant by that. "Uh. Okay?" I figured I could try.

She nodded. "Close your eyes," she said.

I did. And then she began to speak.

"The story of Shakuntala is an ancient one, central to the history of India today," she said softly. "Long ago, the great Rishi Kanva, for whom this ashram is named, was walking in the woods. There he happened upon a crying baby surrounded by Shakuntala birds. The birds, he knew, had been caring for this baby while they awaited his arrival. And so he named the baby Shakuntala after those birds who had kept her safe."

I did my best to picture her story in my head: the birds, the crying baby. To imagine how lonely and frightened Shakuntala might have been.

"Rishi Kanva adopted Shakuntala and raised her as his own. He lived in the wild forest, among the animals and birds, and there Shakuntala lived with him. The deer were her friends, the flowers her playthings. Shakuntala's entire world was the forest and her beloved father."

Outside the curtain, the chanting grew louder, and for a moment the rhythm of the voices seemed to match perfectly with the guru's story. The notes grew softer, sweeter, as she spoke of Shakuntala's adoptive father.

"One day Rishi Kanva went away, leaving his daughter with his words of love and her beloved friend, a deer, to protect her. He did not expect that any mortal human would pierce the forest's protection of Shakuntala. But time soon proved him wrong."

The chanting grew louder, faster.

"The King of Hastinapur, whose name was Dushyanta, came riding near the forest on a hunting trip. He spotted a deer and shot it. The deer, unbeknownst to him, was the beloved friend of Shakuntala. She came running to the deer's rescue, determined to save it."

The intensity of the chant grew, and the quick rhythm felt as though it were tumbling through me.

"Shakuntala surrendered herself entirely to the needs of the deer. Dushyanta had never witnessed such love, and it touched his heart. He dropped to his knees, begging Shakuntala to forgive him for his cruel actions."

The chanting suddenly slowed, relaxing into a more peaceful rhythm. It was starting to feel like the guru and I were the only two people in the room, the only two people in the ashram. As though nothing else existed but the story she was sharing and the rhythmic notes coming from somewhere behind me.

"Shakuntala eventually forgave the king, but only on the condition that he would stay with her in the forest and help nurse the deer back to health. And so he did. I imagine you can guess what happened next."

I could. I smiled.

"Within just a few days, the king had expressed his love for Shakuntala, and she her love for him. Yet Rishi Kanva had not returned from his trip, and so the king had no way of asking his permission for marriage."

The chanting swelled again behind me.

"So Dushyanta and Shakuntala made a choice, and they married without her father's permission. Dushyanta placed a ring inscribed with his name on his lovely wife's hand and promised to love her always, and she promised him the same in return."

The chanting relaxed again, and I found myself sinking into a strange romantic trance as I thought of Kiran standing on the hill, holding the box that held my grandmother's journals.

"The king was forced to return to his kingdom, as he had left it too long already. Yet Shakuntala was loath to leave without first telling her father of her new love and husband. And so she stayed in the forest to await his return. Dushyanta promised his love he would return to her, gain her father's permission for their marriage, and take her back to his kingdom."

I imagined Shakuntala and Dushyanta at the edge of the forest saying their good-byes. And if they looked just a little bit like Kiran and me in my head? Whatever. I figured I was allowed to imagine mythical characters any way I chose.

"And so Shakuntala, with only her forest friends and the trees nearby to keep her company, drifted in her love for days, forgetting and letting go of everything else in the world but her love for this man. Content to dream of Dushyanta and the happiness he brought her, she hardly noticed when Rishi Durvasa came to visit her."

The notes of the chanting lowered suddenly, and it took on an almost forbidding tone.

"The rishi was thirsty and begged Shakuntala for water. Lost in her visions of her love, Shakuntala took no notice of him. The rishi's temper took hold of him, and he cursed the girl of the forest. 'The person you think of,' he told her, 'shall lose all memory of you forever.' The curse woke Shakuntala from her trance. It frightened her and she began to cry."

I couldn't imagine being cursed to have someone you loved so greatly forget you. What kind of life would that be?

"Shakuntala apologized to the sage and begged for his forgiveness. Somewhat chagrined by her upset, the sage agreed to make one small change to the curse: if Shakuntala could show Dushyanta something he had given her, he would remember her once more."

The chanting tapered off just then, and a short silence took over the room.

"As the rishi had promised, Dushyanta lost all memory of Shakuntala, and he did not return to her. After waiting in the forest alone for far longer than she could stand, Shakuntala set out to the kingdom of Hastinapur, determined to make her love remember her. But it was not to be. The journey was long, and along the way Shakuntala dropped her wedding ring while crossing a river. She cried as a fish leaped into the air, swallowing it whole and destroying Shakuntala's hopes for a long life with the person she loved."

Oh, my God. That was terrible. Shakuntala didn't love anyone else but Dushyanta, and now he would never remember her.

Behind me, the chanting began again.

"Shakuntala traveled on to the palace, but just as she had feared, the king had no memory of her. He sent her away, and she wept as she saw the blankness in his eyes when he looked upon her."

The chanting had grown soft. Mournful.

"On her way home, Shakuntala learned that she was pregnant. Ashamed to return to the father she had dishonored, Shakuntala built a new home for herself in the forest. There, surrounded by animals who came quickly to love her, she gave birth to a son: Bharat."

I imagined Shakuntala giving birth alone in the woods surrounded only by the deer and birds to keep her company.

"Bharat grew up as Shakuntala had, a child of a forest that loved him. Shakuntala and Dushyanta, however, each lived on within their own sadness, though only one knew why that sadness was."

Poor Dushyanta. Imagine feeling a loss like that and not even being able to figure out what was missing.

"One day a fisherman arrived at the king's palace. He presented to the king a ring with his name on it, saying he had found it in the belly of a fish. The king only needed to lay eyes on the ring to remember Shakuntala and everything that once had been. He immediately began his journey to her home. Only Shakuntala was not there."

The chanting grew quieter again, and I thought *kirtan* might be nearly over. I wondered if this was one of those myths that ended by making you wish you'd never listened to it in the first place. Dushyanta and Shakuntala had to find each other again. They *had* to.

"Time passed, and the king despaired of his lost love. Until one day he was hunting in the forest when he spotted a young boy playing with lions. Impressed with the boy's bravery, the king asked him who he was. 'I am the son of Shakuntala and Dushyanta,' the boy replied proudly."

The chanting swelled again into a short crescendo.

"And so Shakuntala was reunited with her lost love. Together she and Bharat traveled to the palace, where she would also reunite with her father. Bharat went on to become a great emperor of India, and he is the reason that *Bharat* is the true name of this land."

"Wow," I breathed as the guru finished her story. Behind me the room had gone completely silent. Everyone had moved on to meditation, most likely.

"The story of Shakuntala is a very important one, as I said." Guru Baba smiled. "Your middle name comes with great power and importance, Raya. I hope that understanding this impor-tance will assist you as you continue on your path to your discovery."

I hoped so, too. If only I could be sure of exactly what it was I was supposed to be discovering.

"Thank you," I told the guru. "Thank you for...taking the time to share that story with me." But I was thanking her for more than that, and we both knew it. I was thanking her for taking time to care about me and this confusing journey I was on.

"Of course, Raya." Guru Baba nodded. "Have faith. Have patience. I am certain you will find all you are looking for."

I wish I shared her limitless optimism.

I stayed in my own head the rest of the morning. Anandi and Devin were both quiet at breakfast (to the point where I actually wondered if Devin was sick or something), and Samaira didn't show up for service again. She'd been missing it a lot lately. I ate lunch by myself and then decided to take a walk before it was time to go to the school.

I ended up back at the statue garden, where I spread out on the grass and stared up into the trees, trying to let Shakuntala's story wash over me.

The next thing I knew I was lying next to Kiran while he did something on his phone.

"Where did you come from?" I rubbed the sleep from my eyes and prayed to any Hindu god or goddess who would listen that drool wasn't dripping down my chin.

"You're pretty when you sleep."

"Not an answer." I smiled and sat up. "What time is it?"

"Late afternoon." He slid the phone into his pocket. "I walked over after lunch and found you here."

"The school!" I looked down at my watch. "Damn, I missed going to the school! Why didn't you wake me up? Pihu's going to be so upset!"

"Sorry." Kiran frowned. "You just looked so peaceful lying there, and I started thinking about how we could spend the whole afternoon together. . . . I didn't think you'd be all that upset if you missed school for one day."

All I could think about was Shakuntala ignoring Rishi Durvasa because she was so in love. And Daadee, giving up on being one of the first female gurus because of someone she fell in love with at this ashram. Was I starting to ignore everything else that mattered to me because of Kiran? Logically, I realized that connection wasn't totally fair to him. I'd been the one to fall asleep, and it wasn't Kiran's job to make sure I got to the school on time. But the fact of the matter was that I was with *him* just then, and not where I was supposed to be.

"I can't believe you didn't wake me up." I glared at him. "You don't care about the school at all, do you? Just like you don't care about *anything* at the ashram." I knew what I was saying was somewhat cruel, but I didn't even try to stop any of it from coming out of my mouth.

"Hey." Kiran put his hand on my shoulder. "I really am sorry, Raya. Not waking you up was a mistake—I get that. I don't care about much here—you're right. But I do care about you." He began making slow circles across the top of my back with his hand. "What's wrong, Raya?"

I sighed. "I read some more of my grandmother's journal. I still can't figure out why she gave up on everything she wanted when she first came here, so that's kind of depressing. And then

I heard the story of Shakuntala and Dushyanta today. Talk about *super* depressing."

Kiran laughed. "Did you completely miss the happy ending? Birth of India and all that?"

"Did you completely miss the part where they spent years apart, longing for each other?"

"I've always preferred to focus on the happy side of life." Kiran shrugged.

That was definitely the greatest difference between us. But then Kiran looked down at me again, and I couldn't find it in myself to care.

Maybe Shakuntala and my grandmother hadn't figured out how to have love without giving up on everything else. But that didn't have to be me, right? I could figure out a way to have everything I wanted. A meaningful experience at the ashram. The future I was searching for. Kiran.

There had to be a way. Because I knew this for sure: when a guy looks at you the way Kiran looked at me right then, you kiss him.

So I did. For a very, very long time.

thirteen

SANSKRIT AND SMEXINESS

July 12

I continue to find meaning and strength here unlike any I have ever experienced. But it has not come from the places I expected.

Certainly, a great deal of it has come from prayer. The practice of beginning each day with prayer and meditation has enlightened me in ways I never thought possible. I feel spiritually cleansed. Anew. My discussions with others in satsang have certainly led me to greater understanding of the gods and their purpose.

Yet I realize, fully, that much of the joy and understanding I have gained here has come from the time I have spent with meri jaan.

This terrifies me.

This terrifies me because it was not what was to be. I was to build a better understanding of myself entirely through my prayer and study here, not through a man. Certainly not a man already promised to someone else.

I think often of Shakuntala these days. Of the sacrifices she made, the pain she must have endured, as she waited to discover if she would ever be remembered. The helplessness she must have felt when she realized her limited ability to control her own future.

And all because she could not let go of this man. This man she met in the middle of a forest.

"She has a poem like that." Anandi flipped open Daadee's poetry book as I finished reading the entry to her. We were sitting in the common area after dinner while we waited for *satsang* to begin. "It's the only one with no author next to the title, so I don't know who wrote it. I kind of wonder if Daadee wrote it herself. This line says, 'I see my skies changing / I know not what weather comes next.'" She looked up at me. "She fell for him hard, didn't she? Daada."

"We *don't know* that it's Daada," I reminded her emphatically while she groaned. "But yeah, she did." I sighed.

Devin plopped into a chair next to Anandi. "I have determined that I am going to die alone," she announced.

Anandi's eyes widened. "Aren't you, like, thirty-three?"

"Thirty-two, love. You'll understand when you no longer have the metabolism and skin of a seventeen-year-old." She stared at us both longingly. "Take my word for it, darlings. Use moisturizer every day."

"Oh, I do." Anandi nodded seriously. I did not nod along with her. Mom was always on me about remembering to moisturize and use sunblock. I forgot at least four times a week.

"So, where were you today after lunch?" Devin asked Anandi. "I dropped by the room to see if you wanted to take a swim. I couldn't find you there."

"Oh, I was taking a nap. Not in the room. Outside." I noticed she couldn't seem to look either one of us in the eye.

"But I looked out by the pool, too, and—"

"Look, I was sleeping, okay?" Anandi stood up, an anger written across her face that I'd never seen before. "Stop making such a big deal about it." Then she stormed out of the room.

"What was that all about?" Devin asked.

I had no clue. I was trying to decide whether it was best to keep bugging Anandi about her mysterious afternoon or leave her alone when I saw Vihaan in the corner, holding an older man's face in his hands.

"It's just so weird," I whispered to Devin as I stirred my rice pudding. "Why doesn't anyone else ever think it's bizarre that he does that? They all just go along with it like it's totally normal."

Devin squinted at me and sipped her tea. "Didn't you tell me once that normal is all relative?"

Oh, yeah. That did sound like something I'd say. Well, sure... but even then, there had to be some kind of *baseline*.

"I'm thinking of going back to England," Devin said suddenly.

"Huh?" I finally looked away from Vihaan in time to see the miserable expression on Devin's face. Her lips were dropped into an extreme pout, and her eyes were darkened by black circles. It occurred to me that for as much time as Anandi and I spent around Devin, I rarely thought of her as a real human being with actual *feelings*. Most of the time she was just the sometimes-annoying comic relief of my time at the ashram, whose stalker-ish stories I followed with half interest.

It's not a great feeling to realize you're treating someone who probably considers you a friend like a glorified prop. I inwardly winced and vowed to do better. For all of Devin's faults, she really wasn't a terrible person. And it wasn't like I'd tried very actively to help her fix the things she did that *were* actually terrible.

Maybe it wasn't too late. "Devin," I said, gathering some serious bravery, "can I tell you something?"

She looked up at me, interested. "Of course, love."

"You say really insensitive things sometimes. Racist stuff. Stuff that's hurtful. And you're not great at giving people space."

I took a breath. "But I think if you worked on that—if you tried harder to think about how what you're doing and saying makes people feel—people would be a lot happier around you. And you'd be happier, too."

Devin looked like I'd knocked the wind out of her. "But I've just always thought people should say what they think. You know, get to the point and get on with it. Why beat around bushes?"

I nodded. "Okay. But even when it hurts others to say whatever you want? Or makes them uncomfortable?" I shrugged. "I get not wanting to be polite just for the sake of being polite. But empathy's not a bad thing, and it's not hard to get the hang of. Before you say or do something, just think for a second about how it might make the other person feel."

"Huh." Devin frowned. "I'll have to think about that."

"Okay." It was a start, at least. Then something occurred to me—a question I had never asked Devin. "Why did you come here, exactly? I know you've said you had some bad relationships right before you left England and you had an addiction problem, but why come here? To a Hindu ashram?"

"I had *all* the bloody bad relationships, darling." Devin shook her head. "And rehab was hard. I suppose I felt it was time for a change. My friend Rina did the whole *Eat, Pray, Love* thing and said an ashram changed her life or what the fuck ever. Thought maybe it would change mine, too."

"Maybe it still could," I told her softly. "But that doesn't have to be because you meet the love of your life here. It could be for other reasons."

"Oh, sure, I get that all this prayer and happy is supposed to make me an infinitely better person," Devin said drily. "I suppose that works for you and Anandi; you're both all in touch with your Hindu sides or bloody whatever and actually *like* those morning prayers. I'd much rather be back in bed with a cup of coffee. Or a hot video gamer, really."

"I don't think this place is the path for everyone," I told Devin as images of Kiran beat my mental walls and flashed through my mind against my will. "But don't go home just yet, okay? Give it another chance. Maybe without worrying about John? Just try to make the experience all about you."

Devin groaned and dropped her head onto the table. "Darling, I can't imagine you haven't noticed, but *everything* is already about me."

But I wasn't sure that was true.

By the next morning, Anandi was back to her usual self, acting like nothing strange had happened after dinner the night before. I decided not to say anything to her about her secrecy—at least not yet. Instead, I spent the morning's *kirtan* studying Devin and tried to figure out why these rituals meant so much more to me than they did to her. Wondering why it was so easy for me to pray to Hindu gods for insight, why I always left this time feeling phenomenally at peace and content. After all, I hadn't exactly been raised in a super religious environment, and I still wasn't sure exactly what I believed about life and death and the purpose of the universe and all that. I'd never thought it would be so easy for me to feel connected to my spirituality. I wasn't ready to call myself a full-on Hindu yet, but I knew that praying at the ashram and following its practices woke up something inside me. Was it because Daadee had been my connection to this place, these practices? Because she had meant so much to me?

I sucked some air deep into my chest and released the vibrations from my body with the rest of the room. My hands, digging into the carpet below me, seemed to pull those vibrations back out of the floor until they were coursing through me nonstop.

It felt powerful. Like as long as I was in that room, surrounded by so many others who felt the same power I did, there was nothing we couldn't conquer. Nothing we couldn't fix in the world or at least make better.

I said that to Pilot on the walk to the school that afternoon. "Sounds like someone's been sniffing the plants around the back of the garden area," he told me. But he was smiling. I knew that if anyone understood what I meant, it would be him.

"Does it work that way for you?" I asked him. "Do the prayer and rituals help?"

He shrugged and frowned, stopping to play with a tiny purple flower growing at the edge of the bridge. He reached down and plucked it out of the ground before handing it to me.

"You really don't know what I did, do you?"

I rolled my eyes. "Ah, no. How many times do I have to say it?"

"It's just hard for me to believe sometimes. Seemed like everyone knew, I guess." He sighed. "So, listen. I was out as a gay actor, and it was no big deal. But I was dating this guy who wasn't out. He was in the Hollywood scene, too. His career was bigger than mine. I was in love, but maybe he wasn't. I dunno."

I definitely didn't like where this story was heading.

"I did something dumb. We were hanging out together one night, and I was all happy to be with him, and I decided that I'd had enough of us being in the closet. So I posted a bunch of pictures of us...together."

"Oh, shit." Pilot had *outed* someone? When they didn't want to be outed? I remembered when Lexi came out, how she used to say that the most important power she had was the ability to decide when and how people got to know. "Oh, Pilot..."

"As soon as I did it, I knew it was a mistake and I wanted to take it back. But you can't take the internet back, you know? Everyone knew, and it was my fault. I outed a guy I loved." He shook his head. "He sure didn't love me after that."

"I'm so sorry," I told him.

"Why are you sorry for me? I did it. I was the bad guy, and the world let me know it." He laughed bitterly. "The world let me have it so hard I had to erase myself from existence for a while and come here. So yeah, the prayer helps. *Kirtan* and all that, it helps. But mostly because when I'm doing that, I'm not thinking about anything else. I'm not thinking about how he hasn't answered a text or call from me since that day. Or how my agent can't get me any decent roles anymore. Or how much I hurt someone who meant a hell of a lot to me. I'm not thinking about how I maybe wrecked someone's life because I cared more about what I wanted than what he wanted. Not thinking about what a selfish asshole I am."

"You're not a selfish asshole," I told him. "Selfish assholes don't read to kids every afternoon. Selfish assholes don't answer people's questions about Nick Jonas for hours on end just to make them happy."

"Or maybe that's exactly what they do when they're trying to repent." He pulled another flower out of the ground and handed it to me before he walked off in the direction of the school. I didn't even try to keep up, because nothing I could say would make any of what Pilot had just told me disappear.

I started off our service at the school unable to get Pilot's story out of my head, but Pihu quickly distracted me.

"Raya," she announced as we sat down together on a bench to read the next chapter of our book together, "I wanna read to *you* today."

I wasn't super surprised. Pihu never backed down from a challenge, after all. But I wondered what had brought this pronouncement on. Pihu often asked to read aloud in our small reading group, but when it was just the two of us, she usually preferred to listen to me read the story to her. The book we were reading was pretty far above her level, and she knew it.

"Are you sure?" I asked.

She nodded. "I practiced while you were gone yesterday." She took the book from my hands and nodded confidently at me.

And then she read to me—three whole paragraphs. From a *chapter* book in English. A book she definitely could not have even read several sentences in a row from on the day I first came to school. Yeah, sentences were choppy and rough, and it probably took her twenty minutes to get through those three paragraphs, *but she read them.* By herself.

"Pihu!" I squealed as she finished. "I'm so proud of you!"

"I'm proud of me, too!" She threw her arms around me. "Thank you so much for helping me, Raya. I never would have done this without you."

I was buzzing with excitement as I finished reading the rest of the chapter to her, and I still had that buzz going when I met Kiran by the footbridge and immediately told him what had happened.

"And then she read, like, three paragraphs by *herself!*" I finished my story with a squeal, clapping my hands and laughing like a little kid as we walked to the statue garden. Kiran grinned wildly.

"That's fantastic, Raya," he said. "Really. You must be so proud of her. And yourself, too."

If I was being honest, I was. Listening to Pihu read aloud from our book that afternoon had given me a sense of accomplishment like none I'd ever felt. It was the first time in my life

I could be absolutely sure that my existence *mattered.* That I had done something no one else had done before or would again.

I'd helped Pihu learn to read.

"You're amazing." Kiran and I both dropped to the grass as he nibbled lightly on the top of my earlobe.

I squealed again. No shame. Having someone nibble at your earlobe is *hot.* I couldn't wait to tell Lexi.

I laughed as he rolled over and pinned me to the ground, his body suddenly heavy and looming over me in a way that made my skin tingle from my neck all the way down to my toes. Lust wasn't something I'd easily recognized in myself before. Sure, I'd gone through the phase where posters of Joe Jonas (Anandi had nothing on me back when we were twelve) could leave me craving touch in a way I couldn't explain without seriously blushing. But I wasn't like Lexi, who seemed to be horny 100 percent of the time and sometimes talked about girls' and guys' bodies like they were hanging in a meat market. *What I'd give to break off a piece of Lila's ass....* And yes, she actually meant it. Lexi was definitely one of a kind.

But these afternoons with Kiran were starting to make me actively aware of what *real* lust felt like. All my animal instincts kicked in, and my mind couldn't focus on anything other than getting his clothes off and feeling exactly what was underneath them.

I'd always been one of those people who mocked others when they claimed they got caught up in the heat of the moment or whatever. When Noah Bunkmen knocked up Farren Holloway in eleventh grade, my first thought had definitely been about their poor planning.

But now I was starting to see that *caught in the moment* could actually be a real-life thing. Of course, Farren and Noah still should have had condoms handy for that moment.

Kiran pressed his mouth to mine and my body upped its quivering considerably. Too bad my brain is still my brain and refused to be silenced by all that hotness. Here are just a few of the thoughts that started flashing through it:

What if underwear came off today?

Speaking of which, I didn't shave my pubes like Lexi does. Should I start?

Has he noticed those weird little hairs that sometimes pop up around my boobs? And how am I supposed to get rid of those?

Should I tell him his shoulder is pressing into mine too hard and it kind of hurts? I don't want to ruin the mood, but ow.

How far will he want to go? Up until now we've only done some under-the-shirt stuff. Will he care that I'm not wearing my cute bra?

Are we ready for under-the-pants? Most of my sexual encounters with other guys haven't been all that sexy, to be honest. Turns out sperm is kind of gross, especially when you're terrified of it getting anywhere near your va-jay-jay. But with Kiran, I have a feeling I'm not going to find it quite so disgusting. Or will I?

My brain was finally forced to shut down momentarily when Kiran's tongue slid deeper into my mouth. Kiran had never given me any indication that he wouldn't listen to me if I asked him to stop, or mock me if he noticed anything less than perfect about my body. This was a really good guy whose tongue was down my throat, and dammit, I wanted to do a better job of enjoying him.

His hands drifted under my shirt and I fully gave into the lusty tingles shouting at me from across my body. Right then I wanted nothing more than for him to keep touching me. I moved my own hands to reciprocate and found his nipples hard, like mine. Just thinking that he was as turned on as I was turned me on even more.

My hands were just drifting down to the top button of his jeans when a voice sounded from across the clearing. We jerked apart, both of us falling back onto the grass like we were magnets repelling each other. There was a tree just behind us, so I grabbed Kiran's hand and tugged him with me until we were both hidden behind it. I didn't particularly feel like answering anyone's questions about why Kiran and I were out by the river together with our shirts half undone. The whole scene didn't exactly scream "celibacy."

"I can't imagine why he won't have dinner with you, Devin," someone was saying. "You're likable and lovely, just like your therapist says. And you're working on this whole empathy thing—you really are! You didn't even tell that girl today that she ought to consider a good wax, and you listened when that man told you why it wouldn't be appropriate to paint your face brown for Halloween this year. You're trying to be the best version of you."

I peeked out from behind the tree and saw exactly what I was expecting: Devin, pacing next to the river, talking to herself. Kiran and I stared at each other for a minute, and I could tell he was trying not to laugh. I was focused more on what she was saying. It sounded like Devin might have actually listened to my advice.

"You can keep doing this. You can keep trying to be better. John will appreciate that. It's like your therapist says. He just doesn't *understand* you, Devin. He doesn't understand what you've been through!"

By that point, Kiran was basically crying he was trying so hard not to laugh. I knew that, objectively, the situation was pretty funny. Our sexcapades, which had probably already hit rom-com levels of weird about three interruptions ago, had now been interrupted by a woman who was doing self-therapy about her love life by talking to herself in the middle of the woods.

But I couldn't bring myself to laugh.

On our walk back to the ashram, after Devin had finally left, Kiran couldn't stop talking about what an amazing movie scene the whole thing would make. "Even better than Protein Bar Man," he told me. "That scene is definitely going into one of my first films."

"Really?" I asked. "That felt like pure comedy to you?"

Kiran stopped walking, confusion written all over his face. "Of course. How was it not?"

I didn't understand how he couldn't see it. How someone as perceptive and imaginative as Kiran couldn't see what was lurking below the surface of what we'd just watched. "Devin's lonely," I told him. "In fact, after watching that, I'd say she might just be one of the loneliest people I know."

Then Kiran's face laced with surprise.

"Oh," he said finally. "I guess I didn't think about that." He frowned as he considered the idea, and then he shook his head hard, like he was trying to get rid of any potential sadness that might have taken over his brain for a moment. He grasped my hand harder and pulled me toward the side of the river. "One more kiss good-bye?" he asked.

I couldn't believe how easy it was for him to let go of things that didn't fit into his perfectly ordered and optimistic worldview. But that was why I liked him, right? Wasn't it? "People might see us," I grumbled, even as I let him press our lips together while his tongue laced through my mouth.

Or maybe *that* was why I liked him. I hoped it could be both.

The next morning Samaira and I watched the elderly couple yell at each other across the pool. *"Nahi! Nahi!"* I could distantly hear the woman call. *No.* Their minion was nowhere in sight; maybe he'd finally given up on getting an invitation to their royal palace. Poor Cinderella.

"Do you think they're happy?" I asked Samaira.

"Absolutely not," she answered as she peeled and chopped

ginger, giving the exact thought that had been floating through my mind.

"I wonder if that's why they're here," I added, because I honestly couldn't think of any other reason why they might have come. Why travel to an ashram with your spouse just to fight with them the entire time?

"Maybe they're not sure why they're here," Samaira said quietly, staring out at the spot where the woman was pointing at the sky while her husband shook his head back and forth over and over.

"Sometimes I'm not sure, either," I confessed. More and more I seemed to be doing exactly what Daadee had done—letting my time at the ashram go in the opposite direction than I'd originally planned. I still had no idea what my time at UCLA was going to look like. No idea what I'd have to say for this ashram experience when it was all said and done.

"Really?" Samaira looked confused. "You always seem so sure of yourself."

"Me?" My eyes widened.

"Well, yeah. The way you talk about your family and your friend Lexi and the school and how much you love the children there ... Teachers always seem sure of themselves to me, I guess."

"Teachers?" I asked blankly.

"You're going to study to be a teacher, right? That's why you're working in the school?" Samaira frowned when I just kept staring at her. "I guess I shouldn't have assumed that. But you just love the school so much you hardly talk about anything else anymore—"

"No," I interrupted her. "That's right. That's what I'm going to study. Hey, I need to take off, okay? I'll see you tomorrow...."

I raced out of the kitchen and down the hallway.

I knew Kiran's schedule by heart at that point, and I knew exactly where he'd be: finishing up his cleaning service at the back doors of the ashram. I darted around the back of the building, not stopping until I saw him sweeping the entrance there.

"Teacher!" I called out as I raced into his arms. "That's it! That's what I'm going to study! I'm going to be a teacher!"

Kiran, being Kiran, didn't look shocked by any of this. "I wondered. Happy for you, babe." Kissing was too dangerous this close to the ashram, but he held me long enough, hard enough, for me to be certain he understood how important this was.

"I figured it out," I mumbled. "I did it. Coming here. It worked!"

"Yeah?" Kiran laughed as we separated. "Is that the only thing coming here has gotten you?"

I blushed. "Stop it. When you look at me like that, I forget we're in an ashram."

"Yes, no canoodling in an ashram." Pilot's voice had me moving another few steps back. "You two wouldn't be up to no good, would you? Raya, Samaira told me you came this way. I'm heading over to the school now if you want to come with me."

"Absolutely!" I answered, still high on the new future laid out in front of me. The one lined with Pihus and first-time readers and the feeling of importance and meaning that always filled me when I was working with the students. "Same usual place?" I asked Kiran.

"Of course." He leaned down to kiss my hand.

"You two aren't even subtle." Pilot rolled his eyes. "Good thing you're cute."

"Congratulations!" Kiran called as we walked away.

"Congratulations? For what?" Pilot asked.

"I finally figured out what I'm gonna study next year," I told him. "Education. Samaira helped me decide, actually."

"Yeah?" Pilot grinned at me. "Raya, that's fantastic. World needs more teachers like you." He slapped me on the back, hard. I did my best not to fall over. "Hey, thanks, by the way. For being so cool about what I told you yesterday."

I rolled my eyes. "You're a good guy, Pilot. I don't like you any less just because you made a stupid choice."

"Really?" Pilot look unconvinced. "I appreciate the sentiment, Raya, but there's no way I'm the exact same guy I was yesterday in your eyes."

"Right, you're not." I could tell he was surprised—and a little hurt—by my answer. "But that's true every day, because the more time I spend with you, the more I learn about you." I shrugged. "You're more than one mistake, Pilot. We all are."

"Yeah? That's deep, Raya." His grin got wider. "Maybe some-day you'll go that easy on yourself."

Huh. Good point. "Maybe today's a start. It was so crazy, Pilot. I was just talking to Samaira and it was like all of a sudden it all just made *sense*. Like she clicked in the last piece of this puzzle I haven't been able to solve."

"She's kind of awesome like that. I like Samaira a lot."

"I wish I knew more about her. One minute she's ready to selfie with me—not that we're allowed to have phones here—and the next minute she's acting like I have the plague."

Pilot looked vaguely uncomfortable. *Uh-oh.*

"I've been saying things that piss her off, right? And I haven't even noticed. Great, I'm the new Devin. Do you know what I said? I wanna at least apologize, tell her—"

"Raya," Pilot interrupted, "not everything is about you."

It wasn't the first time I'd ever heard that. Still. "What's going on, then?"

Pilot looked uncomfortable. "Not my story to tell. Just trust me when I say that Samaira has her reasons for acting the way she does."

I forced myself not to groan. The struggle of the Rishi Kanva ashram was real: uncover two secrets, four more appear.

Pihu read another few paragraphs to me that afternoon, so I was in a fairly excellent mood when Kiran met me on the footbridge afterward. I had my grandmother's journal with me, so I decided to treat myself to another entry or two. Kiran sketched and played on his phone while I read.

The first entry for that day was all Daadee's thoughts on what it took to achieve moksha—frankly, it didn't hold my attention all that well. But the second entry? *That* quickly got my attention.

❦

July 20

Today I had a most difficult conversation. It was not a conversation I wished to have, but it was of great necessity.

I told meri jaan that it is time for us to let go of each other. Make no mistake, dearest journal: we have no physical ties to each other. We have never broken our vows of true chastity. But emotionally, we are far more connected than we should ever have let ourselves become.

And so, with great difficulty, I pulled him aside today. He will be leaving soon to return to his home, where I know his family has already arranged an impressive marriage for him. Lately he has hinted that I should leave with him when he goes, that he would happily end his marriage arrangement and spend his life with me.

Today I assured him that was not possible. I told him in no uncertain terms that when he leaves next week he is to forget me. His path is laid out before him and mine before me, and I will not see my path derailed.

He must forget me, dearest journal. It is the only way. I cannot lose myself in my love as Shakuntala did—I simply cannot. And if the tears that fall down my face right now speak otherwise, then these tears are simply one more thing I must dismiss from my life as it exists.

I will become a guru. It is all I have ever wanted . . . until now, at least. It must become that again.

He must forget me.

"Oh, my God," I whispered.

"What?" Kiran looked up from whatever he was writing.

"She ended it with him. She left him, even though she knew she loved him. That's how much she wanted to become a guru. How much it mattered to her." I buried my head into my chest. "She loved him, but she ended it anyway."

Kiran squeezed my shoulder. "Your grandmother really left him? The guy she met here?" he asked. His voice sounded timid, almost frightened.

" 'I told him in no uncertain terms that when he leaves next week he is to forget me. His path is laid out before him and mine before me, and I will not see my path derailed.' " I read the passage aloud, slowing down to emphasize the word *derailed*.

"Wow." Kiran let out a deep breath. "But they're going to get back together, right? I mean, Anandi thinks this guy is your grandfather. They have to get back together, don't they?" Now his voice sounded even stranger—maybe a little frantic.

"I don't know. Maybe I've been right all along, and she met another barrister from Varanasi. Maybe she became a guru first and she just never told us! Maybe she didn't give everything up!" I dropped the journal on the ground, excited by the possibility. "Except...that means she left behind whoever *meri jaan* was."

Kiran shifted uncomfortably. "Isn't that what you wanted?"

"I don't know. I thought I wanted her to dedicate her life to getting what she always wanted—being a guru. But now it's like my heart is breaking for her. I feel like I'm listening to Shakuntala's story all over again, even though they made the opposite choices. It just feels like now Daadee's going to end up alone and forgotten." I shuddered.

"Hey, calm down." Kiran hugged me tightly. "You know *that* doesn't happen. History says so. She ends up with your grandfather, remember? Somehow, it all works out. She ends up happy, remember? Just like Shakuntala and Dushyanta."

"That took years," I reminded him.

He brushed some hair back from my face. "I think they'd both say it was worth the wait."

We lay down together, and I tried my best not to overthink what came next for my grandmother. Finding out what the rest of the story looked like was as simple as turning a page—but I couldn't bring myself to do that.

If Anandi was right, and this man was Daada, she was going to change her mind and go back to him. She'd never become a guru.

The other option was that she did become a guru before she married my grandfather and she just never told us. But that meant she'd first abandoned the love of her life for who knows how long.

I didn't want to know just yet which path she'd taken. Either one seemed horrible in its own way.

"I still can't quite believe she sent him away like that," I finally told Kiran. "She was in love with him. I know she was. That must have been one of the hardest things she ever had to do. Can you even imagine how hard that would be? To let go of someone like that, knowing that you didn't have to? To let go of love?"

"No," Kiran answered. He took a strand of my hair and curled it around his finger while he studied me. "I really can't." He sighed. "Damn *anurkati*," he added softly.

"Huh?"

"*Anurkati*. It means 'love' in Sanskrit. At least, it's one of the words that mean 'love.'"

"What are you talking about?"

He smiled and gently kissed my cheek. "There are ninety-six words for love in Sanskrit. I can't believe you didn't know that, Research Girl."

"Funny. Are you going to tell me what they are?"

He nodded. "If you want me to."

I think I nodded back. It's possible I just stared. His eyes were dark, almost burning, with that same kind of focused thrill he'd just described me as having.

"*Vena*." He brushed his lips against my cheek.

"*Pranaya*." Mouth.

"*Titha*." Neck. At this point, my heart was pounding so hard I was surprised Kiran couldn't hear it beating out of my chest. I wondered if his was just as drumlike in his body, and I reached over to place my hand across his right rib. To find out.

He pulled up my fingers and kissed my palm. "*Vanati*," he whispered.

And then we both stopped talking.

Sex with Kiran wasn't magically better than my other sexual encounters just because it was the first time I had gone all the way or because I had much stronger feelings for him. But it was different. It felt higher, more intense. More meaningful than any sex I'd ever had before. And even though I didn't achieve the orgasm dream, I was certain I could get there with Kiran. We just needed to keep practicing.

When it was over, when we were both lying on our backs catching our breath, Kiran reached over and drifted a finger across my cheek. "*Rasa*," he whispered.

"*Rasa*," I whispered back. Because whatever variation of "love" that particular Sanskrit word meant, it felt like exactly the right thing to say.

"I don't ever want you to forget me," I told Kiran softly.

He kissed my neck. Gently. Slowly. As though he was savoring having his lips on my skin. "I never could," he answered. "No matter how many rings of yours I lost."

fourteen

IMPERMANENCE AND ILL-CONCEIVED NOTIONS

I did my best not to float into the dining hall that night. I kept all wide grins to a minimum and even managed not to hum as I wandered past the buffet table, basically putting food on my plate without even paying attention to what it was. Who cared if my mouth burned? Kiran and I had finally made love. *Nothing* could get me down.

I was pouring myself some tea when I saw Devin sitting at our table, listlessly stirring some *madras,* a local dish made of lentils cooked with yogurt. Poor Devin. The scene Kiran and I had watched the day before played through my mind in stark contrast with the beauty of what I'd just experienced. I wondered if Devin would ever figure out how to get out of her own way. I still couldn't believe that she was even trying—that she'd actually listened to me.

Maybe she'd never fully get out of her own way. But I could try to push her out of it.

I located John the video game designer sitting with a mixed group of older and younger ashram attendees at a table toward the back of the room and marched over to them. "Hello," I said, sitting down next to John. "I'm Raya. Thought I'd try sitting somewhere new today. How is everyone?"

John looked slightly wary, and I realized he'd probably seen me around the ashram with Devin. Great. I was going to have to play this slow.

"We're very well, thank you," said the woman sitting next to me. Kathy, I remembered her name was. She was from somewhere in America, and she'd introduced herself to me during *satsang* once. "How has your service within the community been? You mentioned once that you were working at the school."

"Amazing." I started telling her and everyone else at the table all about the work Pilot and I were doing at the school and Pihu and the other kids, and by the time I'd finished talking I'd forgotten I was basically infiltrating the table on a secret mission. Education definitely wasn't going to be a hard calling to answer.

"It sounds like a wonderful experience," Kathy said as I finished telling them all about how awesome the students at the school were and why they should volunteer. "John, maybe we should join them sometime. We were both just saying that we'd like to see more of what's outside the ashram while we're here."

"Maybe," John answered. And I didn't think I was imagining

that he was staring at me like I was a snake who could reach out and poison him at any moment.

I figured it was probably time to just lay everything on the line, so I leaned over to whisper in John's ear. "If you're worried I'm just here to get you to talk to Devin, it's not like that," I told him.

He almost choked on his *madras*. "Excuse me?"

I shrugged. "I know she's probably been driving you nuts. I get it. She drives me nuts sometimes, too. I'm not eating with you to set you up or anything like that. But you should probably know that Devin's actually a fairly decent human being once you get to know her, and she's trying to be even better. Not everyone's exactly who they appear to be, right?"

John was still staring at me as though he were in potentially imminent danger. "So what do you think the topic for *satsang* will be tonight?" he asked the table, quickly changing the subject.

Ah, well. At least I'd tried.

During *satsang*, the guru brought up a quote from the *Bhagavad Gita* she wanted us to discuss. "The nonpermanent appearance of happiness and distress, and their disappearance in due course, are like the appearance and disappearance of summer and winter seasons." She finished reading and cocked her head at us, smiling slightly. "Do you accept that? Do you believe that to be a truth of the world?"

An older man I didn't recognize started speaking about how much he wanted that to be his own truth, even though he had trouble believing that distress doesn't stay with us forever. As he spoke, I found my eyes drifting to Samaira. She was sitting across the room from me next to an Indian girl about my age who I knew was her roommate. Were she and Samaira friends? Did Samaira even have real friends, or did she randomly stop talking to them whenever she felt like it the way she always did with me?

Whatever Samaira had gone through to make her act the way she did, it didn't seem possible to me in any way that that type of pain could just disappear. I ended up staring for so long that eventually Samaira looked my way and our gazes locked. I shifted, uncomfortable under her own sharp look, until she eventually nodded and turned away.

I pulled my own eyes away and floated them around the room, determined not to be caught staring at Samaira again. That didn't turn out to be hard, because a moment later I found myself staring at someone else: John.

Who was sitting with Devin.

"Wow," Anandi remarked next to me. "He's not running away. He even looks like he might be...smiling."

He did, actually. Not surprisingly, Devin was smiling, too.

Maybe everything really was impermanent.

"I don't understand." Pihu frowned as she ran her fingers back and forth over the word on the paper below her. "How can letters in English make different sounds every time I have to read them?"

It was definitely a legitimate question. "Many others have wondered exactly the same thing," I told her sagely. "It's just the way things are," I added, trying out the line my mother used to use on me whenever I asked a question she didn't know the answer to.

Pihu eyed me skeptically.

"Anyway," I said, "I found another book we can read when we finish the last chapter of the dog book. It was in the ashram library, and I thought you might like it." I rummaged through my shoulder bag, looking for the children's book with the adorable kitten on it. I'd found it buried under stacks of some much more advanced volumes of literature, and I doubted anyone would miss it if I gave it to Pihu.

"Oooh, what's that?" Pihu asked as more books, tubes of mascara, and even a stray tampon all came falling out of my bag. I smiled when I saw the particular item she'd picked up: my grandmother's journal.

"That's a journal my grandmother kept when she was just a little older than me," I told her as I scooped everything else back into my bag. I must have forgotten the kitten book in my room. "It's the treasure I was looking for. You helped me find it when you showed me where that shrine was. Do you want me to read the next part to you? I was going to read another entry today." Maybe I'd be able to handle whatever came next in Daadee's story better if Pihu was with me when I read it.

Pihu looked up at me with wide eyes. "You mean you haven't read it all yet?"

I shook my head. "I've been reading it slowly, a little at a time."

Pihu brushed her fingers across the cover of the journal reverently. "I'd love to read it with you," she whispered.

Pihu and I curled up in a corner together with my grand-mother's voice in the back of my head.

July 25

It is done. He has gone.

Since the day he left, I have been more focused than ever on my spiritual practice. I have engaged in deep prayer and meditation, determined to return solely to a path of spiritual enlightenment and discovery. Yet each morning, as I engage in prayers, I find more emptiness than fullness.

My heart is torn. I feel as Shakuntala must have felt when Dushyanta looked upon her face and could not remember her. I feel as though half my reason for being has abandoned me entirely.

I was always certain that becoming a guru would give me all the fulfillment I required in life. So why do I feel this great void? Why do I feel as though I have lost something I can never recover?

Why do I feel as though my path went in a different direction without me on it? Why do I feel as though the ring that would determine my entire future has been lost in a river?

"Why is she so sad?" Pihu whispered.

"She was in love," I told her. "But she told the man she loved to leave her behind and forget her."

"Why?" Pihu looked horrified.

"Because she also wanted to be a guru someday, and she couldn't have both."

Pihu looked absolutely mutinous. "That's silly. I'm going to be a famous actress *and* a teacher *and* marry someone I love when I grow up."

I laughed. "Good for you," I told her. "Should we read another entry?"

Pihu nodded seriously.

August 2

You would be shocked to know where I am at this moment, dear journal. Or perhaps you would not.

I am on a train to Varanasi.

The guru and I had a long talk last week during services. We discussed my confusion as to my path, the directions and discoveries I have made in this ashram. Eventually I told him the truth as it is: that I formed a connection outside of myself and my spiritual world here, and now I cannot seem to let that connection go. I told him of the likeness I feel to

Shakuntala right now. The understanding I have of her pain, her suffering. I told him I could not remain at the ashram.

I expected some level of upset from the guru. There was none. All he told me was this, when I told him of my demand to the man from Varanasi that I be forgotten: "He will remember you when you remember you."

I prayed extensively for days after that, journal. I prayed for guidance. For understanding. For memory. Eventually, I remembered the only thing that mattered: the happiness that I felt when we were together. It was a greater happiness than I have ever felt at any other moment in my life.

I knew then what I must do.

I secured a traveling companion, a kind man who is also returning to Varanasi from the ashram and I agreed that I might go with him. We left early this morning and should arrive late this evening.

I have remembered myself. And here, then, is the only question that remains: will he remember me in return?

Will Raaz remember as I now do?

I jolted back from the diary as though it had smacked me in the face, which it might as well have. *Raaz?*

That was Daada's name. Anandi had been right all along: the man from Varanasi had been my grandfather.

She had fallen in love with Daada in the ashram.

She'd tried to leave him, and she couldn't.

And eventually she had left behind her dreams and plans of being a guru...all for him.

I dropped the diary on the floor, and Pihu reached down to pick it up. "What's wrong, Raya?" she asked anxiously.

"No...nothing," I told her. "Something just surprised me, that's all. Listen, Pihu, I have to go. I'll see you tomorrow, okay?"

I rushed out of the school before Pilot or anyone else could stop me. There was only one person I wanted to see just then, and I knew where he would be waiting for me.

Kiran tried to speak to me when I finally found him at the statue garden, but I wasn't in the mood to talk.

I took his lips by storm while I unbuttoned his shirt, and he caught on quickly after that. Soon everything about us was merged together in a way that made all the sense in the universe and absolutely no sense at the same time.

Afterward we lounged in the grass, barely dressed, not speaking. Kiran had somehow worked up the energy to get the condom off and into a small plastic bag he'd brought along. The guy seriously came prepared.

"Where are you going to throw that away?" I asked. If anyone in the ashram saw that condom, odds were our relationship wouldn't stay a secret too much longer.

It surprised me how much that thought didn't panic me.

227

"Trash duty is part of my morning cleaning service, remember? It's not a problem."

I ghosted my hand over his bare chest, the short, coarse hair there tickling my fingers. "I read more of my grandmother's journal today," I told him.

"Ummm," he mumbled. His attention was somewhere on my upper thigh.

"She gave all this up, you know. For my grandfather. Gave up her dream. She went back to him. Decided she didn't want to be apart from him after all."

Now Kiran looked up, surprised. "So the man she met here was your grandfather?"

I nodded.

"How do you feel about that?" he asked hesitantly.

"More confused than ever," I answered honestly.

Kiran frowned. "Why? She got what she wanted in the end. It was her choice to go back to him, right?"

"Sure, but look at what she gave up." I gestured to the ashram around me.

"Maybe she didn't look at it that way." He nuzzled his face into my neck. "It sounds to me like she just discovered a drive for something more important," he said.

And *that* was almost exactly what I was afraid of. That when you wanted more than one thing, one of them always had to be more important than the other.

I sat up and started pulling on my shirt, which said HEDGE-HOGS NEED TO LEARN TO SHARE THE HEDGE on it. "Kiran," I asked, "have you heard anything from your parents? About how much longer you're going to be here?"

He looked uncomfortable. "I got a letter yesterday. They're coming to visit next week."

"Why didn't you tell me that?" I didn't even try to hide how pissed I was. His *parents* were coming? Now? That meant the end of all this. It meant that decisions I wasn't ready to make were looming over our tree-scraped horizon.

"Raya, calm down." Kiran pulled my body into his. "They're coming to check on me and 'talk.' Most likely they'll decide I'm still too immature and need to stay here longer. And even if that's not what they say, I've told you before, we'll figure this out. Don't worry so much, okay?" He kissed me again, long and hard, and then went back to buttoning his shirt. "I'm not worried. You shouldn't be, either."

I wish I shared his optimism, but I didn't see how we were just going to "figure this out." I lived in California. He lived in Delhi. Skype was great and all, but I had my doubts it could get us through a relationship *that* long-distance.

"But what about—"

"Shhhhh." He laid a finger gently over my lips. "I don't think we should worry about this yet, okay? We've got plenty of time to figure things out."

The obsessive planner in me didn't love that approach, but I sort of forgot to keep worrying when Kiran started kissing me again. Kiran had to be right—we'd figure this out. And of *course* he didn't want to talk about it before we had to. Kiran didn't like worrying about anything or thinking about upsetting things. Not even impermanence.

Kiran and I were on our way back to the ashram when Pilot came running up to us, a horrific combination of fear and hope written across his face.

"Have you seen Pihu?" he asked us, panting.

"No," I told him. "Not since I left the school."

Pilot swallowed so hard I watched his Adam's apple move. "She didn't make it home today," he whispered. "No one can find her."

fifteen
∞

FEAR AND FORGETFULNESS

We searched for hours. We didn't find Pihu.

"She probably just wandered off somewhere near the village and got lost," Khatri assured me when Pilot, Kiran, and I returned to the school to report that we still had no idea where she was. "It does happen. Everyone in the town now knows to be on the lookout, so I'm sure we'll find her."

I couldn't decide if I believed her.

"Oh, and Raya," Khatri added, "this is a terrible time to tell you this, but you left something here earlier. A small notebook? Pihu took it with her for safekeeping.... I'm so sorry I don't have it to give to you. But as I said, I'm sure she'll be back. We will find her."

I dug my hand into my bag to make sure it wasn't there, even though I already knew it wasn't.

My grandmother's journal was gone. It was with Pihu.

Who was also gone.

"Do you think Khatri is right?" I asked Kiran anxiously as we walked back to the Rishi Kanva. A huge majority of people from the ashram, including Anandi and Devin, had gone out to help look for Pihu, but almost everyone else had gone back already at the insistence of Khatri and others leading the search. They said we'd looked everywhere there was to look in daylight, and the area around the village was too difficult to search at night. We'd all start together again in the morning, Guru Baba had been quick to remind us when several of us protested. "Will we find her?"

Kiran squeezed me around the shoulders. "I'm just as new to this part of India as you are, Raya," he said softly. "I don't know."

Oh, yeah. Asking Kiran to explain the intricacies of the area around the ashram was as ridiculous as him thinking I'd seen a ton of apple trees in my life.

But at least thinking about the apple trees made me smile for a moment.

I found Devin and Anandi back in our room at the ashram, huddled together on Anandi's bed. Anandi slid something underneath it when I walked into the room.

"What was that?" I asked. Okay, growled. Pihu was missing, nobody would let me look for her again until morning, I'd lost the journal I'd come all the way to India to find, and now Anandi was hiding something else from me? With *Devin*, of all people?

"I'm so sorry about Pihu," Anandi said in a rush. "We'll find her tomorrow. I know we will."

"Yeah, so everyone keeps telling me." I eyed the bed again. "Seriously, what's going on? Why are you shoving things under the bed the minute I walk into the room?"

"Really, love, it's nothing," Devin interjected. "John and I were just talking while we were looking, about some music for this video game he's designing, and—oh, bollocks, I've just blown the secret, haven't I?" She winced when she realized Anandi was glaring at her.

"What secret? I knew there was something sus about you and music." All my frustrations—Pihu being gone, *meri jaan* being exactly who I didn't want him to be—felt like they were bubbling over as I walked over to the bed and pulled out the object Anandi had just stuffed under it.

It was a guitar case. Or some version of that. It looked smaller than any guitar case I'd ever seen.

"I'm learning to play the sitar," Anandi said. Almost challengingly.

"That's it? That's what you've been hiding?" I popped open the case, half expecting to find it filled with cocaine.

Nope. Just a triangular-shaped guitar-type thing. Nothing else whatsoever.

"Well, I think I'll take myself to dinner, then," Devin interjected with absolutely zero subtlety. "Must meet John. See you loves later." She kissed us both on the cheeks and left.

"Why wouldn't you tell me you were taking sitar lessons? What's the big deal? Where the hell *are* you taking sitar lessons, anyway?" I didn't mean to sound quite so angry. But all the stress of the last few hours suddenly seemed to be bubbling to my surface and all over Anandi's instrument case.

Anandi pushed the case in question back under the bed. "Raya, you know how seriously my father takes his work. He's been talking about me becoming a barrister like him since I said my first words. He's never let me take music lessons before because 'they'd become a distraction.'" Anandi air-quoted the last four words. "But I've wanted to learn how to play an instrument for a really long time now. Ever since I heard my first Jonas Brothers song, back when you first visited, I wished I could make music like that. I wanted to create music that would make people happy, the way Nick's music makes people happy."

I guessed it did make *some* people happy.

"When we decided to come here to visit the ashram, I found out that a well-known sitar player lives in this village. So I contacted him and asked if he would give me lessons."

"So why hide it? What's the big deal?"

Anandi drew in a deep breath. "I was afraid you might accidentally tell someone in your family, and that it would get back to my father."

I laughed, but the sound was far hollower than I ever intended. "Your father would be *that* upset about you taking sitar lessons? Like no lawyer in history has ever learned to play the sitar?"

Anandi bit her lower lip. "Raya," she said softly, "you have no idea how seriously my father takes my future. A year ago I made the mistake of telling him I might want to study music in addition to law." She drew in a deep breath. "He told me he would disown any daughter of his who studied anything as frivolous as music."

Whoa. That was seriously harsh. I remembered Anandi's words in Barog: *Sometimes mistakes are costly.*

But *still.*

"Why would you think you couldn't trust me?" I practically growled at her. "I would have kept your secret. Jeez, Anandi, I came to an *ashram* with you. And you didn't even trust me enough to tell me you were taking sitar lessons?" The tension that had already boiled over from within me was starting to permeate the room now, and I was certain Anandi felt it just as heavily as I did.

Her eyes narrowed. "It's not that simple, Raya. All it would have taken was for you to mention something to your mother by accident and for her to mention it to my mother. And, just like that, I'd lose everything."

I rolled my eyes. "Oh, don't be so dramatic. I'm sure he wouldn't *actually* disown you."

"Like you understand anything about how my parents operate." She slammed the sitar case shut again and shoved it back under the bed. "Raya, sometimes you amaze me. All you do is walk around here bitching and complaining about how you have no direction, no idea what you want to be." She turned up the notes on the last words in her sentence, mocking all the whining I apparently did all the time. "You have no idea how lucky you are to have that freedom. My whole future's been laid out since I was in the womb. You can't even fathom what that would be like, can you?" She scoffed when I didn't answer right away. "Nope, I didn't think you could. So I kept the music lessons a secret. So what? Who cares?" She stalked to the edge of the room and pulled the door open. "Don't even try to pretend you're not keeping a much bigger secret from me."

And then she flounced out the door, leaving me with my eyes wide and no idea how to answer any of that.

There was no way I was going to dinner after *that* argument. Who the hell would I sit with? Vihaan?

I ignored my growling stomach and went to sit in the great hall, waiting for *satsang* to start. I couldn't sit around all night thinking about Pihu's disappearance and my fight with Anandi—I needed to get my mind onto something else for a while. If anything could do that, it was probably *satsang*.

"Hello, beautiful," a voice whispered in my ear.

Or possibly Kiran.

"Don't be cute," I mumbled. "I can't be cute back right now."

"I know you're worried about Pihu. I'm so sorry, Raya." He

sank down next to me. "The guru said she's ending services at first light tomorrow so we can all go out and look. We'll find her, Raya."

"You don't know that." I felt the tears welling in my eyes as I studied the statue of Bharat. So much sadness had to be created in the world in order for him to exist. Why did so much good in the world always have to be surrounded by terribleness?

"It's not fair," I whispered. "I don't know why Pihu has to be missing or why Anandi can't just play the damn sitar or why she and I can't just switch places. That would be a better solution."

I'm sure Kiran had zero idea what I was talking about, but he didn't interrupt me.

"And now your parents are coming to visit next week," I added in a whisper. "What do we do if they say you can go home? You can't stay here; you've got things to do. I know how much you miss being able to do what you love. I'm going to lose Pihu. And then I'm going to lose you."

A little voice in my head added: *But you were always going to lose him anyway. You're supposed to go back to California and study to become a teacher, remember?*

"You're not going to lose me, Raya." Kiran avoided touching me—we both knew people would start coming into the great hall for *satsang* at any moment—but he did gently rub the fingers on his right hand over mine, where they lay across the floor. So many emotions, complicated and simple, were written into that touch.

"There's no way I can keep you," I whispered. "Not without giving so much else up. Just like Shakuntala. Just like Daadee."

He sighed. "Raya, I told you, there's no point thinking about it, okay? I don't even know what my parents are going to say, so why spend time now thinking about it? Why worry when we don't have to?"

I couldn't even fathom how he could feel that way—not when my brain could go for ten minutes without stopping on this kind of topic. "How can you say that?" I asked. "Doesn't any of this matter to you?" I gestured to the room around us, but we both knew what I mean. Him. Me. Us.

He frowned. "Of course," he said. "Which is why I know we'll figure things out."

For the first time since I'd met him, I did not find Kiran's optimism charming.

"Kiran, I can't be okay with that." I shook my head. "You know I don't work like that. I need a plan. I need to know what's going to happen if you leave."

Kiran groaned. "Look, Raya, I get that you think you can plan out your entire life in one month-long session at an ashram—"

I cut him off. "What's that supposed to mean?"

"But you have to understand that my parents have plans for me, too. And until I know what those plans are, I can't say exactly what's going to happen next."

"Sure," I mumbled. "We'll just wait on your parents to decide both our futures." My thoughts floated briefly to Anandi's sitar case.

He rolled his eyes. "Like you chose UCLA completely by yourself?"

Okay, fair point. "Maybe, but at least my parents aren't picking out my future spouse," I shot back.

Kiran sighed again. "Look, we always knew we were on borrowed time here. We'll find a way to make this work—I promise." He pulled my hand fully into his, and I didn't resist. If someone wanted to walk into the room and report me to the guru for holding Kiran's hand, they could go on ahead and do that. "Tell that whirling brain of yours to shut down for two minutes and give you a break. Have some faith in us."

I wanted to. I really did. But between Pihu and Anandi and all the confused futures and pasts swirling around in my overtaxed brain, I was starting to find that the Rishi Kanva ashram was a tough place to have faith.

sixteen

∞

PARENTS AND PROBABLYS

I ended up leaving *satsang* early that night and falling asleep before Anandi even got to the room. I was determined to be at my very best the next day. Pihu needed all my energy.

So Anandi and I didn't speak again until the next morning, as we were getting ready for rituals.

I wanted to stay mad at her. I wanted to stay mad at her *so badly.* She'd kept a secret from me, as if I were some gossipy bitch who couldn't be trusted.

Except maybe she had some decent reasons. I was close to my mother, and Anandi knew it. Anything could slip out once I was home and talking to my mother again. And while I wanted to believe that Mom would keep an important secret like that on Anandi's behalf, she was close to her cousin.

Daadee used to say that secrets are like leaves in a windstorm: they have a way of taking on their own travels.

"You're right," I finally mumbled. "I have secrets of my own. You know about Kiran, right? I should have told you about him."

Anandi looked up from where she was tying her sneaker lace, clearly surprised. "It's okay that you didn't," she told me. "You're allowed to have secrets from me." Her implication was clear behind her words: *And I'm allowed to have them from you.*

I nodded. "Thanks," I told her. "Did Daadee used to say that thing to you? About secrets being like leaves?"

A slow smile spread across Anandi's face. "I used to love that saying."

"Me too." I sighed. "For what it's worth, I wasn't really mad at you, Anandi. I'm just worried about Pihu. Sorry for taking it out on you."

Anandi crossed the room and hugged me. "I know. I understand."

I swear, the world isn't worth the amount of empathy and forgiveness built into someone like my cousin.

As promised, Guru Baba ended morning rituals at first light so the majority of the ashram's residents could walk over to the school together and rejoin the search for Pihu. Anandi and I walked together with Pilot, and I was surprised when Samaira joined us. I hadn't seen her join the search party yesterday.

"Thanks for helping," I told her.

She didn't answer. Just nodded.

241

At the school, a large group of community members and fellow students of Pihu's had gathered. The crowd was impressive, especially considering it was the middle of the week and a lot of people probably should have been at work. Samaira and I ended up being paired up together to walk the perimeter of the woods closest to the school. We walked off together as Khatri was reassuring Pihu's tear-stricken mother that surely she couldn't have gone far.

Samaira was clearly back in a silent mode, and I didn't feel much like talking, so the first hour we spent together essentially just involved the two of us calling Pihu's name while we walked on the edge of the trees.

We had just looped back on the same part of the forest when Samaira cried out suddenly and sat down on the ground.

"What is it?" I fell to my knees next to her. "Did you see something?"

"No!" she all but shouted at me. "Don't you understand? We haven't seen anything! She's gone, Raya!"

A lump dug itself into my throat. "She isn't gone," I informed Samaira. "Khatri said students wander off. We'll find her. We'll—"

"Don't be an idiot!" Samaira was *really* shouting now, her words loud and clear for anyone nearby to hear. "That's what they always say!" She shook her head hard, tears running down her cheeks. "She's been taken, Raya. All the signs are there. We're not going to see her again."

A cold crept over me with the same speed that nasty lump had invaded. "You're wrong," I told her. "Why would anyone take Pihu?"

Samaira looked up and caught my eyes with hers. They were dark and distant. "The same reason why they took me. For the money."

Fear choked my body. "You were..."

She nodded. "I was taken. From a village about the size of this one, but in the South. My parents had no money to look for me, just like Pihu's parents won't. Her teacher and the police and the others here won't be able to help, just like people couldn't help my parents. She'll be gone, just like I was. I was gone for almost two years." Her voice was soft now, her tone more neutral than anything else. "That's why I'm here, you know. The people who found me, who sponsor me, thought this place would help me heal."

I thought for a minute my throat was going to close up around the sobs that were threatening to break through. *Not Samaira. Not Pihu.* "I'm so sorry," I whispered, shaking my head. "All that time we've spent joking about that married couple, all the time I've spent whining to you about my problems—I can't believe we talked about any of that now, knowing what you've been through."

Samaira rolled her eyes. "You seriously don't get it, do you? Raya, I *liked* that you whined to me about your problems. I liked wondering about that couple with you. Everyone else here treats me like I'm made of glass. You never have. Please don't start now."

The whole situation did explain a lot about the *you make me feel so normal* comment.

She stared off into the distance for a moment. "If Pihu is ever found," she finally said, "she'll need people like you. People who treat her like she's normal."

The words hung over me for a long time. I think they hung over both of us. As we finished another loop of the woods. As we walked back to the school, both of us searching earnestly in Khatri's face for any kind of good news.

But there was no good news lurking in that school. Only Pihu's mother's shaking shoulders, and Khatri telling us her daughter was still nowhere to be found.

We spent the whole day looking. Eventually the search was called off.

"We believe the young girl is no longer in the area," Guru Baba told those of us who had gathered from the ashram to help. "The authorities are searching for her using…other avenues. Now we can only pray that she finds her way toward moksha."

I couldn't be sure, but I had the sense that was the Hindu equivalent of America's beloved phrase "Our thoughts and prayers are with you." A phrase I hated with all my heart.

Thoughts and prayers were nice. Necessary. And I wasn't one of those people who thought prayer was meaningless—I was living in an ashram, for goodness' sake.

But they were just words. Words that were said all too often with nothing behind them. And while I knew the guru didn't intend for her words to feel hollow, they did. In every possible way.

So I ran. I ran away from the guru's words, as far and as fast as I could.

Kiran found me in the statue garden, sobbing.

"She can't be gone," I begged. "She can't be gone, Kiran."

He wrapped me in his arms next to the statue of Bharat, the statue where my grandmother had hidden pictures for me to find.

"I'm so sorry, Raya." Kiran kissed my hair.

"I just...I can't believe this can happen. That someone can just disappear like that. And be gone. Samaira says she's probably been..."

Kiran sighed. "I know. I heard. Listen, though, Raya, you can't let this be the last and only thing you remember about that school or Pihu. India isn't just full of sex traffickers and Bollywood movies—you know that. Bad things happen everywhere, but so do good things." He kissed me gently. "Like people reading to little kids just because they want to do some good in the world."

I scoffed. "Helping out at the school was as much for me as it was for those kids, Kiran. You know that."

"Yeah. I do. Raya..." Kiran said hesitantly. "I have an idea. Something else we could try."

"I'll do anything. I can't let her be out there all alone like this. I just can't." Suddenly I was sobbing again, and I wasn't sure how I'd ever stop. Eventually I pulled my face out of his shirt, likely leaving a very unattractive trail of snot behind. "Whatever it is, we have to do it. I don't care."

"Okay, then." Kiran stood up and started walking out of the statue garden.

"Where are you going?" I called after him.

"To call my parents. I'm going to tell them they can't wait until next week—they need to come to the ashram now."

Oh.

They arrived in a swirl of high-priced perfume and elaborate pantsuits. Actually, it was just Kiran's mother. With her assistant, of course, who looked like he was trying desperately not to be bored to death.

"*Namaste.* Good to meet you," Mrs. Parashar said briskly, hardly making time to meet my eye. "Kiran, lovely, I was so pleased you called. It's just terrible what happens to children in these rural areas." She shivered. "Your father and I feel so lucky that you've been safe here."

I decided not to mention that Delhi was basically the capital of the India sex trafficking industry.

"Can you help?" I asked. We were standing in the middle of the great hall, with the guru and Khatri next to us. Apparently, Mrs. Parashar liked to arrive to an immediate and captive audience.

"One can never be sure." Mrs. Parashar frowned. "As I'm sure you all know, these people operate quickly and efficiently. But I do believe we can expand your search beyond what the police would be able to do on their own. We've already contacted the organization we work with that has sometimes been able to recover victims of such horrific events."

I assumed, based on all the Prada she was wearing, that "work with" meant "give large sums of money to." Not that I was complaining. Not if all that money would help get Pihu back.

"And of course we've asked all your father's friends in law enforcement to move this case to the top of their lists." She nodded at Kiran, and I decided not to even ask myself what that nod probably meant. "All we need is a picture to start sharing with our network. It's likely the girl is somewhere near Delhi, and if we hurry, we still have a chance to find her."

Khatri produced a picture Pihu's mother had given her, and Mrs. Parashar passed it to the assistant. He glanced at it and nodded.

"Kiran, my darling, we will return home immediately, of course." Mrs. Parashar took his cheeks in her hands. "If you're calling me to beg for help for others, this place has done exactly for you what we hoped it would. Clearly it's accomplished a world of good. It's time, then, to leave. Raya, it was lovely to make your acquaintance. Pack quickly, please, Kiran."

And on that note, she spun around and left the room, with the guru and Khatri talking quietly as they followed behind her.

"Your mother is intense. You know that, right?"

"Since I was three." Kiran laughed, but there wasn't any kind of amusement in the sound. "Still, she's not a bad person, and she does know how to spread around her money. Bringing her into this will hopefully increase the chances that Pihu can be found. That organization she works with sponsors some of the people here, you know. She's gotten lots of them back to normal lives."

Ah. Samaira. So that was where this new version of "normal" had come from. I realized it probably wasn't a coincidence that Samaira and Kiran were staying in the same ashram.

Except that Kiran wasn't staying here anymore. Because he'd called his parents to come to the ashram early, all to help Pihu. And now his mother was going to take him away.

"Are you really leaving?" I asked, as Mrs. Parashar's words finally registered in my head. "You're really going to go home with her?"

Kiran shifted uncomfortably. "I think I have to, Raya," he told me. "What else am I gonna do? Tell her I don't want to leave because I fell for a girl in a chaste ashram?"

I tried not to get stuck on the words *fell for a girl.* What did those words matter if Kiran was leaving?

"But Pihu's still missing, and we still haven't talked about what's going to happen to us. What's... going to happen now?" I asked lamely.

Kiran took a breath. "Pihu's search is in better hands now, Raya. My mother really will make sure all her resources are on this. I know it's hard, but we need to have some faith while these people do their jobs."

So that answered one of my thoughts. But not the other. Kiran was quiet for several long moments before he said, "I don't want to lose you, Raya."

"I don't want to lose you, either." Kiran had become so wrapped into the fabric of my universe that I could no longer imagine a world without him. It didn't seem even remotely possible that my time with him could be impermanent. I *knew* we should have already talked about what was going to happen when one of us finally had to leave the ashram. But no. Ever-optimistic Kiran just kept insisting that things would somehow work out.

Now here we were, about to be separated, with no plan whatsoever to keep that from happening. I did my best to push down the feelings of frustration that were swelling inside me.

Kiran twisted a lock of my hair around his finger. "What if you stayed in India or something? You have family here. Maybe you don't have to leave?"

I frowned. "Kiran, you know I can't do that. I'm starting at UCLA soon. And I finally know what I'm going to do there—you know how much it meant to me to figure that out. I can't give up on getting a degree in something I love before I even start."

"You wouldn't have to give it all up. You could still find a way to study teaching. You might just have to . . . compromise a little."

I narrowed my eyes as the frustration I'd felt a moment earlier suddenly grew. Compromise? Like Daadee had? "Why do I have to be the one to compromise? Couldn't you come to America or something?"

"Yeah, right." He rolled his eyes. "You just met my mother. You think that woman is going to let her only child—the family heir—abandon everything she and my father have built in India so I can go live in another country? It'll never happen, Raya." He reached for my hand, but I pulled it away. "Maybe we could try to do this long-distance. You're leaving the ashram soon. Between Skype and messaging, we could talk all the time...."

His voice trailed off. Even the ever-optimistic Kiran seemed to realize, just then, that the odds of us making a relationship work across that many time zones were slim to none.

"We should have talked about this," I muttered. "I knew we should have talked about this sooner. But you just kept saying everything would work out. You never want to talk about anything that might be even a little bit upsetting or bad. Well, not everything always works out, Kiran," I added, a little snottily.

"Oh, so this is my fault? Raya, the reason I didn't want to talk about me leaving is because I always knew this would be where we ended. That you'd just let us go without a second thought." His voice grew lower, almost angry.

"Excuse me?" I whispered. He thought I cared about him that little?

"I saw the way you talked about your grandmother's story. How much you wanted her to give up on the guy she loved rather than give up on her dreams." He shook his head. "I always knew you'd let me go in a heartbeat when we had to make this choice."

I swear, I saw red. *How dare* he put this all on me? "I never wanted her to leave him!" I all but shouted. "I just didn't want him to be the reason she gave up on everything else she wanted." I paused. "Just like you're asking me to do right now."

"Raya, listen to me." Kiran tried to take my hands again, but I still wasn't giving them up to him. I crossed my arms over my chest. "I meant what I said when we first met. I don't ever want to be the reason you give up anything. You can still be a teacher if you stay—we'll figure it out." Now his words sounded almost desperate. Because he *was* desperate, I realized.

There was no way for us to stay together, and maybe there never had been. One of us would have to lose sight of everything else in our lives—just like Shakuntala and Daadee.

Shakuntala had let herself forget the rest of the world for love, and all that forgetting had brought her was pain. Daadee had chosen to forget everything else for the love of her life, and she'd never become what she'd always intended to be.

I took a step backward. Away from him.

"Then you have to forget me, Kiran. Just like I have to forget you."

His face hardened. "Just like that? You're really going to let everything we have go? You're really telling me to *forget* you? Forget everything we had together here? Everything we've become together?" The desperation in his voice was hard now, and sharp in its enormity. It seemed to fill every corner of the room.

Even so, I didn't answer him. I couldn't. A combination of fierce anger and the greatest sadness I'd ever felt was building more steadily in me, taking over every single part of me. If I tried to speak just then, I couldn't be sure what would come out.

I knew what I needed to do, and I was doing it.

Kiran shook his head. "So that's it, then," he said bitterly. "Just like I knew it would be. I guess you think you have to make the choice your grandmother couldn't." He glared hard at me, his face taking on an expression I'd never seen before. It was so chilling and dark that I wrapped my arms further around myself, almost as if I could keep out the cold his look was radiating. "Don't worry, Raya," he said softly. "I'll make sure I forget all of this. And I sure as fuck won't need a lost ring to do it." With that, he turned and stormed out of the room.

I stayed in that room for a long time. Not thinking, for once, about anything. Just standing there, staring at the paintings around me. The colors in them. The people. The stories that lay there. The stories of sadness and happiness and everything in between.

When I finally left that room, I was careful not to look back. If I had, I would have broken into a million pieces of pain.

seventeen

∞

DREAMS AND DIRECTIONLESS TRIPS

For the next week, I threw myself fully into two things: ashram life and looking for Pihu.

I got up at 4:30 a.m.

I forced myself to meditate with a focus so strong that Pilot accused me of trying to start "competitive meditation." I told him that if people could turn yoga into a sport, then anything was possible.

I worked at the school every single afternoon, staying long after the children had left to help Khatri clean up and plan lessons for the next day. The more I worked with her, the more I was sure I was making the right choice to study education. I loved dreaming up new ways to get her—our—students excited about lessons. I loved finding new books I thought they'd enjoy.

I hadn't told my parents yet that I was planning to major in education at UCLA, but I was pretty sure they'd be supportive. Dad would probably bitch about how there was no money in that field, but he'd also be proud of me for taking on work that supported communities.

Like Anandi had said, I was lucky. And I planned to thank my parents a lot more often for all that luck.

Every afternoon I looked for Pihu, walking endlessly around the village and the ashram. Past the stores and houses and apple orchard and statue gardens and the river. Everyone told me I was wasting my time and that Pihu was definitely miles away by now. But I had to do something, and searching was all I could do.

That was all my days consisted of: meditation, teaching, looking. It was all I *let* my days consist of. I was doing my best to forget, just like I'd told him to forget. Anandi and Devin never brought his name up, even though they both knew we'd had a thing and they must have realized he was gone. Pilot never mentioned him, either, making me all the more thankful I had that particular Disney Channel star on my side.

"I'm not ready to go back to California," he told me one day on our walk back from the school to the ashram. Anandi and I still had another ten days in the ashram, but Pilot only had eight. Devin's sixty days at the Rishi Kanva were finally almost up, and she was scheduled to leave right after us. Everything was coming to an end soon.

"I thought you said your agent landed you some big auditions when you got back." I still remembered how excited he'd been when he'd shown me that e-mail.

"Yeah, but Twitter will still be there, too." He groaned. "Lasting evidence of all my wrongdoings, preserved until the end of time."

It was too bad Pilot couldn't just throw out his ex's ring to get the guy to forget him. "Have you tried talking to him?" I asked hesitantly. I couldn't exactly imagine Lexi forgiving someone who outed her to the world without her permission, but I also couldn't imagine not forgiving someone like Pilot for what he'd already acknowledged had been a terrible mistake.

"I tried texting him, but he wouldn't answer me." Pilot shrugged. "Not that I blame him."

"Maybe you should try writing him. Like, a letter. With actual stamps." I cracked a smile as I thought of Lexi again. "Tell him everything you haven't been able to say. You screwed up, Pilot, for sure. But it's not like you don't deserve forgiveness. He was keeping your relationship in the closet, and that's tough. He put you in a hard position."

"I knew what I was getting into when we got together," Pilot said. "But you're right—it was hard. Doesn't excuse what I did. But still..."

"The least he can do is read a letter from you."

Pilot rolled his eyes. "Jeez, wasn't I the one who was supposed to drop truth bombs on you? Who's in charge of this mentorship? You gotta just swoop in and take all the glory by being helpful."

"Feel free to clean the chalkboards at school tomorrow in return."

"Please. Like you don't owe me for keeping your sordid affair a secret all that time."

Truth. For just a moment I allowed myself to remember.... Nope, terrible idea. I shook my head hard, as though my memories were on some kind of Etch A Sketch that could be erased like that. "Good thing I have you, Pilot."

He rolled his eyes. "I *guess* I'm not mad you came here, either."

I just laughed.

"You ever gonna tell me?" he asked. "What happened to you and him?"

So much for Pilot not going there. "Probably not, no," I told him.

Pilot grinned. "Right. I get it, though." He shrugged. "I ever tell you why they call me Pilot?"

"No, but I'm sure we're about to have some movie-magic moment where you tell me a story and it inspires me to grow and change in some super obvious way," I groused. He completely ignored me and kept talking.

"I had this aunt growing up who was a flight attendant and I used to spend a lot of time with her. I thought I wanted to become a pilot. I talked about it so much that she and my grandma started calling me Pilot. One day I came home from school mad about something. My grandma looked right at me and said, 'You might be piloting that plane someday, child, but there's always going to be weather.'"

Was that supposed to make me feel better? I tried not to glare at him. "That what you told yourself after you accidentally outed your ex?" I asked, trying not to sound too sarcastic.

"'Course not. I was a hot mess. Didn't leave the house for almost three days. But I'm hoping you'll be smarter than I was." He leaned over and kissed me gently on the forehead. "Sorry about the bad weather," he said softly.

We finished our walk without talking, and I was totally fine with that.

He was there. Over and over again in my dreams. And in every single one, he had no idea who I was.

I woke to a dark room and my snoring cousin. Leaning over to look at the clock, I realized it was still only 1:00 a.m.—hours before I had to be up. But I already knew I wasn't going to be able to go back to sleep.

I pulled on slippers and padded to the doorway, careful to open it as slowly as possible so I didn't wake Anandi. I slipped down the silent and darkened hall of the ashram, eventually stopping in front of the statue of Bharat in the great hall.

Kiran's blank face, the one I'd just seen in my dreams, the one void of all memory of me, haunted my mind.

"Raya, it is good to see you this morning," a soft voice said behind me.

The guru was there. Because of course she was.

"You are not yourself in prayers lately." She moved to stand next to me, and I did my best not to shift away from her. "I know how saddened Pihu's disappearance has left you. But this is something more, isn't it?"

I squirmed. I wasn't ready to admit that I, a perennial rule-follower, had laid total waste to the ashram's strict policy of chastity.

"I…" I couldn't figure out how to finish the sentence.

"You have lost yourself," the guru told me.

What? Like hell I had. "No," I told her. "Not at all, actually. I think I finally found myself. That's what I came here to do," I added.

The guru nodded. "And there, perhaps, is the problem. You were looking for something that did not need to be found."

Huh?

"Have you prayed to Sarasvati for wisdom?" Guru Baba asked.

"Not lately. I found the wisdom I've been looking for—I promise. I'm going to be a teacher," I told her proudly.

"I see." The guru nodded at the statues around us. "But that only means you have found what you are going to *do*, Raya. It does not answer the question of who you are going to *be*."

A sort of mild terror washed through me as her words rang true in my head.

"You are leaving the ashram soon," the guru reminded me. When I didn't answer her, she leaned over and placed her hand on my shoulder. "Raya," she said, "your journey here is not over, I am sure of that. But this is not the place for you now. Your path to discovery is elsewhere. You will complete it; I am confident of that. All journeys are completed in their own time."

Bharat's face, locked somewhere behind a smile and a frown, stared imposingly at me. I couldn't decide if this was the most or least helpful conversation I'd ever had in my life.

The guru took her hand off my shoulder, and even though I wasn't looking at her, I could hear enough of her soft footfalls to know she was leaving the room.

"Raya." Her voice, soft and strong from the doorway, wasn't something I could stay turned away from. I moved my neck in her direction.

"He will remember you when you remember you," the guru told me.

A jolt ran through me as I remembered Daadee's journal. "Where did you hear that?" I called after her. Maybe it was just something all the gurus here were trained to say.

She kept walking away, though, and I never got an answer.

I was still thinking about those words hours later, when Anandi met me outside the school after her sitar lesson to help me with my daily search.

"How's the sitar stuff going?" I asked.

"Good." She shrugged, and I couldn't help but notice how

unusually downcast her usually upbeat expression was. "I'm going to miss my lessons when we leave."

I sighed. "I think you need to talk to your father again."

Anandi rolled her eyes. "Maybe I'll just write him a letter and everything will be fine?"

"Hey!" I said indignantly. Clearly someone had been talking to Pilot. "I stand by that advice. And maybe you *should* write a letter."

She shrugged. "I keep reading Daadee's poetry, trying to figure out if I can find more answers in there. But I've read every word now, and I still don't know what to do. I wish you still had the journal, you know?"

"Believe me, I know," I agreed as we started walking. "I think there was a lot in there we missed out on, even if there weren't many entries left." I tried to focus my thoughts solely on the journal itself and not on the person it'd disappeared with. "Today I was thinking we'd walk up to the shrine. You know, the one Pihu first showed me? I know plenty of people already searched there, but I haven't looked there yet."

"Okay," Anandi agreed easily. I knew she—and likely everyone else at the ashram—thought I was slightly delusional for thinking I'd somehow find Pihu on one of these afternoon searches. But she almost always came with me anyway. Talk about friendship goals.

We made the climb to the shrine huffing and puffing. "Good thing Devin's not with us," I remarked. "She'd have made all kinds of comments about all her missed Pilates classes by now."

"You think she and John will stay together?" Anandi asked in between breaths. "Good matchmaking work on them, by the way. I meant to tell you ages ago."

"Thanks." I didn't even try to hide my pride just then. I'd managed to set up a socially incompetent Brit with an introverted American gamer; that was definitely a feat to be proud of. "Honestly, though? I don't know. I don't know John well enough. And they don't live near each other."

"I guess." Anandi shrugged. "But I like to think that love conquers distance, you know?"

"Yeah, right," I barked out. *Don't think about him. Don't think about him.* "The optimism is sweet, Anandi, but that's not reality." *Don't think about how optimistic he was. Don't think about all that beauty he saw that you always seem to miss.*

"I guess. But what's the point of any of this if you can't be optimistic about where it's all going?"

I opened my mouth to answer her. No sound came out.

"Good, we're here," Anandi announced as we arrived at the top of the hill. "Can we sit, please?" Anandi collapsed to the ground, and I wasn't far behind.

"Breathing in Varanasi is going to feel so easy after this." Anandi reached over and squeezed my hand. "Raya, I know not everything about our visit here has been good, but I'm glad we came anyway. I'm glad we did this together."

"Me too." I squeezed her hand back while the statue of Bharat looked on. "Pray with me, Anandi? Pray for her? For Pihu?"

So we did.

We prayed for minutes. Lots of them. Maybe even hours.

When I looked up again, the sun was starting to drop in the sky. Soon it would be time for dinner, and then bed, and then morning rituals. And soon after that this place would be miles and miles away from me.

Anandi stayed bowed in prayer, but I stood and took a quick walk around the shrine, trying to memorize every inch of it. Every statue, every piece of dirt.

My eyes locked on the statue of Sarasvati, so secure in her knowledge and understanding of the world. Maybe someday I'd stop being jealous of her.

"Raya," Anandi whispered behind me. "There's something tied to her hand. What is it?"

What was she talking about? There'd never been anything tied to that statue before. I looked more closely. Sure enough, a piece of pink cloth was tied around Sarasvati's third finger.

I untied it slowly. Wrapped into it was a piece of paper.

With Daadee's handwriting across it. My heart thumped. "Anandi! Get over here!" I screamed as I pulled the paper open the rest of the way.

On one side was the first journal entry of Daadee's I'd ever read. The first page of that book we'd found here weeks ago.

"Turn it over," Anandi urged. So I did. And there, in tiny

letters covering only the very first inch of paper, I saw something, written in Hindi in Pihu's messy handwriting.

"What does it mean?" I asked Anandi desperately. It had been eight days since Pihu had disappeared. How long had this message been tied to Sarasvati's hand, unnoticed by everyone who'd looked for her here?

"It means 'The Castle.'" Anandi frowned. "What's that?"

"I don't know, but we'll find out!" I called as I raced back down the hill at lightning speed.

eighteen

∞

DISCONNECTED CONNECTIONS AND DISAPPEARING ACTS

W e have to talk to them!" I urged Guru Baba. "We have to talk to the Parashars!"

"Raya, calm down," she replied. "We've already called the police. They are not sure what the words 'The Castle' even mean, but they're adding the information to their case file."

"The police won't be able to help," Samaira interjected. "They have too much on their plates."

The guru nodded again. "Well, be that as it may, I have no way of contacting the Parashars directly now that Kiran is gone." She looked uncomfortable. "When he left, Kiran requested that we remove all his contact information from our system."

She might as well as have added *because he was so fucking*

pissed at Raya and didn't want to talk to her ever again to the end of that sentence.

"We can't just look up their contact info? Find them on social media or something?" I begged.

Samaira crossed her arms angrily. "We could try, but the odds of them seeing the message soon aren't very good. The Parashars are practically famous. They probably get hundreds of unsolicited messages a day; I bet they have assistants go through them. Who knows when they'd get it or if they'd even pay attention to ours."

This was unbelievable. Thanks to the internet, I could meet people from eight different time zones within five minutes, but I couldn't even get a simple message about a lost kid to someone who was a car ride away?

"This message has to be passed along right away." I'd never heard so much urgency in Samaira's voice. "The people the Parashars work with, the ones who found me, will know what to do. But they need the information now. Too much time's already gone by. It's been several days already." Her voice dipped. "So much can happen in so little time."

"Kiran!" I announced. "Pilot, you must have his number, right? Did he friend you on Facebook or Insta or something?"

Pilot, who was standing next to me, looked uncomfortable. "So, before he left, I gave him my number and my info. He was gonna reach out to me in a few weeks when I left the ashram. I just walked somewhere where there's cell service so I could check my phone, and he hasn't yet. I tried friending him and messaging him on a few apps, but still no answer."

I couldn't believe what I was hearing. "Are you kidding me? Is there seriously no way to get Pihu's message to the people who are looking for her until Kiran or his parents happen to check their DMs?" Anandi patted me on the shoulder reassuringly. It didn't help.

Samaira shook her head. "For their own safety, this group is very secretive. They have no name. No phone numbers, no addresses. The Parashars know how to find them, but very few other people do. I only know where they are located because..." She hesitated. "Because I've been to their headquarters."

I could not imagine what that trip had been like for her. "So what do we do?" I demanded again.

"We wait," the guru said, her voice ever soft but still firm. "Pilot, continue to send more messages to Kiran and the Parashars through any site you can. I'm certain it won't be that long until someone sees them. We wait for the Parashars to get our messages and then tell them of the note so they can make sure the information finds its way to the proper channels. You did well, Raya and Anandi, finding this. Now we must leave the rest to prayer. Prayer has gotten us this far." She smiled at each of us and then left the great hall.

"I can't thank you enough for finding that letter, Raya." Khatri, who had come over to the ashram with us after Anandi and I stopped at the school to show her what we'd found, engulfed me in a hug. "Finally, Pihu's mother has some hope. I'll go tell her about this right away."

"Anandi found it," I told her, even though I was certain my cousin wouldn't care about the credit. Anandi clearly didn't. She kept her gaze on the floor, her eyes dark and sad.

"Thanks to both of you." Khatri kissed both me and Anandi on the cheek. "I'll see you tomorrow, okay?" She left the room, her bright-purple sari swinging elegantly behind her.

Samaira frowned.

"You don't seem very hopeful this clue will help," I said.

"I don't know." Samaira shook her head. "It's pretty amazing this note even exists. I never thought—or had a chance—to leave something like this behind. But you don't understand how quickly the people who have Pihu will move. How intelligent they are. Do you know why they only take one child at a time, when they could easily abduct more at once? Because it's smart. People think the child is just lost, or wandering, or they'll come home soon. They take their time looking—just like we did. Just like everyone does." Samaira dropped her head into her hands. "Whatever this 'castle' place is, they won't keep Pihu there long. We may already be too late. If the Parashars take even an extra day getting this message to the people who saved me...we may run out of time."

Oh, Pihu. All the hope I'd started to build up in the last hour or so began to slip away again. "And you don't have any idea where we can contact those people? The ones who helped you?"

"No." She ground a bare toe into the floor. "All I remember is the building and the street where it was. I could possibly find it again if I were in Delhi. But I don't know the address."

I stared at one of the bazillion paintings etched on the wall of the great hall. It was a person reaching out to another person, holding an arm out from a long distance. "I don't know what it took for Pihu to be able to leave this note behind," I said, "but we can't let it be for nothing. We have to get it to these people right away. The ones who can help her."

"We do," Samaira said confidently. "So you're coming, too, then?"

As if she needed to ask. "Of course I am." Delhi wasn't that far. So what if the train ride there was so notoriously dangerous that Anandi's father had sent us with a chaperone to take it the last time? We could handle it ourselves. We had to.

Pihu's life possibly depended on it.

"Fuck, by yourself?" Devin asked. "Hasn't one of you already been kidnapped once or something?" So much for Devin's new understanding of empathy.

To Samaira's credit, she just snorted. "So the odds are probably with us, then, aren't they? Raya and I will be fine. We don't have a choice in this. Until we get in touch with the Parashars, there's no way for the necessary people to get this message. And every moment they don't have this information is a moment when..."

"Terrible things can happen. Shit." Pilot scrubbed his face

with his hand. "Fine. Whatever. But I'm coming with you. Like hell the two of you are taking the train alone. Like hell we're taking a train, period. We'll rent a car. It's much faster to drive to Delhi than take the train."

"We're going to drive on these roads?" As desperate as I was to find Pihu, I couldn't help but hope someone else wanted to be behind that wheel. I had no desire to try my hand at navigating the tiny curved roads around the ashram that all seemed to be built on the side of a cliff.

"Why wouldn't we?" Samaira answered. "Okay, it's settled, then. We can grab a taxi to Shimla and then rent a car there."

"Great," Anandi interjected. "So we're all going to Delhi. When do we leave? Someone needs to call the cab." Devin looked immediately alarmed, which was more than fine with me. I had a feeling Devin's presence on a trip like this would be anything but calming.

"Samaira and I are going. With Pilot." Anandi started to argue, but I immediately cut her off. "Listen, when people realize we've left, the shit is going to hit the fan. They'll probably call my parents. You have to be here to calm everyone down and to be our eyes and ears, Anandi. Make sure they know I haven't left for good and that I'll be safe."

"You promise?" Anandi's voice wavered.

"I'll make sure of it," Pilot growled.

Samaira rolled her eyes. "You're not an Avenger," she informed him.

RACHEL ROY AND AVA DASH

"Hey, I could totally play Tony Stark's sidekick. Maybe even Stark if they'd cast a few more black guys as comic book heroes in Hollywood."

And that was how I ended up sneaking out of the ashram in the early morning hours with a girl who was probably still supposed to be a high school sophomore and a wannabe Tony Stark.

To go back to the city where I'd sent the boy I loved with orders to forget me.

We'd all done some serious phone charging before leaving the ashram, so once we had decent cell service, we were able to check for missed calls from angry gurus and parental figures on the way to Delhi. There was nothing but radio silence, though. "Either no one's noticed or Anandi's doing a great job of keeping everyone calm," I observed as my phone stayed quiet. "If my parents knew about this, someone would already be calling me from an airport. They would probably get to Delhi before me."

Pilot focused on navigating around a sharp curve in the road and laid on his horn when another car's headlights came into view. I closed my eyes. "Pilot, can we check your phone again? See if Kiran got any of your messages?"

"Of course."

Samaira handed me the phone from the backseat, and I unlocked it with the code Pilot had given us when we'd decided that he'd do the driving while we stayed in charge of communication. "Nothing, still," I growled as I looked through every app Pilot had used to either friend or message Kiran. "I can't believe this. I was sure he'd be on his phone twenty-four/seven once he got it back."

Pilot glanced over at me and I willed him to put his eyes back on the road. At least we were driving in the dark. Pilot probably didn't like that very much, but not having to look down every cliff we were driving on the side of was helping me keep up my sanity. "Maybe he's not really feeling being social these days. Maybe he's still trying to get over someone."

I closed my eyes again. "Please. Someone like Kiran Parashar has definitely already moved on to greener pastures."

"I don't think so," Samaira said quietly behind me.

"What? You knew Kiran and I were together?" I whirled around in my seat to stare at her.

"Please." Samaira rolled her eyes. "The way he would stare at you across the room during basically every single meal? Anyone who didn't notice had to be blind."

"Damn," I murmured as I turned back to face the front. "So much for our secret relationship."

"I think the point Samaira is trying to make," Pilot said, "is that there's no way someone who looks across a room like *that* just forgets about another person. You mattered to him, Raya. He mattered to you, too—I could tell. You finally ready to tell me what the hell happened?"

I traced a finger over the Smart car's tiny window. "I wasn't ready to give everything up for him. Home, my future, my plans. And he wouldn't, either. So I told him he had to forget me."

Neither of them said anything for a few minutes. Finally Pilot spoke up again. "And that was it? You guys didn't even try to figure something out? Compromise or figure out a Skype schedule or something?"

"Please, Pilot. Compromise just means someone always has to give something up." I thought of Daadee. Shakuntala. Of the sacrifices they'd both made.

"Of course it does. *To get other things*." Pilot pulled the car around another fast curve while I clutched my seat. "Shit, Raya, if you ever want anything in life, you gotta give other things up. That's just how the world works. Do you want to be with Kiran or not?"

"Do you love him?" Samaira added softly.

There was a lump lodged deep in my throat. I couldn't answer her.

"You always have to compromise something, no matter what choice you're making, Raya," Pilot told me. "So this time, ask yourself if you compromised the right things."

I didn't know what to say to that. What if Shakuntala hadn't been wrong when she allowed herself to get lost and immersed in her love? Maybe it was Rishi Durvasa who had been unfair. What if my grandmother wasn't wrong when she made her own compromises and went back to Daada?

It was hard not to remember the sheer happiness Daadee and

Daada glowed with every single time they looked at each other. It was a look they'd both had every day I ever saw them together, right up until Daada's last breath.

I couldn't imagine one of them without the other. I still wasn't sure why Daadee had left behind all her other goals after she went back to her *meri jaan*, and maybe I'd never know. But she'd lived a life full of happiness and contentment. It was strange to realize that I'd forgotten that.

I nodded off for a while after that. I woke up to Samaira shaking my shoulder. "Raya, guess what!"

I rubbed the sleep from my eyes and studied my surroundings. I could tell from the large buildings ahead and the smog lacing the sky that we were just outside Delhi. "What? What's going on?"

"Kiran got Pilot's DM on Instagram! He has the address of the place we need to go. He's going to meet us and take us there!"

Relief flooded through me. *Pihu, we're coming,* I thought.

And then all that relief contracted again as an image of Kiran's smiling face filled my vision. What was I going to say when we saw each other again?

I decided to focus on other things. "I can't believe you're still awake and driving," I said to Pilot as we moved farther toward the city and traffic tightened. "Aren't you exhausted?"

"Adrenaline," he informed me as he swerved around a minivan. "Someone had to take charge after you both fell asleep," he informed Samaira and me. "Tony Stark, my ass. How does the black guy *always* end up being the sidekick?"

"In your story, we're the sidekicks," Samaira pointed out. I fist-bumped her. Sometimes it was hard to remember this girl was only a little older than my brother.

"Yeah, whatever. Samaira, where are we meeting Kiran?"

"Near the place where Gandhi was cremated," she said. "The Raj Ghat. I used to take walks there when I needed to get away."

I opened my phone's map app so it could help get Pilot through the traffic, and the three of us fell quiet as the computerized voice told him which turns to take.

We moved deeper and deeper into the city as the sun rose over us. Soon the sights and sounds of Delhi were everywhere around me, and even though I'd never set foot in this place with Kiran, I saw him everywhere I looked.

He was in the sun peeking through the windows of the taxis waiting in the street. He was in the colorful saris dotting a store's exterior. He was in the delicious-looking breakfast samosa I drooled over when I saw someone eating it next to a food cart.

I wondered if I'd ever get to read the story of what had happened to my grandmother after she left the ashram to travel to find my grandfather. She probably had stopped in Delhi on her way to Varanasi. Like Shakuntala, she'd traveled all the way to him, uncertain of what she would find when she arrived. That was how badly she'd known what she wanted.

Not what she wanted to *do,* but what she wanted to *be.* She wanted to be a person in love for as long as the world allowed it.

There was a jarring sensation in my chest. And I knew then, for sure, what compromises I needed to make.

"You have arrived at your destination," the GPS lady announced. Pilot miraculously found parking in a crowd of cars, and we stepped out of the car and into the stifling Delhi air.

"I think I miss the Himalayas," Pilot informed us, coughing slightly as he rolled up his shirtsleeves. I guessed it was probably already almost ninety degrees out. "Also, for the record, driving on the left side of the road isn't bad. Maybe I'll take that road trip in England after all."

I was glad he hadn't minded it, since I was pretty sure I would have driven us off the side of the road if I'd been behind the wheel.

"There it is." Samaira pointed to a large park to our right that seemed to stretch for acres upon acres. "This is the area where I used to walk. He said he'd meet us at one of the footbridges."

I took a breath. Looked over at the park, at the people milling across the walkways there. Looked down over the street we'd just come from, and then over to the footbridge—the one where the boy I'd let go of was about to be meeting us.

He will remember you when you remember you.

So who was I, then?

I was Raya Liston. Lover of ridiculous T-shirts and little girls who liked books about dying dogs. Cousin to secret music aficionados and daughter and granddaughter of some of the most wonderfully driven people the world had ever produced.

But now I understood that drive wasn't just about figuring out what you were going to get up in the morning and give back to the world every day for the rest of your life. It was a lot more than that.

I was starting to understand that it was about figuring out what you were going to give yourself.

nineteen

RAJS AND REUNIONS

Kiran met us on the footbridge that operated as the overpass to Gandhi's resting place. It was a very different kind of footbridge from the one where we met at the ashram, and yet the whole scene felt fitting. My heart burned inside my chest as his face came into view, and all the memories of the moments we'd spent together flooded through me.

Apple orchards. Sweet and lazy hookups next to Hindu statues. The way he'd rushed to the top of that hill with me, determined to help me find whatever Daadee had left behind. How had I ever convinced myself I could forget him?

He and Pilot bro-hugged; Samaira and I just got nods. It was painfully awkward, but that was to be expected. "I'm sorry it took me so long to get back to you. I was doing other stuff," he said lamely.

"Thanks for being here now," I told him.

He couldn't seem to look directly at me, so I only caught half his eye as he nodded. "So what was in that note you found?"

I stayed quiet while Samaira poured out the story. "You'll take us to the headquarters?" she finally asked.

"Of course. I don't know what 'The Castle' means, but hopefully someone there will."

We walked, with Pilot and Kiran leading the way, while Samaira and I stayed behind them.

"Do you have hope?" she asked. "That you'll get back together with him?"

Hope? Shakuntala had hope all those years ago. So had Daadee. But I had never been the hopeful one in this relationship. No, any optimism in us had always belonged to Kiran.

And he wasn't looking particularly hopeful these days. I couldn't even get him to look me in the eye. I didn't know how to answer her.

We followed Kiran and Pilot around a corner to an apartment building. The door was wedged between a grocery store and a clothing shop, and it was so tiny and discreet it was amazing the people who lived there ever found it. Kiran hit a button on the panel, and when it buzzed he said, "It's Kiran Parashar. You knew I was coming."

It occurred to me that without Kiran, these people might never have let us in the door even if we had found the place on our own.

Someone buzzed Kiran in, and we followed him up a long flight of stairs to a nondescript door.

The guy who let us in looked sleepy, and I had to wonder what sort of hours he kept. "Kiran, man," he said as they engaged in a bro hug. Then his face moved over to Samaira. "No way," he whispered. "Samaira?"

For the first time since we'd walked in, I looked at Samaira's face. This was the place where she'd first found rescue, refuge. It hadn't even occurred to me what coming back might be like for her. "Amal," she answered. "I wasn't sure if I'd ever see you again."

They hugged so hard, and for so long, that I started to think maybe it wouldn't be so difficult for Samaira to find her normal after all.

"Do you know what this means?" Samaira pulled the note we'd found out of her pocket and showed it to him as she told him the story of where it had come from.

I swear, the guy did a double take when he saw the note. "We already had the police check this place out." He shook his head and read Pihu's words again. "But maybe they missed something. Maybe someone got to them first and paid them off. Maybe we weren't careful enough."

"So you know what it means?" I asked, grabbing for Pilot's hand as hope filled every single part of me.

"I do. It's a spot where they like to stash people before they do transports—I bet she heard them talking about it." He nodded at me and Pilot. "You did well, whoever found this. We'll have it checked again. And we'll make sure it gets done right this time."

"Do you think there's still a chance?" I asked. I wondered if he could hear the desperation in my voice.

"I don't know," he answered honestly. "All we can ever do is try."

"You must be going back to California soon."

I was standing with Kiran on the Raj Ghat footbridge, looking out over the monument that marked Gandhi's cremation site. I didn't want to think about leaving India, so I just shrugged.

Amal and Samaira were at the other end of the bridge laughing together. Amal, it turned out, had been the one who rescued Samaira from her captors, along with a bunch of other girls. He'd helped her adjust back to life in Delhi before arranging the Parashars as her sponsors.

And just a few minutes earlier, he'd gotten an entire network of people moving to find Pihu. All because of one note she'd thought to leave behind on a statue. Now all we could do was wait and hope.

Unfortunately, the hope for my relationship with my parents was a bit shakier. Anandi had just texted me to say the jig was up. Our disappearance had been noted by the people at the ashram, and my parents were *not* pleased to say the least.

Anandi said she didn't realize gurus could actually clench their fists.

Pilot was talking to the ashram now, telling them that we'd be on our way back soon, while I tried to figure out exactly what I wanted to say to Kiran.

"Why is there a fire down there?" I asked, leaning casually over the bridge. Kiran had basically refused to engage in conversation with me the entire time we'd been standing there together, so I had no problem resorting to small talk about the landscape.

"They light it to mark the cremation spot," Kiran told me. "It stays lit like that all the time."

"Oh." He still wouldn't look at me when I spoke. It was time to bring out the big guns. "I can't forget you," I told him. "I haven't been able to. I don't want to try anymore."

He rolled his eyes. "That's nice for you, isn't it?"

The sarcasm wasn't a great sign. I focused on the flame below. "I didn't mean to hurt you, Kiran. I just thought—"

"I know what you thought, Raya." The tone of his voice hadn't changed, and it was becoming clearer and clearer that getting back together with Kiran wasn't going to be a matter of me just waving my hair at him and telling him I wanted him. "And you weren't wrong. One of us was always going to have to give something up—or a lot of things up—if we wanted to stay together. I wasn't being realistic when I said we could make it work. It's like you always said, you know? I spend too much time focusing on what's positive and good and beautiful and not enough time paying attention to what's actually in front of me."

"Maybe you do," I answered, and I could tell from the look

on his face that he was surprised I'd agreed with him. "But I like that about you. I like that you make me want to see more of what's possible in the world." I looked up from the fire so I could make sure he was really seeing me when I said, "I wish I'd stopped to think about all the ways it could be possible for us to stay together."

"Raya, you told me to forget you." I could hear frustration and resignation in his voice. "And I won't lie—it hasn't been easy. But it's what you told me to do, Raya. So I've done it. You can't come back now and tell me you've changed your mind. That you realized you were wrong about this important future you have to plan every single minute of. And I still can't promise you that I'll be able to magically get my parents to let me go to America. We're still exactly where we were. Nothing's changed."

"You're wrong." I made sure I said it with every ounce of conviction I had. "*I've* changed. I realize now that some compromises are worth it, and I'm willing to do what I have to do for us to stay together. That probably means you'll have to make some compromises, too, but I think we can both do it, Kiran. It might suck. It might not always be fun or easy, and maybe we won't make it in the end. But don't we owe it to ourselves to try?"

He shook his head and took a step back. Away from me. "It's too late," he said. "The ring is gone, or whatever the fucking story says. You told me to forget you, and I did." His voice shook. "But it wasn't easy, and I can't do it again. So that's it, Raya."

He started back down the path, away from the bridge.

"A fisherman found the ring," I called after him. He turned around and glanced back at me.

"Huh?"

"A fisherman found the ring," I told him. "It took a long time, right? He didn't find it right away. But he did, eventually. I know what I want to be, Kiran. Who I want. So I can wait."

Kiran turned quickly and started walking away, but not before I caught the expression I needed to see on his face.

Hope.

twenty

SARASVATI AND SORRYS

Well. Let me tell you how *not* easy it is to talk your parents out of flying all the way to India to kick your ass after you disappear with complete strangers (to them, anyway) in the middle of the night.

You know what else isn't easy? Convincing them to let you stay in India after you do that. But here I was, two weeks later, still apologizing to my parents from the front step of the village school that I'd come to think of as my second home.

"I'm sorry sorry sorry," I told Dad. Again. "You want me to send over some of my blood or what?"

"Like that's the only thing you need to be sorry for," he grumbled. "Should be sorry I'm not moving you into your dorm room next week."

I rolled my eyes. I'd heard this speech enough by now to know he didn't mean it. Somewhere underneath all his gruffness and panic that something bad was going to happen to his baby girl, he was proud of me. I was sure of it.

It helped that my mother had confirmed that fact a few times.

He keeps telling all his friends how his daughter's out saving the world and when she's done she'll come back to college and save the world some more, she'd told me a few days before. *But this is all a lot to get used to. He'll get there, baby.*

In my father's defense, all the recent changes in my life *were* a lot to get used to.

Hell, I was still getting used to them. After all, I'd just spent the last three days throwing up.

As it turned out, the water in the ashram had been filtered. The water in the village was not. So my recent move into the village had been just a bit of shock to my poor body.

Along with many other things.

I'd arrived back at the ashram with Samaira and Pilot with more than just two pissed-off parents who were annoyed I hadn't been answering my phone. I'd gone back knowing what I wanted to do *and* who I wanted to be. Finally. And once I had that knowledge, I wasn't about to give it up.

So I'd decided to double down on my parents' shock and horror. I'd announced to them that I wanted to stay in India for a semester and work at Pihu's school, and that I'd moved out of the ashram and into one of the rooms in Khatri's

285

apartment. She was quick to offer me a job—after all, I'd basically told her I'd help her out for nothing but room and board. Plus more students had come to the school while I'd been gallivanting around down in Delhi, and Pilot was leaving soon. She was more than excited to have a full-time teaching assistant.

Once I'd laid out the plan, my parents were surprisingly accepting of it. Mostly my father was just annoyed and worried that I'd arranged the whole thing on my own and therefore wasn't going to be getting recommendations from any fancy programs that placed Americans abroad.

So I'd moved out of the ashram. Khatri's apartment didn't have a pool in sight, and the room I was staying in was the size of a closet, but I loved it. I loved being here and I loved the purpose I felt; it was truly exciting to wake up each day filled with hope at the changes I could make in my young student's lives. The view from my window looked out over Daadee's favorite shrine. I visited there almost every day, waiting.

I had a feeling that if he ever came back, that's where he'd go to find me.

"Anyway, you stay safe," Dad told me. "Still don't know if you're okay in that damn village anyway, especially if people can get taken there. You have your pepper spray?"

I did. It wasn't a crazy concern. Something terrible had happened to Pihu here, and I would always be cautious. But terrible things could happen anywhere.

"Yes, Daddy. Plus you and Mom are coming to visit in just a couple weeks, remember? So you'll be able to see for yourself that I'm fine." My parents hadn't even wanted me to move out of the ashram until they could come to India to ensure that I was still living and working in a safe place they approved of. Luckily, Anandi's mother had checked both out and vouched for them to my mom—although she did make a comment under her breath about "parents having to let their children make their own absurd choices." My parents had still insisted on visiting, but at least they'd trusted me and let me pursue my dreams first, before college.

"I remember. Love you, Raya baby. You have fun saving the world."

He hung up, mumbling something about existential crisis, and I realized I still didn't know what the hell an existential crisis was.

I slipped my phone into my pocket and rubbed at one of the bright-yellow flowers on the wrist of the jacket I was wearing. Anandi's mother, Prisha, had brought something with her when she'd come to take Anandi home and to see my new place: a beautiful jacket and skirt covered with floral embroidery in every color of the rainbow. "Your Daadee had it made years ago," she told me. "I thought you might like to have it now."

At first I couldn't stop looking at it, touching it. Trying to feel Daadee through every fiber. Of course, after Lexi saw a photo of me in the outfit she made me take it to a tailor to have it fitted and modernized. I'd worn it for my first official day of teaching and almost every day since.

I found myself rubbing more of the beautiful embroidery as I left the front steps of the school and started the walk up to the shrine.

Teaching without Pihu was difficult. Every day I saw the empty spaces where she wasn't sitting. It seemed to me that going two weeks without any news of her was a bad sign, but Amal had been sending Samaira regular updates on their search, and up until a few days ago, all of those updates had been hopeful. Then the updates had disappeared. Samaira insisted that was a good sign, that they needed to rescue girls in complete secrecy because the rescues were so dangerous. "They probably found something," she kept telling me. "He'll be in touch when he can be again."

I hoped she was right. The periodic visits Khatri and I made to Pihu's mother got harder each time. Her younger brothers were starting to realize that maybe she wasn't coming back, as they'd been told. They kept asking why we wouldn't let her leave school.

I sometimes wished I had Anandi or Pilot or even Devin to make these daily walks to the shrine with me, but they were all gone now. Even John had left, and only Samaira was left at the ashram. Anandi was starting law school next week. Her last WhatsApp said she still hadn't figured out how to talk to her father.

Try the letter!! I'd texted back. Worked for Pilot.

And it had. Sort of. He'd written a letter. Sent it. When he'd gotten back to the States, he'd learned that his ex had "publicly forgiven him"—on Twitter, eye roll. But he still wouldn't speak to Pilot directly.

It was a start, though. And Pilot had a callback to play the Flash, so who knew what was possible? I never wanted to be Tony Stark anyway, he'd texted me. Flash is way doper.

Whatever you say, I'd answered. I had no real loyalty to any comic book character. But bantering with Pilot and Lexi, of course, was becoming one of my favorite parts of the day. I missed them a lot.

Devin had left the ashram with plans to try doing things long-distance with John, but I honestly had no idea if that was working out or not. Even as I'd hugged her good-bye, I'd known Devin and I weren't destined to stay in touch. I'd miss her, but in that way that you miss people exactly at the same time you know you never need to see them again.

I hit the bottom of the shrine's hill and started climbing. Once my ravaged intestines had recovered from the beating they'd taken the week before, I'd realized the altitude in the village wasn't bothering me as much as it used to. Every day this climb got a little easier.

I reached the top and sat down next to Bharat and Sarasvati, where I proceeded to tell them about my day. I still tried to meditate regularly, but slowing my mind down was never going to be my strong suit. Lots of days it was easier just to let out the stream of consciousness.

"So this boy, Umid? He reminds me a little of Pihu, you know? He's not afraid to try *anything*. Today he wanted to try multiplying, even though the kid can barely add. I love him. I can't wait until he figures out addition. I think he's going to get it soon. I—"

There was a rustling behind me, and I realized someone was coming up the hill to the shrine. Weird. I never saw anyone here.

I didn't want everyone in the village to know the American girl came up here every single day to talk to herself, so I shut up. And waited.

The rustling grew louder, and I swear a giggle followed it. A giggle I knew.

No. No way. My mind rejected the very possibility. But there was no denying I knew that sound.

And then a small head covered in a pink hat peeked out over the top of the hill, and I didn't have to deny it anymore.

Pihu ran into my arms.

"You found it," she shouted. "They told me you found it, my note!"

I held her tight, close, determined not to let her go. Tears ran down my face and into her shirt, and what did any of that matter, because Pihu was here again. In my arms.

"I can't believe you're here," I told her. "I prayed so much, Pihu, I hoped so hard, but I never..."

"It's okay, Raya." She squeezed me again. "I'm okay. The people found me, and then Kiran brought me home."

Kiran. I jerked my head up, out of the warm comfort of Pihu's shoulder.

And there he was, standing right in front of me. Recording my reunion with Pihu on his phone. Smiling in that way only Kiran ever could.

Of course.

twenty-one

ENDINGS AND ENDLESSNESS

We didn't talk right away. Not about us, anyway. We were too busy having dinner with Pihu's family, where her brothers talked nonstop and her mother never stopped crying once.

Everyone called Pihu's recovery miraculous—especially when they learned she hadn't been seriously physically harmed. The people who had taken her had stashed her in a hiding place they called "The Castle" while they waited for authorities to lose her trail before they transported her. But Pihu had been smart. She'd heard them talking, and when they were first moving her, she'd found a way to leave that note on the statue of Sarasvati.

"I knew you'd go there," she told me. "Because your Daadee did."

Personally, I didn't see Pihu's return home as a miracle. Pihu was home because of a whole lot of luck and some serious quick-thinking and bravery on her part. Maybe that did all add up to make a miracle, but I thought people were giving far too much credit to fate and not enough to Pihu herself.

After hours of food and laughter and hugs and crying, Pihu finally passed out in her chair, and Khatri gave me and Kiran a sly signal with her eyes suggesting it was time to leave.

I woke Pihu up to say good-bye. "Don't worry," I told her when she wouldn't let go of me. "I live here now, remember? You can see me every single day."

"Good," she answered. "Oh!" Pihu clapped her hands excitedly. "I forgot! I have something for you." She ran out of the room and came back holding something—something that looked very familiar.

I think I actually stopped breathing for a minute. "You kept this?" I asked in a strangled voice as she handed me Daadee's journal. "The entire time that you were..."

"Of course! Sometimes I read it when I was really sad and lonely." She shrugged. "I couldn't read all the words, but it made me feel better." She smiled up at me, her grin bright and almost completely unblemished by everything she'd been through. "I had to keep it safe for you."

I hugged the book to my chest. "Thank you, Pihu," I whispered. "You have no idea how much this means to me."

"Of course I do. You told me. I need to go to bed. I'm tired." Pihu yawned widely, and all of us laughed.

Khatri stayed behind to quickly talk with Pihu's mother—she said she had information for her about survivors' resources they could access—while Kiran and I walked home together.

"I'm staying at the ashram," he told me as we moved together through the dark and quiet main road of the village. "You're staying with Khatri now?"

"Yeah. Will I see you again?" *Please say you're not leaving right away.*

He hesitated. "You really decided to live here? Give up UCLA? That's a big commitment, Raya." I saw the look of fear in his eyes, and I knew where it came from: it was a fear that I'd given too much up. Fear that he could never match my compromise.

"I didn't give up UCLA," I told him. "I'm just starting my teacher training here, you know? I just deferred for a semester. I'll start UCLA in January."

"Oh." He shifted his feet, looked up again as a cow mooed softly in the distance. "I talked to my mom. Told her I was thinking of applying to USC. She didn't love the idea, but I finally got her to agree to at least let me apply."

"You did?" I thought of the crazy-intense Mrs. Parashar and what it must have taken for Kiran to even get his mother to consider USC. "I...I can't believe you did that."

"Yeah, well." He shrugged. "I didn't want you to be the only one making compromises, you know?"

There was hope written all over that statement. "Wow," I said. We walked in silence for a few minutes before he spoke again. "I couldn't forget you," he finally said. "I tried so hard. But I guess your curse didn't work, Raya Liston. Because I remembered everything."

I laughed and took a risk: I grabbed his hand, and my whole body flooded with warmth when he squeezed mine back. "I'm happy it didn't work. So happy!"

"You were right, you know. I don't like to be uncomfortable. I don't like sadness or fear or anger, and I was so determined to avoid them that I didn't try to really figure things out with you until it was too late. But you know what? After I left you, I couldn't really avoid shit like sadness and anger. For once I had to let myself feel them." He shrugged. "For a while I hated you for that. It was terrible."

I curled my fingers around his, horrified that I'd made someone I cared about feel so much pain. "I'm sorry."

"I'm not. Because you were worth letting myself have all those feelings. You're the first person in my life who ever has been, you know? After a while I couldn't ignore that. Couldn't ignore how much less beautiful things were when you weren't around."

"You've been so good for me, too," I told him. "You help me spend more time in the present and less in the future. You help me quiet my brain, Kiran. You're probably the only reason I've gotten anywhere with meditation at all. And you don't even like it!"

He burst out laughing. And when he didn't stop, I took advantage of his surprise to lean over and kiss him.

"I think I might *anurakti* you," I told him when we finally came up for air.

"Oh, yeah?" He pulled my body into his, and in that moment I saw the world the way he did: as beauty and perfection without limits. "Me too," he added softly.

"That's probably not how you say that, though, huh?"

"Not at all." And then he kissed me again.

A week later, I was sitting in front of Pihu, listening as she sounded out the word *becoming*.

"You've got it," I encouraged. "Just add on the last sound."

"Oh, I get it!" She beamed. "Let's keep going. I like this story."

Of course she did. She liked all of them.

Pihu had returned to her "normal" life with surprising ease. Her mother told us that she still woke up sometimes screaming with terrible dreams, but they were getting better the more she worked with the counselor she'd been assigned to at the survivors' organization. And no matter how bad her dreams were, every day she got up and came to school. Every single day she begged me to read with her.

We were reading a story about Sarasvati, my favorite Hindu goddess. I was trying to learn Hindi, so every day after I helped Pihu with her reading in English, she helped me practice my Hindi.

The Hindi was coming slowly, but at least I knew more than basic phrases and curse words now.

When Khatri called out that the school day was over, Pihu

leaped up and gave me a huge hug. "I like that I see you every single day now," she told me.

"So do I." I kissed the top of her head. I spent a lot of time trying not to think about how close we'd come to losing her. If this was even half the hell parents went through, then I could understand why my parents alternated texting me once every three hours. And called in panic if I didn't answer.

I left the school for the footbridge. Kiran and I met there every day after school was out, always without fail. "Kiran!" I rushed up to him. "I learned six new words today."

"Oh, yeah? *Ab mein kya keh rahi hoon?*" he said.

I rolled my eyes. "Those were not the six words. How'd your interviews go?"

Kiran was staying at the ashram while he shot footage for a documentary he was filming about trafficking. He'd been interviewing Samaira almost every day for weeks. I knew that soon the footage he needed to shoot here would be complete and he'd have to go back to Delhi, but that was okay. He'd started an application to USC. I knew he'd get in, and it wouldn't be long before we were together again in California.

There was a future before us. I was trying to accept that I couldn't always be sure exactly which direction—or directions—it would take.

"Good. Samaira's amazing to do this. I can't imagine what it costs her to tell those stories." He shuddered. "Raya, Pihu's so lucky you and Anandi found that note."

"She's amazing for finding a way to leave it." I sighed. "She's amazing on basically every level. Left a note so she could be rescued, got out reasonably unharmed, *and* saved my grandmother's journal in the process."

"She's pretty fucking phenomenal," Kiran agreed. "Hey, you never told me what happened to your grandmother after she went to Varanasi. Did you finish reading the journal?"

I shook my head as I pulled it out of my shoulder bag. "Not yet. I'm almost... afraid to? That's not the right word, though. It's more like I'm apprehensive about it, I guess. I don't know if I'm ready to see how everything ended."

"Raya." Kiran laughed as he kissed me. "You *know* how it all ended. Happily ever after, remember?"

He was right, of course. Daadee had gotten a pretty happy ending, just like Shakuntala. It wasn't perfect, for sure—but it was definitely happy.

We sat down next to the statue of Bharat, and I started reading out loud.

September 10

My life today looks entirely different than I expected it to look merely four months ago. Every path I laid out for myself has shifted, every dream and purpose I was certain of has become uncertain. And yet I am nothing but happy.

This was not the case when I first arrived in Varanasi. Finding Raaz here seemed nearly impossible at first: a city full of training barristers—where was I to start? I knew that his father's office was near the Ghats, so I traveled there first, but the number of barristers' offices near the Ghats in Varanasi is nearly staggering. All but ready to give up, I sat beside the Ganges River, in tears.

You would never guess who approached me then. I still remain shocked by what happened then, although perhaps I am foolish to feel this way. Because this is an old story, older than time. Far older than me. Older than Shakuntala and Dushyanta, I suspect.

A fisherman approached me and asked what was wrong. Normally I would have been wary of a stranger seeking to help me, but I thought of the fisherman in my most beloved tale. How he found the ring that united two forgotten loves.

The fisherman listened to my story of my lost love. And then he informed me that he knew where the office was, and he led me directly there.

This story is, truly, older than time.

I am living in Varanasi now. Raaz and I have been promised to each other. He is attending law school and working at his father's office, as he always intended. I am spending a great deal of time at an ashram near the Ganges, *studying with the guru there. It is still my intention to study Hinduism with all fibers of my being, and Raaz supports me entirely. We have come a long way from our first encounter in the ashram.*

Only lately I have begun to wonder if perhaps my future lies elsewhere. When I close my eyes in prayer and think of the impermanence of all this, I see different paths. Paths with young ones and family and nights spent around the table helping with schoolwork, not sitting in halls of prayer. My faith will always be an important part of me, but I am more certain than ever it is only one part of me.

Once I was certain where my path led. This uncertainty I live in now has given me peace unlike any other, and I thank the gods each day for it.

I flipped through the empty pages that came next. "That was the last entry," I told Kiran as I lay down in the grass next to him. "Huh."

"*Huh?* That's all you have to say?" He rolled over on his elbow, laughing at me. "We break up because you think your grandmother gave up her dreams for your grandfather, and all you have to say is 'huh'? We could have avoided so much shit if you'd just read this last damn entry before the journal disappeared," he teased.

"That wasn't the whole reason we broke up," I told him haughtily. "And you know it. Plus we got back together, so that's all that matters."

He draped his body over mine, kissing me gently.

"I should never have thought I could forget you," he told me. "Dushyanta was a moron."

"Sure, you say that now. Just wait until someone curses us."

"Uh-huh." He kissed me again. "Fuck 'em. They can curse us if they want to. Won't work."

I thought of the documentary he was making. It was such a different project from the ones he used to talk about that I'd almost thought I'd heard him wrong when he first described it. This wasn't the same Kiran who'd opened the door for me that day at the ashram. I loved this Kiran just as much as I'd loved that one, only in different ways, new ways. I hoped he never stopped changing, because I was sure I'd always love every single side of him.

We made love in the statue garden, the place Kiran had found for both of us. Then he held my hand and we walked to the ashram for dinner.

Even though I wasn't technically a resident of the ashram anymore, no one seemed to mind me showing up to eat there. Kiran and I didn't flaunt the fact that we were dating, but it must have been obvious to everyone that we'd gotten together during our time there. So much for chastity, but no one ever said a word to us.

I'd just sat down with our food and was waiting for Kiran to get us some tea when Vihaan sat next to me.

"Am I ever going to see you at the school?" I asked him.

He didn't answer me. Instead, he placed his tiny hands on my cheeks and stared at me for a long time, and for the first time I understood why everyone always stared back. You couldn't help but look back into those eyes—they were so deep, so intense, so different from anything else a person can see in the world.

Then Vihaan nodded and smiled, as brightly as if I'd just laid everything he'd ever wished for right at his feet. He dropped his hands and walked away from my table.

Kiran came over and set a teacup down next to me. "Everything okay?" he asked.

"Everything's perfect," I told him. "This place. This moment. You."

He grinned. "Are you saying you still *anurakti* me?"

I couldn't kiss him like I wanted to—not there, in the middle of the Rishi Kanva ashram. But I did lay my hand over his. "I am. And I can't wait to learn the other ninety-five ways to tell you I love you."

Authors' Note

There is no quick fix for the problem of child sex trafficking in India, which impacts at least 12 percent of the Indian population and is rooted in systemic poverty.

UNICEF reports that more than a quarter of India's population lives below the poverty line and nearly half of all children in rural areas are underweight. Only half of girls attend secondary school, and 35 percent of women are illiterate, according to UNESCO.

We believe one person can make a difference; choices both big and small are effective and helpful in changing lives. That's why some proceeds from our novel will go to the World of Children organization, a global recognition and funding program for people specifically serving the needs of children.

For more information, visit worldofchildren.org.

Acknowledgments

Anytime Ava and I have accomplished something of worth or of value, it has been because we either overcame a difficult circumstance or because talented, wise, and insightful souls have helped us on our journey. In the case of *96 Words for Love*, we accomplished bringing this love story to life because a team of ingenious and creative minds supported us. When a gifted writer like James Patterson chooses your work and gives it a platform, it is among the kindest of gifts and it makes us (Ava and I) want to do better, to tell a better story, to live up to his belief in us. We thank you, Mr. Patterson.

Aubrey Poole and Kirsten Neuhaus—how grateful we are to have the opportunity to work with such imaginative boss ladies like you! Carey Albertine, Saira Rao, and Johanna Parkhurst, your indelible support and enthusiasm for this project from the start was the missing link we needed to tell our story the way we believed in so passionately! Amy Rapawy—the true definition of that lasting and permanent leader that holds up the structure. We have so much gratitude for our entire team at Jimmy Patterson books: Sabrina Benun, Erinn McGrath, Julie Guacci, Tracy Shaw, and Linda Arends. Ava and I thank you. What started as a love story from mother to daughter, of wanting to pass down part of our Indian heritage, turned into a love story to the world. This book represents all that is possible, all that lies within us all along. You must first look within before you can see what's ahead. Cheers to those who believe in themselves, who believe that leading with love in all that you do will make a difference, one soul at a time.

About the Authors

RACHEL ROY is the daughter of an Indian immigrant father and Dutch mother. She is mother to Tallulah and Ava. Rachel is the founder and creative director of her eponymous brand and a tireless activist for using your voice to cultivate change in the world and to design the life you wish to live. Rachel founded Kindness Is Always Fashionable, an entrepreneurial philanthropic platform to help women artisans around the world create sustainable income for their families and communities. In 2018, Rachel was named a United Nations Women Champion for Innovation and works for the UN advocating gender equality and other critical women's issues. In 2015, Rachel published *Design Your Life.*

AVA DASH is the daughter of fashion designer Rachel Roy. She attends college and works and lives in Los Angeles. Ava works with young adults that have aged out of the foster care system, as well as former sex trafficked girls in India. Inspired from her travels with her mother, Ava hopes to start a give-back business that provides critical resources to educate and empower the girls she has met on her travels to India.